The
FINDERS
KEEPERS
LIBRARY

The FINDERS KEEPERS LIBRARY

ANNIE RAINS

FOREVER

New York Boston

Cover design by Sara Congdon
Cover photographs © Getty, Shutterstock
Cover copyright © 2024 by Hachette Book Group, Inc.

Forever
Hachette Book Group
1290 Avenue of the Americas, New York, NY 10104
read-forever.com

@readforeverpub

First Edition: April 2024

Forever is an imprint of Grand Central Publishing. The Forever name and logo are registered trademarks of Hachette Book Group, Inc.

The publisher is not responsible for websites (or their content) that are not owned by the publisher.

The Hachette Speakers Bureau provides a wide range of authors for speaking events. To find out more, go to hachettespeakersbureau.com or email HachetteSpeakers@hbgusa.com.

Forever books may be purchased in bulk for business, educational, or promotional use. For information, please contact your local bookseller or the Hachette Book Group Special Markets Department at special.markets@hbgusa.com.

Floral Book chapter opener art © Shutterstock

Library of Congress Cataloging-in-Publication Data

Names: Rains, Annie, author.
Title: The finders keepers library / Annie Rains.
Identifiers: LCCN 2023051337 | ISBN 9781538710111 (trade paperback) | ISBN 9781538710135 (ebook)
Subjects: LCSH: Book clubs (Discussion groups)—Fiction. | LCGFT: Romance fiction. | Novels.
Classification: LCC PS3618.A3975 F56 2024 | DDC 813/.6—dc23/eng/20231102
LC record available at https://lccn.loc.gov/2023051337

ISBNs: 9781538710111 (trade paperback); 9781538710135 (ebook)

Printed in the United States of America

LSC-C

Printing 1, 2024

For Savannah Barwick Lambert—the original Savannah.

Chapter One

Savannah

Not all those who wander are lost.

The Fellowship of the Ring, J. R. R. Tolkien

Am I at the correct address?

Savannah Collins was well aware of the phenomenon where houses that had once seemed so big as a child became smaller in adulthood. But her aunt Eleanor's home wasn't just smaller than she remembered; it was also overgrown with flowering vines to the point that she could barely make out the house's mauve-colored siding.

Savannah reached up to press the doorbell but stopped when she noticed a sign hanging in the paned glass window.

NO NEED TO KNOCK. COME RIGHT ON IN.

The invitation took a moment to register. Surely her aunt didn't just allow people to walk into her home without permission? As Savannah pondered, the door opened, and a girl looked up at her. She was maybe eleven or twelve and had long strawberry blonde hair and big blue eyes. She looked familiar even though Savannah was certain she'd never seen her before.

"Who are you?" The girl cocked her head to one side, looking put off by Savannah's mere presence. One side of her lip drew up in a snarl. "And what's with the humongous hat?"

Savannah reached up to touch the wide brim of her hat. Out of habit, she'd taken it off her dashboard before stepping out of her car. There was no cure for lupus but staying away from certain triggers like sun exposure helped. Not that the day was sunny. Instead, clouds had been rolling in for the last hour, creating a thick and stormy gray sky. "I'm Savannah. And you are?"

Instead of answering, the girl said, "Are you here for books?"

Savannah remembered that her aunt had a small library in the garden out back. Savannah's uncle had built it for Aunt Eleanor many years ago, and neighbors loved to stop by to chat and check out a book. "Actually, I'm here to see Eleanor. She's my aunt."

As Savannah waited for the girl to respond or step aside, the stray kitten that Savannah had somehow adopted in the last week wiggled around inside the large straw bag hanging from her shoulder. Savannah couldn't leave it in the hot car, which is exactly what she'd done with the thirty or so plants she'd traveled with this morning.

Savannah had always had an interest in plants, which was why she'd gone to college to study botany. A lot of good that degree had done her so far in life. Currently, she had a modest online store where she sold plants, and she also ran a vlog and social media page with the same name—Late Bloomer. Those things didn't pay the bills though. At the moment, nothing was paying the bills.

"Ms. Eleanor is in the kitchen," the girl said, still not stepping aside. "You weren't about to ring the bell, were you? Because Ms. Eleanor doesn't answer the door anymore. Just walk in."

Savannah shook her head. "What do you mean Eleanor doesn't answer the door anymore? Why not?"

"I thought you said Ms. Eleanor was your aunt. You don't really know much about her, do you?"

Ouch. The truth was that Savannah hadn't kept up with her aunt the way she should have. She'd called, of course, but Eleanor was a widow now. She lived alone. And short of Savannah's parents, Eleanor didn't have any other family to check on her.

Done with the conversation, the girl bounded down the porch steps, hugging a paperback copy of *Anne of Green Gables* to her stomach. The book was worn, and Savannah wondered if maybe it was the same copy that Eleanor had given her to read when she was a similar age. Aunt Eleanor was always doling out summer reading lists when Savannah had come to visit every June and July as a girl.

Growing up, Savannah had spent every summer at Aunt Eleanor and Uncle Aaron's home here in Bloom, North Carolina. The summer months had always felt magical in a way that Savannah hadn't experienced since she'd stopped coming at nineteen years old. At twenty-nine, she wondered if it was even possible to feel that childlike magic again. She certainly hadn't felt anything extraordinary with her ex-fiancé, which told her a lot about the relationship.

Wasn't true love supposed to feel magical? Or was that just a lie that fairy tales endorsed?

Peering through Eleanor's open front door, Savannah hesitated before stepping inside. "Aunt Eleanor? Hello? It's me, Savannah." When no one immediately called back, worry gathered inside her chest. Eleanor's home was overrun by books. They were everywhere, covering every surface and piled up on the floor. Her aunt was a retired librarian. She'd always loved to read but her home was usually neat and tidy—never like this. "Hello? Aunt Eleanor?"

"In here!" Eleanor finally called from the kitchen at the end of the hall.

Savannah picked up her pace and found her aunt standing behind the far counter with two mugs in front of her.

"Oh, there you are! I was just about to make some tea. Would you like a cup?" Eleanor asked as if it hadn't been years since seeing Savannah in person.

Savannah hugged her bag with the contraband kitten to her hip. "A cup of tea would be amazing. Thank you."

Eleanor pointed at a tall wooden rack near the back door. "Take off your hat." Her gaze dropped to Savannah's bag. "And let whatever it is in that tote of yours out to breathe. Poor thing."

Nothing had ever gotten past Aunt Eleanor.

Savannah nibbled at her bottom lip. "I should have asked if I could bring the kitten with me. I honestly wasn't sure if I was even keeping her. Fig is a stray. *Was* a stray."

"Fig, huh?" Eleanor chuckled softly.

"Short for Figaro," Savannah explained, although she was certain her aunt knew exactly where the name had come from.

"*Pinocchio* was one of your favorite stories when you were young. That puppet's growing nose always made you laugh."

4

Eleanor watched the black-and-white kitten squirm in Savannah's arms. "Well, it looks like Figaro decided to keep you. It happens sometimes."

Yes, it did. And sometimes fiancés decided not to keep the person they'd vowed to love forever.

Savannah stopped her thoughts in their tracks. She was over Randall, she was—even if the way he'd left her still stung. There was no time to dwell on her broken engagement though. Her focus now needed to be on a job that offered a livable income and a place to start over. And she needed both those things ASAP.

She'd had a few interviews, and some had already contacted her to respectfully decline. Coming to Bloom was just a stop on her way home, which, truthfully, was the last place Savannah wanted to go. Her mom would inevitably tell her for the millionth time what a mistake getting her master of science in botany had been, and Savannah's dad would lament over the cost of college just to buy Savannah a useless degree that left her homeless and jobless.

Please let a job pan out soon.

"I'll start the kettle to boil and get a saucer of water for your friend. Then we'll have tea, and you'll tell me all about what's new in your life," Eleanor said.

"Oh, I wouldn't want to bore you." Savannah lowered Fig to the floor. At least Savannah was no longer pet-less. That was something. Although she was sure her parents would have something to say about that as well. They never did enjoy pets when Savannah was growing up. A fish was about the extent of what they'd allowed.

Eleanor glanced back at Savannah, giving her a thoughtful look. Then she raised a finger in the air. "Love is or it ain't. Thin love ain't love at all."

"Toni Morrison. *Beloved*," Savannah said without missing a beat. Eleanor had assigned that book to both Savannah and the boy next door the summer after tenth grade.

Eleanor looked pleased. "That's right. Your breakup with that young man tells me he was nowhere near good enough for you. We should celebrate."

"Celebrate my broken engagement? I'm not sure I'm there yet, Aunt Eleanor. But maybe we can go out to toast something different. I am up for a drink." Even though alcohol was on the long list of things Savannah's rheumatologist had advised against.

"Oh, no, I don't think so." Eleanor visibly stiffened. "Everything I need is right here in this cottage." She placed a saucer of water on the floor beside the fridge, looking on delightedly as Fig padded up to it. After a moment, Eleanor returned to the counter and retrieved two mugs of tea, carrying them to where Savannah was seated on one of her barstools. "Talking to you is a nice change of pace. I usually talk to the roses in the evenings."

Savannah nearly choked on her first sip of tea. "You talk to the roses?" Okay, *now* she was concerned. "Do they, um, talk back?" *Please say no, please say no.*

Eleanor gave her an amused look. "Don't look at me that way. You were the one who started it, Savannah. Don't you remember?"

Savannah furrowed her brows as she pressed a hand to her chest. "Me?"

A quiet laugh bubbled off her aunt's lips. "Oh, yes. You would sit under that rose arbor out back and talk to the roses for hours when you were younger. That's where I learned to talk to them. Why, you made it look like so much fun."

Savannah blinked as a fuzzy recollection that could have been a dream came to mind. "I was just a kid."

Eleanor clucked her tongue. "We could all stand to have more of that childlike innocence if you ask me. I've found that the roses are good listeners. Maybe you should give it another try while you're here."

That evening, Savannah stepped off the back deck of Eleanor's house and walked along the stepping-stone path. The air was as sweet as she remembered from spending her childhoods here. It was also heavy with moisture. The soft, barely audible rumble in the sky told her that a storm was brewing.

It would be exactly her luck to get caught in one of Bloom's summer downpours, she thought as she walked past a wall made of lattice with roses weaving in and out of its openings. It stretched across half the backyard, ending with a deep arbor that had a variety of roses reaching across the structure's bow. Underneath, there was a garden bench, where Savannah used to sit and read.

It was the ultimate sensory experience. The colors. The fragrant air filling her lungs. The buzz of bees and the sounds of birds. Every year, Aunt Eleanor would give Savannah and the boy next door summer reading lists, and this was where she'd devour books like *Bridge to Terabithia*, *The Secret Garden*, and *Where the Red Fern Grows*. She must have read *A Wrinkle in*

Time half a dozen times sitting under this magical waterfall of roses.

"Have you missed me?" she asked the roses, feeling slightly foolish. "Apparently, you and I used to talk often. We were good friends," she said. Since she only came to Bloom during the summers, she didn't have a lot of friends. There were two, mainly: the boy next door and an energetic girl who lived down the street. Then there were these roses. If Savannah's memory served her, she'd even given some of them names. "I'm not even sure what I'd tell you these days. Maybe that life is a lot harder than I'd realized. It certainly isn't a fairy tale."

Love wasn't a fairy tale either. She was supposed to be getting married this summer but all those plans had shattered when she'd gotten sick earlier this year. Savannah had naively thought her illness might bring her and her ex closer, but instead, it had been a wedge that drove them apart.

Randall had gotten more and more distant, throwing himself into the start of his golf-pro business—the one that Savannah had intended to help him with while keeping her gardening passion on the side. Then one day three months ago, Randall had sat her down.

"It pains me to do this, Savannah," he'd said with a heavy sigh.

She'd looked at him, suddenly worried. "Do what?"

He had leaned over his knees and clasped his hands in front of him. That's when she'd noticed he wasn't wearing the promise ring she'd given him. It was symbolic and meant that Randall would soon be a married man. "This just isn't going to work."

Her mind had searched for meaning. Somewhere deep inside she thought she knew exactly what was happening but she was in denial. "What? Your business? Starting up a business is always hard. Don't—"

"Not the business," he'd said, cutting her off. "Me and you. I'm an ambitious guy, Savannah. You know that. It's one of the things you've always loved about me."

She'd nodded numbly, hoping she was wrong about the direction the conversation was heading. "It is."

"Now that you're sick, that changes things. I'm sorry, but I don't think I'm up for that kind of lifestyle."

"What kind of lifestyle?" Tears filled her eyes, spilling over onto her cheeks. She hated crying in front of others but this conversation had taken her by surprise. They'd just gone to look at wedding venues the day before. Randall had chosen a prestigious golf course, which she'd only agreed to because she'd wanted him to be happy.

"I'm not up for a life where you're sick and I have to put my own needs on hold to take care of you."

For a long moment, she was too stunned to speak. She had lupus. It wasn't ideal but it didn't mean her life was anything less. She and her physician had come up with a plan for her to stay healthy. There'd be lifestyle modifications, and yes, there might be times when she was sicker than others, but they could get through this—together. "We can weather this storm. We can do anything, remember?" That's what he'd always told her.

What he'd meant, she'd discovered after the fact, was that they could weather his storms. Not hers.

Randall stood. To his credit, his facial expression really did look as if he'd gotten a golf swing straight to the head. "I'm sorry, Savannah. I don't want to get married anymore."

She'd lost her fiancé, her job as his right hand in their golf business—his business—and her home, all in one fell swoop. "I just need a small break from all the stress," she told the roses now. "I need someone to throw me a lifeline. Is that too much to ask?"

As if on cue, her cell phone vibrated inside her pocket. She pulled it out and her pulse jumped as she read the screen. She had an email about a job opening she'd interviewed for last month. The position was for an assistant professor in the botany program. It was a long shot, and accepting the position would require her to move to South Carolina, which was maybe a bigger change than she was looking for. But it was employment.

Who am I kidding? There was no way she'd get the job anyway. She wasn't nearly qualified enough. Most universities wanted their professors to have PhDs these days. Bracing herself for the third rejection this week, she tapped the email and her eyes skimmed quickly.

Dear Ms. Collins,

We are delighted to offer you employment at South Carolina University. Should you accept, the position would begin September 15 of this year, under the terms previously discussed. Please let us know your decision no later than August 1.

Sincerely,
Chancellor Smith

Savannah let out a soft squeal. *A job! A new beginning!* It didn't start for a couple of months, which meant she'd still have to stay with her mom and dad for a few weeks, but at least she'd have a plan—something to tell her parents when they openly disapproved of her life choices.

Throwing her head back and her arms out to her side, she did a twirl under the arbor in the same way she used to as a child, watching the colors of the roses swirl above her.

The sound of a branch crunching on the ground stopped her girlish twirling. Dropping her arms, she zeroed in on someone walking down the stone path. He was tall and broad shouldered. It had gotten dark since she came outside and she couldn't make out anything else about him. "Hello?"

The man headed toward her, his walk slow and deliberate. "Look who finally decided to return to Bloom," he said, his deep voice rumbling just like the thunder above them.

He stepped into a patch of moonlight, and Savannah gasped at the man's familiar features. Black hair. Angled jawline. It'd been years since she'd seen the boy who'd lived next door. The one who'd shared the same reading lists from Aunt Eleanor during those long, hot Bloom summers.

Savannah's heartbeat quickened as he continued walking, stopping once he was standing a couple feet ahead of her. The boy she remembered had always been smiling. The man in front of her now wore a subtle frown, his blue eyes glinting in the moonlight. And, unless she was mistaken, he didn't look happy to see her.

"Evan Sanders, is that you?"

Chapter Two

Evan

Life changes in an instant. The ordinary instant.

The Year of Magical Thinking, Joan Didion

Evan had thought he was imagining it when he'd seen Savannah Collins standing under the rose arbor the way she used to when they were younger. He still came out here sometimes to clear his mind, and he often found himself remembering the girl he'd crushed on every summer.

He wanted to be happy to see her right now, but instead, resentment flared in his chest.

After Eleanor's fall this past winter, Evan had expected Savannah to show up at least to check on her aunt. The accident was months ago though, and as far as Evan had seen, no blood relatives had come to check on his elderly neighbor at all. It was criminal.

"It's good to see you, Evan." Savannah's dark blonde hair was shorter than it had been the last time he'd seen her. She'd kept it midway down her back and braided loosely when they were teenagers. Now her golden locks fell just below her shoulders.

"You too. Although it would have been nicer to see you before now," he said.

Savannah's smile faded. "Oh. I, um, well, I guess I've been busy." Her hands came together, and she interwove her fingers, looking nervous but no less beautiful.

"Too busy to check on the aunt who cared for you every summer as a child? Wow." He shook his head. "That's not the girl I used to know."

"Excuse me?" Her brow furrowed over her puzzled expression. "Are you upset with me right now?"

Maybe he was being hypersensitive but family took care of family. When his father had gotten sick, Evan had moved back to Bloom to care for him until he'd died last year. When the mother of his child had unexpectedly passed away in January, he hadn't hesitated to take full custody of June, despite the objections of her maternal grandmother. Family was the most important thing.

"I call Aunt Eleanor all the time." Savannah folded her arms over her chest. "And, really, my relationship with my aunt is none of your business."

"It is my business." Evan was doing his best to keep his tone neutral. He wasn't mad at Savannah. Just disappointed. "Eleanor is like family to me, and—"

Thunder punched the quiet of the evening, stopping Evan short and making Savannah jump.

She looked upward for a moment and then back at him as smaller rumbles of thunder filled the air. "Maybe I should go inside."

Evan nodded, some part of him already regretting this brief interaction. "Eleanor needed her family, Sav. She needed you."

The little divot of skin between Savannah's brown eyes deepened. She opened her mouth, but before any words came out, there was another boom. This one was louder and so forceful that the ground vibrated.

Savannah's hand flew to her chest, which was rising and falling in quick motion. "I should—" A drop of rain hit one of her cheeks and then the other.

More drops splashed across Evan's forearm. "You should—" Before he had a chance to finish his sentence, the sky broke open.

They were standing under the arbor but rain still made its way through the tiny openings between the roses.

"I need to check on my daughter," Evan said. "She's afraid of storms." He wasn't sure why he told Savannah.

"You have a daughter?" she asked. "I didn't know."

Evan had to read her lips to hear her over the summer storm that had arrived as unexpectedly as Savannah. Once upon a time, he'd wanted to do so much more than read her lips.

"A lot has changed," he said, wishing he didn't mean for the worse, in some instances. He couldn't help being disappointed in her lack of attention to her aunt after her fall last year. Eleanor's injuries had been serious. The Savannah of his youth would have been here as quickly as possible. He'd once caught Savannah crying her eyes out over a butterfly with a torn wing.

She'd been embarrassed when he'd walked up on her but that moment was one that had sealed his first love.

Maybe that was another reason he was upset. After Eleanor's injury, part of him had been secretly excited at the thought of Savannah returning to Bloom. He was ashamed to even think so selfishly, considering how much pain Eleanor had been in, but he had. It didn't feel like Savannah had only rejected her family; he also felt rejected.

"Count of three. You run that way and I'll run home," he said.

"Just like old times," Savannah said with a small smile.

His heart thumped uncomfortably against his ribs, the way it had all those years ago.

"Goodbye, Evan." She seemed to suck in a breath as if she were about to dive underwater, and then she sprinted out from under the rose arbor.

Evan thought he heard her squeal as the rain drenched her in quick order. He was about to run out into the storm as well when he noticed Savannah's shoe lying on the stone path. It must have fallen off as she'd run. "Savannah! Hey!" He darted into the rain and dipped to grab the gray athletic sneaker. He was about to chase after her when he heard a loud crack directly above him. Instinctively, he knew that a tree was coming down, hard and fast.

Instead of chasing after Savannah, he veered left, in the direction of home, and ran as fast as he could.

Light flashed in the window as Evan sat at his kitchen table an hour later, waiting for the storm to pass. He glanced down the hallway toward June's bedroom, wondering why she'd kept her door shut all night. She used to come running at the slightest rumble of thunder.

It was a good thing June wasn't afraid of storms anymore. A positive. He should be glad, but instead, he felt even more like he was losing his baby girl. June had grown up so fast since her mother had died. She'd finished out the school year living with her grandma Margie in California and had officially come to live with Evan last month. The transition hadn't been easy so far. June was quiet and sullen. And she didn't keep it a secret that she wanted to return to California to live with her grandmother.

Evan was her father though, and he'd always wanted June to live in Bloom with him. Growing up without a mother himself, however, Evan had been adamant that June live with her mom for most of the year, which left him taking June part-time during the summers. Now she was here to stay but she seemed miserable.

Another flash of light in the window illuminated the drops of rain on the glass. As soon as the storm stopped, Evan planned to walk outside and see what the damage was. He'd already called Eleanor and made sure the tree hadn't hit her home. It hadn't; but it had definitely hit the garden. Hopefully the damage would be minor. Eleanor's backyard was the venue for a wedding that was happening this summer, and after all that the bride-to-be had been through, she deserved a perfect day.

"Dad?"

Evan bolted upright from where he was resting his head on the table and faced his daughter. "Hey. You okay?"

June's face scrunched up. "Why wouldn't I be?"

He motioned outside the window. "You hate storms."

"Maybe when I was little. Not anymore."

Evan's heart dipped. "Right. Need anything?"

June continued toward the fridge. "A glass of water. Why are you sitting at the table?"

In case you need me. "Can't sleep," he said.

June turned and gave him an assessing look. "Do you need a glass of water too?"

"No, thanks. I'll be fine." He watched her fill up her glass from the water dispenser on the fridge's door. Then, without looking back, she retreated to her room. The door shut and he heard the lock click. He sighed. Then he laid his head back on the table and closed his eyes, just for a moment.

"Dad?" June asked.

Evan startled, lifted his head off the table, and groggily blinked his daughter's face into focus. "Hm? What's going on?"

"Someone's at the door. It's a weird lady with a big hat. I saw her yesterday at Ms. Eleanor's."

Savannah. Evan instantly felt more alert. He checked the time on his phone's screen. It was already 6:00 a.m. "Did you let her in?"

June gave him a sideward look. "You told me to never answer the door for strangers."

"Right." Evan scooted back from the table and got up. Then he headed toward the front of the house, grabbed a gray athletic shoe off his staircase, and opened the door to find Savannah standing there. It had been dark when he'd seen her last night. This morning, in the light of day, she was even prettier than he'd remembered. In the decade since he'd last seen her, she'd grown into those huge brown eyes of hers.

"Hi." Savannah avoided meeting his gaze. "Um, Aunt Eleanor asked me to assess the damage from last night's storm. She suggested that I might ask you to go with me just in case there's some hidden danger out there. Like a downed power line or something."

"Sure. Good idea." Evan held out her shoe. "Did you lose something last night?"

Savannah laughed, her entire demeanor shifting from nervous to bubbly. "Yes, I did lose my shoe." She gestured to her feet. "Luckily, I had a spare pair packed but this one happens to be my favorite."

"The right one, not the left?" Evan teased.

"Both. This pair is my favorite." She looked away and pulled her bottom lip between her teeth. "Thank you."

"No problem. I'm sure you would have eventually found it but it might have been waterlogged." Evan gestured behind him. "Give me a minute to put on my own shoes."

He would have invited her in but Savannah was already lowering herself to the front step of his porch.

Evan quickly pulled on a pair of sneakers and then stepped outside.

Savannah stood when she saw him approaching. Then she matched his pace, walking beside him. "I don't live here, Evan. I'm an adult with responsibilities, including a job. Kind of."

He wondered what she meant by that but asking would only take away from what he really needed to say. "Eleanor has needed you. You didn't even come back last winter." He stopped walking and faced her, watching as confusion tightened her features. Her eyes searched his, her gaze bouncing back and forth as if the answer she was seeking was written on his expression.

"She didn't tell you about the fall?" he asked, before shaking his head. "Of course she didn't." Eleanor was stubborn and independent to a fault. "Eleanor probably didn't want to interrupt your very important life."

Savannah rolled her eyes, reminding Evan of his preteen daughter. "That's not fair. I call Aunt Eleanor all the time. She's never once mentioned any falls. What happened last winter?"

It was Eleanor's story to tell, and it should come from her. But Eleanor hadn't told Savannah, and it seemed that she wasn't going to. "Eleanor was out shopping after Thanksgiving. She had bags of presents. You know how she is."

"Very generous," Savannah said.

Generous was an understatement. "While she was out shopping, she tripped and fell. The impact shattered her pelvis. It was pretty serious. Until last month, a physical therapist was coming out to her house. She's gotten better, but as far as I can tell, she's still not getting around the way she used to." Evan couldn't remember the last time he'd even seen Eleanor's car leave the driveway.

Savannah blew out a breath. "I wish she would have told me."

"Would you have come?" He was aware that his tone was hard and judgmental. He felt protective of his elderly neighbor though. Eleanor was like a second mother to him growing up. After his own mother had passed away, Evan had turned to Eleanor for all the things a mom would normally do for her kid.

Heat flashed in Savannah's eyes. "You're not being fair, Evan."

"It's an honest question."

Savannah hugged her arms more tightly over her chest. "Of course I would have come."

He shrugged. "I don't know. From what I hear, you've been busy planning a wedding. That takes time." He knew how much went into wedding planning, because he'd been helping Eleanor prepare her backyard garden for the wedding taking place there in three weeks. Eleanor's garden was beautiful but it had been neglected since Eleanor's husband passed away. Evan had recently trimmed back the unruly roses along the garden path that led up to the back deck where the bride and groom would recite their vows.

Savannah shifted between her feet, looking uncomfortable. Evan noticed now that she wasn't wearing an engagement ring. "I wasn't aware of Aunt Eleanor's fall, okay? As far as I know, my parents weren't informed either." Savannah continued walking, leaving Evan a few strides behind.

He had to practically jog to keep up. "Listen, I'm sorry if I came off strong yesterday."

She glanced over her shoulder. "It's fine."

The tone of her voice told him it wasn't fine though. He caught up to her and walked, refocusing on the garden as they crossed into the backyard.

They walked in silence for a few moments, and then Savannah stopped in her tracks.

"Oh, no." She pressed a hand to her chest.

Evan was speechless as he took in the scene in front of them. The rose arbor had toppled over in the wind, pieces of it scattered among the broken tree limbs, and the decades-old roses were a disarray of vines and flowers on the ground.

"Aunt Eleanor is going to be so upset. These were my uncle's roses. They're nearly forty years old. Older than me."

"They're still alive," Evan said, stepping toward the mess. Granted, he knew virtually nothing about plants and flowers. Could they survive this kind of trauma? He turned back to Savannah, who looked shell-shocked. She had said Eleanor would be devastated but he thought Savannah looked equally upset. Maybe she hadn't distanced herself from everything in Bloom like he'd thought.

The loud sound of the tree cracking and falling last night came to Evan's mind, and he wondered if there was more damage in the garden than just the fallen rose arbor. Heading forward, he looked for a missing tree. He could hear Savannah's footsteps behind him, crunching the broken limbs on the ground.

"Where are you going?" she asked.

"I'm positive I heard a tree fall last night."

"Me too. That's when I lost my shoe. I was going to turn back but the sound sent me running for shelter."

Evan glanced over his shoulder and down at her feet as he continued walking forward. Today she was wearing a pair of pink hiking boots. "You're a regular Cinderella."

A small smile bloomed on her face, and for a moment, he felt like he'd scaled Mount Everest. He'd chased that smile every day during the summers of his youth. No sooner than it had come, it vanished, and her eyes widened as she looked beyond him. "Oh, no! The Finders Keepers Library!"

Chapter Three

Savannah

Where you tend a rose, my lad, a thistle cannot grow.

The Secret Garden, Frances Hodgson Burnett

Savannah faced the library that Uncle Aaron had built for Aunt Eleanor many years ago.

While Little Free Libraries were popping up all across the country, Aaron had created something on a much grander scale for his wife. They'd named it the Finders Keepers Library, and it was open for anyone looking for a good book to read. If they found a book that they would like to read, they were free to keep it. But most also brought a book to give away in return. People in town were free to take the path around Eleanor's home and come and go as they pleased, but most of the time, they also stopped in to visit.

"Poor Aunt Eleanor," Savannah whispered.

Evan rubbed a hand behind his neck. "It's just the back corner. I can call someone to pull the tree off."

"What about the roof? Do you think you can fix it?"

He chuckled humorlessly. "I'm great with my hands but I can't say that I've ever fixed a roof before. I'm sure I can call around and find a handyman though. That shouldn't be too hard."

Evan headed toward the structure and opened the door. Then he stepped to the side to make room for Savannah to come in as well.

"Noooo. The books." Savannah hurried over to the corner that had been crushed by the fallen tree, bending to pick up a couple of soggy books. She held them away from her body to prevent her clothing from getting wet. "I need to box these up and get them out of here. Maybe I can save them." She really wasn't sure if that was possible.

"Good idea." Evan pinched his chin between his forefinger and thumb. "I'll get my daughter to help. Maybe Mallory will be willing to stop by if she's not working at the hospital."

"Mallory?"

Evan looked at Savannah. "I'm guessing you've lost touch with her too."

Savannah shrugged. There wasn't a particular reason she'd lost touch. Childhood best friends just drifted apart sometimes. Savannah didn't spend her summers in Bloom anymore, and this was Mallory's home. After Savannah had gone away at nineteen, they'd kept in touch by email for a while, and they'd sent a text here and there. Eventually, the communication had become less and less frequent, and they'd both gone on with their busy lives. "It'll be great to see her again while I'm here."

"I'm sure." Evan faced forward. "But first, we need to break the news to Eleanor. She's waiting for us inside."

Savannah grimaced. "Good luck with that."

"Me?" Evan chuckled dryly. "Why me?"

"Because I'm apparently a crappy niece and friend. I might as well go with this reputation that I've formed in the last few years."

Evan gave her a long, assessing look, his gaze lifting to her hat that she never went outside without. "It's good to have you home, Sav."

Bloom wasn't her home but it had always felt more like home than Burgersville, where she'd spent the rest of the time growing up. Evan was part of what made it feel like home here. Mallory too. At one time, the three had been inseparable, riding their bikes through the streets while chasing the ice cream truck and swinging off ropes to drop into the local swimming hole.

"It's good to be home." She exhaled with a heavy sigh. "Best to get this over with sooner rather than later."

"Yeah." He turned and stepped out of the library and then waited for Savannah to catch up.

Eleanor was sitting at the dining room table when they walked through the back door, a book open in front of her. She looked up, wrinkling her brow as her gaze jumped between them. "How bad is it?" she finally asked.

"Um, well…" Savannah shifted back and forth on her feet. She looked to Evan for assistance.

"Nothing we can't fix with a little time and some help. A lot of help."

"Time?" Eleanor's voice was shaky and threadbare. "The wedding is in three weeks. How much time?"

Evan shoved his hands in his pockets. "I really can't say. Hopefully just a couple weeks. We'll clean up the garden, and I'll make some calls for the roof."

"Three weeks is plenty of time," Savannah said, even though she really had no idea how long the repairs would take. Working outside was not ideal for her right now. Her first big lupus flare was only a few months behind her. Her rheumatologist had advised her to stay out of the sun as much as possible and to listen to her body. Those limitations were exactly what had run her ex-fiancé off, however.

"Are the books damaged?" Eleanor asked.

"Just a few," Savannah said.

Eleanor pressed a hand to her chest, looking pained as if they'd told her someone had died.

"I'm sure we can dry them out though," Savannah added.

Eleanor's brows lifted high on her forehead. "We? I thought your visit was short-lived. Aren't you going to see your parents this summer?"

Savannah could feel Evan watching her too, probably ready to jump right back into thinking she was shirking her familial duties. Eleanor needed her. The garden needed her. And maybe she needed Eleanor and the garden too. "There's no rush. I can stay, Aunt Eleanor. My new job doesn't start until September fifteenth anyway."

"New job?" Eleanor looked delighted.

Savannah hadn't accepted the position yet but she really didn't have other options on her horizon. Not yet at least. There were a few more potential employers that she was waiting to hear back from—one in particular that she'd love to accept if they came back with an offer. Otherwise, like it or not, she'd be moving to South Carolina next month.

"Well, that is a bright side to this mess. If this storm and its damage means you'll be spending another Bloom summer with me, then I can't complain, now can I? As long as everything's ready for Madison's wedding."

Savannah blinked. "Madison? Madison Blue? Mallory's sister?"

Eleanor's eyes sparkled with excitement. "Yes. Isn't it wonderful?"

She was happy for Madison, and Savannah was truly glad she'd found out that her fiancé was wrong for her before they'd said "I do." But she still struggled not to feel hurt.

"Yes, it is wonderful." Savannah tried to muster a smile. Then she caught Evan staring, as if he could see right through her.

Later that afternoon, Savannah had filled one box with damaged books and was working on filling a second. The books needed to go inside to dry out and hopefully be salvaged.

The door to the library opened, and Evan peeked his head inside. "Hey, have you seen my daughter, June?"

Savannah looked up from the box of books. "Nope. I've been in here for the last half hour."

Evan wiped sweat from his brow. His T-shirt was soaked through as well, sticking to his body and revealing a chiseled waistline.

Savannah pulled her gaze from him, working hard to ignore the little jump in her pulse. She and Randall had dated for years, and she hadn't felt that jump for at least the last two of their relationship.

"Lately, she's always running off," Evan said. "I wish I knew how to reach her."

Savannah had so many questions, like where was the girl's mom? Why was Evan struggling with his father-daughter relationship? She didn't ask because she didn't want to pry.

"I know kids. I work with kids for a living, and for the most part, I understand them," he said. "I felt like I understood June too, right up until she moved down here last month. Now we're butting heads at every turn."

"That sounds painful." Savannah wasn't sure what else to say. She couldn't relate to having a child but she and her ex had been the same way during their last months of the relationship, mostly after she'd started getting sick. Nothing she could say or do had been right in Randall's eyes.

"Everyone says to give her space and time. That's what I'm doing. I just need to know that she's okay."

Savannah was struck by the emotion in Evan's face and voice. He was obviously a good father. She wasn't surprised, because he'd always been a gentle and caring friend.

"Sorry to unload on you."

"No, it's okay. It's fine." Savannah hesitated. "Where is her mother?"

Evan's expression told her before he had a chance to answer. "She died earlier this year. Cancer."

"Oh. I'm so sorry." Savannah covered her mouth with one hand.

"Me too. No child should have to grow up without their mom."

Evan had grown up without his mother though. Savannah was sure it was painful for him to know his own daughter would have the same fate. She just wanted to stand up and give him a hug right now. Instead, they stared at one another for a long moment. Then Fig jumped out of the shadows and pounced on Evan's work boots. "Whoa," he said, apparently startled. "Who is this vicious creature?"

Savannah laughed. "That's Fig, short for Figaro."

Evan glanced up, one eyebrow subtly rising. "You hated that puppet."

"Aunt Eleanor remembers it differently. I think it was a love-hate relationship. I never liked liars but Pinocchio redeemed himself. I always did like a happy ending." Even though she was beginning to think those were as ludicrous as a wooden puppet who turned into a real, live boy. "Any luck on finding someone to help with the storm damage?"

Evan sighed. "Everyone I've called is booked up through the end of summer, especially after last night. I'm not done making calls yet though. I'm going to keep looking—just as soon as I locate that daughter of mine."

"I'll tell you if I see June. Or, if I see her, I'll tell her that you're looking for her," Savannah promised.

"Thanks. See you, Fig." Evan looked down at the kitten and then back up at her.

There went her pulse racing again, like a wild horse chasing the wind.

"See you, Sav."

"Bye."

She blew out a pent-up breath once he was gone. "No, Savannah. This is not the time for heart flutters or romance." She reached for another book and loaded it into the box. Most of the books in this corner were beyond repair but she still planned to do her best to salvage them.

The door to the library opened again and Savannah braced herself to see Evan a second time.

"Savannah Grace Collins, why did I have to hear from Evan Sanders, of all people, that you're home?" Mallory Blue stepped into the tiny library and placed her hands on her curvy hips. Her hair was just as dark and long as ever but the fringed bangs that hung in front of her blue eyes were different.

Savannah hopped to her feet and immediately went to hug her old friend. "Mallory! I've missed you so much."

Mallory laughed as she pulled back. "I wouldn't know it, because you never come around. I didn't even get an invitation to this wedding of yours."

Savannah grimaced. "It was a short list of invitees. We were trying to keep the costs low because Randall was starting his own golf-pro business. *Is* starting his own golf-pro business." Savannah looked down. "Anyway, the wedding is off, as I'm sure you've heard."

Mallory poked a finger into Savannah's shoulder, gaining her attention. "His loss. And I'm just teasing you. No hard feelings about the no-invite thing. It's been years. Friendship is like riding a bike; just hop back on and it's like you never fell off."

"Is that so?" Savannah appreciated Mallory's relaxed nature. She could have given Savannah grief the way Evan had last night.

Mallory looked at the caved-in corner of the library, and her smile dropped. "What a disaster. How is Eleanor holding up?"

"Well, Aunt Eleanor hasn't seen this mess yet. There's too much on the ground for her to walk around right now. Not with her recent injuries. She's just trusting me and Evan to take care of it."

"You and half the town, it looks like. I don't mind helping either. That's why I'm here." Mallory looked at her smartwatch. "I have about thirty minutes until I need to leave for my shift at the hospital. I know it's not long but use me while you have me."

"Consider yourself used," Savannah said. "Sit and pack books with me."

"Bossy pants." Mallory plopped onto the floor in front of Savannah. As soon as she did, Fig launched herself onto Mallory's lap. Mallory stiffened and eyed the kitten as if it were a snake about to strike. "Sorry, little beast. I'm allergic." She shooed the cat away.

"That beast happens to be my new life partner."

Mallory narrowed her blue eyes. "I need that story over drinks. How long are you staying in town for?"

"I told Aunt Eleanor I'd stay long enough to fix up the garden for Madison's wedding."

Mallory's eyes lit up. "Can you believe that? My little sister is getting hitched before me."

"Actually, I can believe that," Savannah said, teasing her. "I never knew you to like a guy longer than one summer."

"Nothing has changed there. Ever since Madison got engaged, Grandpa Charlie has been telling me that it's my turn now. He keeps threatening to play matchmaker."

"Maybe you should let him," Savannah suggested.

Mallory gave her shoulder a gentle shove. "I am happily single, thank you very much."

Having been pushed away, Fig climbed the ladder that led to the library's loft.

"So how was it seeing Evan again?" Mallory finally asked.

Savannah felt her cheeks grow hot. Mallory was the only one she'd ever told about that one kiss with Evan when she was nineteen, the last summer she was here. "Oh, it was…" Savannah noticed movement in the loft and then Fig pounced on whatever was up there. Or whoever. Strawberry blonde hair snaked over the hole in the ceiling.

Savannah guessed this was the daughter that Evan was looking for.

"Hello?" Mallory waved a hand in front of Savannah, gaining her attention again.

"Oh, um, well, it was okay, I guess. He's kind of holding a grudge against me for not coming to visit Aunt Eleanor more often. I honestly didn't know about her accident though."

"I guess in hindsight, I should have called you," Mallory said. "I just assumed you knew." She seemed to think for a moment. "Actually, I'm not sure I have your contact information anymore."

"Really?" You knew you'd drifted apart when your childhood best friend didn't even have your phone number. "I don't think I have yours programmed into my phone either."

Mallory made a *gimme* motion, curling her fingers toward her palm. "Here. Hand me your phone and I'll fix that."

Savannah unlocked her phone and placed it in Mallory's hand, watching as she expertly maneuvered to the contacts app and entered her digits.

"There you go," she said, handing it back with a wide smile. "Now you have no excuse not to call me." Mallory tossed a book into the box and stood. "Well, I need to get going. I'll carry this box to the house as I go. Would that help?"

"That'd be great. Thank you. And it's good to see you, Mal."

Mallory lifted the box in her arms, hugging it against her midsection. "Girls' night. Next week. We have so many things to catch up on."

Savannah really didn't want to rehash her recent years, but she'd love to hear how Mallory was doing. "Sounds good. I'll call you," she said, waiting until Mallory left before looking up at the loft again. Should she let June know that she saw her hiding up there? Or should she just ignore the girl? "Your dad's looking for you, you know," Savannah finally called up. "But you already know that, don't you?" The girl had been here when Evan had come in looking for her.

Silence answered.

"He cares about you."

More silence.

"Okay, fine. I'll just keeping packing these books. But I know you're up there."

The girl finally poked her head into the loft's opening. "My dad's mad at you?" June asked.

Savannah shrugged. "It was a misunderstanding. What about you? Why are you avoiding your dad?"

"It's complicated." The girl rolled onto her back, letting her hair fall over the top rung of the ladder. "He's trying too hard. Ever since my mom died, he's been acting like the dad he never was. He used to be the fun dad and now he's...I don't know.

He's different. Everything's different. I just want my life to go back to normal. Does that make sense?"

"Totally." Savannah knew that being diagnosed with a chronic illness and left by her fiancé didn't compare to losing a parent. "I'm Savannah, by the way."

The girl rolled over again. "June. Are you going to rat me out and tell my dad everything I just said? Because if you do, I'll tell him you have a crush on him."

Savannah's mouth fell open. "I never said that."

June grinned. "Didn't have to. I heard you talking to Ms. Mallory and read between the lines. I've also read most of the YA romance in this library. I'm well-versed in the slow burn."

Savannah let out a shocked laugh. "Summer reading lists from Eleanor?" she asked.

June nodded. "I come to stay with my dad every June. Then I return home by August. Not this year though." She sighed as she sat up.

"June?" Evan called from somewhere in the distance.

June's gaze met Savannah's.

"If you don't want me to tell him about your hiding place, I suggest you go out there and make your presence known."

The girl scowled. Then she turned and slowly descended the ladder. Fig followed suit.

Savannah gestured at the book in June's hand. "Books are exactly how I dealt with things when I was your age too."

June looked at the book and back up. "Ms. Eleanor let me borrow it. My dad says she used to make him read a ton too."

"Your dad was a good friend when I was your age. Books, your dad, and Mallory were my lifesavers during those long summers I spent here. Your dad is pretty good for a laugh too, you know."

June scoffed and looked down at her feet. "Whatever. Of course you're on his side."

"I'm not. I don't even know why there's a side to pick. But if you ever want a friend to talk to…"

June looked almost horrified by the suggestion. "You?"

Savannah tried not to take the girl's reaction personally. "I know, I'm old, and I have a humongous hat."

This made June smile.

"But it's me or the roses," Savannah said, "and I'm pretty sure the roses don't talk back."

June gave her a strange look. Then her shoulders relaxed a tiny bit. "Maybe you're cool. Just not the hat."

Savannah hated to break it to the girl but the hat was staying. Better that than blisters and a sunburn.

"June!" Evan called again.

"I gotta go." June looked at Savannah. "Whatever you heard me say a few minutes ago, just forget it, okay?"

Savannah didn't think she could if she wanted to. She nodded anyway. Then without a wave or goodbye, June hurried off.

Savannah listened to Evan continue calling for his daughter for a moment longer. Then his calling stopped.

Fig hopped into Savannah's lap and climbed up her chest to look into her eyes as he meowed loudly. "Hungry?" Savannah asked.

Meow.

"I'll take that as a yes." Holding the kitten against her, she stood and headed out of the library toward Aunt Eleanor's house. It was amazing that one little storm could cause so much damage. Savannah had no doubt that it would all be fixed in the end. She liked to think she was an optimist but she wasn't convinced all the repairs could happen before the wedding.

A line from a book floated into her mind, which hadn't happened in years. Books were a way of life during her Bloom summers. She was nineteen when she'd read *The Silver Linings Playbook*, sitting under that rose arbor and looking up at the sky after reading a paragraph.

If clouds are blocking the sun, there will always be a silver lining that reminds me to keep on trying.

Savannah looked up now, hoping to see a silver lining to serve as a sign of some sort. Instead, the sky looked gray and promised more rain in the coming hours. Considering there was a huge hole in the library's roof right now, that didn't bode well for the library or Eleanor's beloved books.

Chapter Four

Eleanor

Real isn't how you are made...it's a thing that happens to you.

The Velveteen Rabbit, Margery Williams

Eleanor could hear the familiar sound of Charlie Blue's car in the driveway. That Oldsmobile of his was one of his prized possessions, and he kept it in pristine condition. The motor hummed differently than any other vehicle she'd ever known, and Charlie visited often enough that she knew the sound as soon as he turned into her driveway. Consequently, her heartbeat picked up its pace.

He was a friend, although the kind that pushed the boundaries just enough to sometimes make her think about more.

There was a soft knock on the door before Charlie pushed it open and peeked his head inside. "Ellie?"

"I'm right here," Eleanor answered from her reading chair in the sitting room. "Come on in, Charlie."

Charlie stepped inside and held out a bouquet of flowers like he did a couple times a month.

"For me?" Eleanor asked, knowing the answer already. She shifted forward in the chair and then stood to take the flowers from his hand. "Thank you, Charlie. I'll put these in a vase. Care for a cup of tea?" she called behind her, hearing him follow her into the kitchen.

"Not today, Ellie. I'll sit with you while you drink yours though." Charlie had a seat at her breakfast table. "I'm so sorry about the garden, Ellie. Whatever you need, just ask."

Eleanor bypassed the kettle and reached for the crystal vase on top of the fridge. "I appreciate that. I don't know the extent of the damage. I haven't walked out there to see it for myself."

"And you don't need to. The last thing you need is another fall. Unless that fall is you falling for me."

He made it sound like a joke and he didn't make eye contact when he said it. Was he being serious?

"I've spoken to Evan, and I know he's already making calls to get your garden and library back in tip-top shape," Charlie continued.

"I've already had several people in town reach out this morning, asking if they could help," Eleanor said.

"Well, the town loves you. You know that. I want you to know that if you need me to find another place for Madison's wedding, I understand," Charlie said. "Don't hesitate to ask."

Eleanor whipped around to look at him, the quick movement momentarily putting her off balance. "Nonsense. I want nothing more than to host your granddaughter's wedding. It's going to be here, no matter what. This is a big deal for me, you know." Eleanor really wanted to see Madison get married. She'd known the Blue sisters since they were newborns. They were important to her. Due to recent hardships, Madison needed a free venue, and Eleanor wasn't sure she'd be able to attend the wedding if it were held somewhere else. Since her fall last winter, Eleanor didn't feel comfortable leaving her property. "We'll have the wedding here, and I won't hear another word about it. Savannah is staying just so she can help."

Charlie pressed the tips of his fingers together. "I'm sure you're happy about that. What about your library?"

Eleanor placed the wildflowers in the vase and fanned them out. Then she carried the arrangement to the table where Charlie was sitting and pulled out a chair to sit as well. "Fifty-five books were ruined." Her eyes burned. Every time she thought about the loss, she wanted to break down in tears. She'd loved every single book in that building. They were all a piece of her somehow.

Charlie placed his hand over hers. "We'll replace them, Ellie."

The feel of his skin against hers made her breath hitch. A woman in her seventies had no business entertaining such an intense attraction but she couldn't deny that's what she felt. It was a simple crush, that was all. One that she intended to ignore. "We?"

"I've already spoken to the Books and Blooms members," Charlie told her. "We're going to take up a collection at the farmers market next weekend."

The Books and Blooms Club had been inspired by Eleanor

and Aaron's marriage. Eleanor had always loved books, and Aaron loved gardening. For years, they'd been in their own clubs, separate from one another, but many of the members had spouses in the opposite club. It just made sense to merge the two clubs and enjoy the best of both worlds.

"As much as you've done for this town," Charlie continued, "I imagine you'll have more books than you can fit in that library of yours. We'll have to build a bigger building."

Eleanor laughed quietly. "That's so nice of everyone. Thank you, Charlie."

"You know I'd do anything for you."

She looked away, willing her heartbeat to slow down. "Thank the club for me as well."

"You can thank them yourself in person this week. I can pick you up and drive you to the meeting."

The club gathered every other week, alternating whose house they met in. Since her fall, Eleanor had been attending via Zoom except for the weeks that her house was the meeting location.

"I think I'll stay here, Charlie. I'm just fine seeing everyone through my laptop screen."

"We miss you, Ellie. It's not the same without you there sitting beside me."

The thought of leaving home made Eleanor's heart race for an entirely different reason. "Charlie, I … I just … I'm not ready to go anywhere just yet." She saw the worry flicker in his pale blue eyes. He'd been doing his best to lure her out. Every time she turned him down, she realized more and more that her resistance to leaving her property was becoming an issue. This house and her yard were becoming a prison of sorts. One she couldn't escape.

"Maybe it would be less scary leaving your home if you were with me," Charlie suggested.

Eleanor wasn't sure where to start with that statement. "Who said I was scared?"

"You took a fall and hurt yourself last year. It's only natural to worry that something like that might happen again. I got into a car accident with my truck a few years ago, and for the next year and a half, I was scared to drive. I still get rattled behind the wheel if I think about it too much."

Eleanor didn't like to be accused of being afraid. "You never told me that story."

Charlie lifted a shoulder. "I never wanted you to see me as a coward. I wanted you to think I was tough. And incredibly handsome."

This made Eleanor smile. Lately, he'd been more and more obvious about his feelings for her. She wasn't sure what to think about that. But if she didn't think too hard, she liked the interaction between them. "I would never think such a thing about you. The coward part, I mean."

His eyes twinkled. "Ah. But you would think the handsome part."

"You're impossible, Charlie Blue."

"It doesn't need to be for the Books and Blooms meetings. I could take you anywhere you want. I could take you to your favorite restaurant."

"I don't have one," she said.

"Then I could take you to all the restaurants in town until you figure out which one is your favorite."

She watched him for a moment. "That's sweet of you."

"I've been called worse."

A laugh bubbled off her lips. It seemed to be a habit when she was with him.

"Just think about it."

She shook her head. "There's not much else to do, is there? Other than read or worry."

"You have nothing to worry about, Ellie. As you already said, Savannah and Evan are working on your garden and the library. Everything will be fine," Charlie said. "Trust me."

She wanted to trust him. If she were honest, she wanted to go on a date with him too. "Who knows, maybe this whole storm ruining my backyard will be the impetus to finally bring Savannah and Evan together."

Charlie palmed his face before looking at her again. "I should have expected that from you." He looked at Eleanor meaningfully. "If two people are meant to be together, they will be."

Eleanor wondered if he was still talking about Savannah and Evan or about someone else—like him and her. "Not always. Look at Romeo and Juliet," Eleanor countered. "They couldn't be together. Too many obstacles."

"I always hated that story," Charlie said with a sour look on his face. "If I'm going to read a love story, the two lovers best be together by the end. Together and not dead."

"Speaking of love stories, did you read the last one I loaned you?"

"I did. I found *The Time Traveler's Wife* to be..."

Eleanor watched him search for words. She was amused, because she was pretty sure he hadn't enjoyed the book, and she hadn't expected him to. "It wasn't your cup of tea?" she asked.

Charlie exhaled and shook his head. "I did read it cover to cover though. Because you asked me to."

Charlie didn't used to be a reader but Eleanor had fixed that. She'd refused to accept his flowers unless he accepted a book to read in return. What surprised her most was that he actually read them and wanted to discuss them afterward. It was just another of the many things she liked about Charlie Blue.

Liked, not loved. She'd loved Aaron. Still loved him to this day. That's why she and Charlie must remain strictly friends. The best kind.

"You didn't cheat by watching the movie instead, did you?" she teased.

"No, but I thought, to reward my efforts, perhaps we might watch the movie together one night." He didn't wait for Eleanor to answer. "Just think about it." Charlie stood. "I need to get started on collecting books for you."

"Books are the way to my heart," Eleanor joked, perhaps not thinking before she spoke.

"I'm hoping that's true." He winked and headed toward the door. "Talk to you later, Ellie."

Eleanor felt flustered on top of all the other emotions she was feeling about the storm and its damage.

Figaro hopped down from her lap and looked at her expectantly with large green eyes.

"Are you hungry?" she asked, eager for a distraction from all her thoughts and worries. She wasn't able to help Savannah or Evan outside but she could help this little kitten. Shifting and scooting to the edge of her chair, she leaned forward and rocked her weight onto her feet. Her hips were still stiff and sore from last year's fall.

Steady on her feet, she started toward the kitchen to get a

can of cat food. Figaro ran ahead of her, glancing back to make sure that Eleanor was coming.

Eleanor laughed with amusement. Then, in the blink of an eye, one foot slipped out in front of her, and her body was falling in slow motion—just like it had that day last winter.

No, no, no. Not again.

Chapter Five

Evan

*It's no use going back to yesterday, because I was
a different person then.*

Alice's Adventures in Wonderland,
Lewis Carroll

Evan had no idea what he was doing. He was great at teaching
English literature to his students, and he could carve a wooden
bowl or spoon masterfully. Fixing a roof though? Yeah, this
wasn't in his wheelhouse.

A dog barked a few feet away, grabbing Evan's attention. He
tugged his ball cap lower on his head to shield his eyes as he
noticed the pet's owner approaching. "Hollis Franklin. Is that
you?"

"The one and only." Even at a distance, Hollis was hard to
mistake. He was an intimidating, burly man until you got up
close and saw his gentle eyes and smile.

Evan laid his hammer down to take a small break. "When did you get back in town?"

"Late last night."

Hollis had been one of Evan's closest friends since childhood. He'd left town at the beginning of last month to visit his out-of-state grandmother.

"How's your grandma?"

"Sweet and sassy as ever." Hollis continued walking in his direction. His chocolate-colored lab turned and sprinted back to escort its owner toward the library. "Your little girl told me I could find you back here."

"That little girl of mine wasn't supposed to answer the door for anyone."

Hollis held out his hands. "I'm not just anyone though. I'm Uncle Hollis."

Hollis wasn't a blood relative, of course, but Evan's family had never done godparents. Instead, they chose honorary aunts and uncles. Although vastly different in age from Hollis, Eleanor was June's honorary aunt. "Well, Uncle Hollis, your niece is a lot more work than I bargained for this summer." Evan lowered himself down the ladder propped against the side of the library. "She's spent half the summer trying to convince me to send her back to California."

Hollis grunted. "Why on earth would she do that?"

"Because Bloom is a town stuck in time and none of her friends are here. Or her grandmother."

"Ah, she'll come around," Hollis said. "She's always enjoyed being here."

"For short durations," Evan retorted. As soon as his feet hit the ground, he was greeted by Hollis's lab as it propped itself up on Evan's thighs, tail wagging. Evan patted her head and then took another swig from his water bottle. Then he gestured at the library. "As you can see, I'm out of my element in all aspects of my life right now."

"You're fixing the library's roof?" Hollis looked beyond Evan to the gaping hole that the fallen tree had left behind. Then he looked at Evan again. "Why on earth are you doing it? As far as I know, you've never even been on a roof before."

Evan blew out a breath. "I've called around. Everyone I've called is busy until next month. Apparently, there were several roofs damaged with the storm."

"Okay. Put a tarp over the hole and wait it out," Hollis suggested.

Evan wished it were that easy. "Madison's wedding is in two and a half weeks. Eleanor wants everything perfect, and Maddie deserves perfect."

Hollis's eyes seemed to agree. "She's been through the ringer, that's for sure." He looked at the damaged roof again. "I can help you."

Evan hadn't even considered that option. Hollis had been out of state visiting his grandmother, and Evan hadn't known when his friend was coming back. "Really?"

"I can ask a few of the guys I work with to pitch in too." Hollis looked at the roof again, walking around to get a better assessment of the damage. "We'll need to cut out the damaged wood and replace it with new wood. Since it's a tin roof, we'll have to tear off the dented portions and lay down new sheets. The supplies will be pricey. Then there's the cost of labor. I'll work for free, of course, but I can't ask the others to."

Evan nodded. "I appreciate it. That'd be great. Thank you."

"And by free, I mean to say that I'll work for food." Hollis patted his stomach. "Assuming June is the one doing the cooking."

Evan grinned. "June might give me a hand behind the stove. I know she would love to see more of her Uncle Hollis."

"Give me a day to get my guys on board."

Evan was so relieved. A day was much better than the month that all the others he'd called had quoted him. "Text me and tell me all the supplies you need. I'll go to the hardware store tomorrow and get everything."

"Perfect. We'll aim for Friday," Hollis said. "I'll help out here and then stay for dinner. What are the odds that Ms. Eleanor will be so thankful that she'll make the meal? Ms. Eleanor's cooking is about as good as my grandma's."

"The odds are pretty good." Evan wasn't sure he wanted to divulge the next piece of information but Hollis would hear about it eventually. "You'll never guess who's back in town," he said.

Hollis raised a thick brow. "Who?"

"Savannah Collins."

Hollis's eyes widened as a full grin formed on his lips. "*The* Savannah Collins?"

"As far as I know, there's only one."

"At least according to you. You had a huge crush on that girl every summer when we were growing up," Hollis said.

"And you had a thing for Mallory Blue."

Hollis grunted. "Yeah, well, we've both matured, haven't we?" He narrowed his eyes, still grinning. "Or maybe we haven't. You and Savannah hanging out?"

"Not exactly."

Hollis offered a low laugh. His dog barked playfully, taking interest in whatever its owner was enjoying. "So, this summer is going to be just like the ones when we were growing up." He rubbed his hands together. "Glad I came back for this."

"Don't get too excited. Nothing's going to happen between us."

Hollis ran his fingers over his neatly trimmed beard. "Famous last words, buddy. Famous last words."

Evan and Hollis chatted for a few minutes longer. Then Hollis hitched a thumb behind him.

"I have to get going. See you Friday. Will work for food."

Evan watched his friend head back down the garden path with his lab playfully running ahead. Then Evan pulled out his phone to check the time. He hadn't heard it ring but he'd missed a call from June's grandmother. Margie hadn't left a voicemail—but she never did. She just expected Evan to see her missed call and dial back immediately.

Deciding to get the call over with instead of letting it hang over his head, he tapped her contact.

Margie answered after two rings. "There you are. I was wondering when you were going to call me back."

It had only been twenty minutes since she'd tried to reach him.

"Hey, Margie. How are you?"

"Quite frankly, I'm concerned."

Evan braced himself. "Oh? Why is that?"

"Because your daughter woke up alone in the house this morning. She texted me when she couldn't find you."

"I was right next door doing some work for my neighbor," Evan explained. "I left June a note on the kitchen counter letting her know."

"Well, she must not have seen it. She was scared. A girl who just lost her mother doesn't need to feel abandoned."

Evan reminded himself that Margie was grieving her daughter. "I assure you that June doesn't feel that way. She has a large support system in Bloom. And after she called you, she called me, and I told her exactly where I was."

"So you answered your phone for her?" Margie asked, needling him. "Or did you make her wait twenty minutes like you did me?"

Evan massaged his forehead. "Everything here is fine, Margie. You would be the first one I'd call if it weren't."

"I would hope that's true. I'm June's grandmother. My daughter died six months ago, and I owe it to Juliana to make sure June is not only surviving but thriving. I promised her that I would look after her, and I intend to do so."

Evan was still gaining traction with his daughter. The last thing he needed was for Margie to attempt to sway June's opinion and feelings even more. He couldn't very well cut Margie out from June's life, and he would never want to. She was her grandmother, and Evan was grateful for everything Margie had done for his family. He just wished that Margie could see that constantly calling June and subtly disparaging him and the town of Bloom wasn't helping June's emotional or mental state right now.

"Evan, I always respected you. You never fought Juliana for custody rights. You knew what was best, and you did it. For your daughter. I always admired that," Margie said.

Evan could read between the lines of what Margie was insinuating. "I'm still doing what's best, Margie. I think Juliana would agree." In fact, he knew Juliana would agree. Before she died, Juliana had told Evan that she wanted June to live with him once she was gone. June should be with her father, and Juliana knew that he would raise their daughter well. Evan wasn't sure if Margie knew that though.

"Evan, I don't like secrets. I believe in being open and honest about things."

Evan wasn't sure where Margie was going with this conversation. "I feel the same way."

"Good. So I want you to know that I'm keeping a close eye on June's new living arrangement."

Evan wasn't sure how that was even possible from California.

"Give me any reason to think my granddaughter is suffering in any way, and I won't hesitate to contact my lawyer."

"Lawyer?" Evan asked, feeling like the wind had been knocked out of him.

"I have June's best interests in mind. I want what's best for her," Margie said.

Evan wasn't sure whether to laugh or start yelling. "So do I, Margie. Living with me is what's best."

"I just wanted to give you notice."

Should he be appreciative that she warned him? Instead, he felt blindsided and insulted. He didn't even have a lawyer. If Margie decided to act on her threat, he'd have to hire one.

"That's all, Evan. Please make sure June knows where you are from now on."

The line went dead before Evan had a chance to respond. He slid his phone into his pocket and released a slow, pent-up breath. He did his best to keep things with Margie cordial but she'd just threatened to take his daughter away from him. He wasn't sure how long he could play nice with that threat hanging over him.

Wiping the perspiration off his brow, he started walking toward his house. He needed to check on June. He was starving, and he guessed she probably was as well.

"Dad! Dad! Help!"

Evan's blood ran cold at the sound of June's scream. He'd never heard her sound so frightened. He took off running, tracking the cries for help. They were coming from Eleanor's house.

He ran as hard as he could down the garden path, practically tripping on a cracked stepping stone. He took the steps of the back deck two at a time and burst through the back door. "June? June, where are you?"

"Dad! Come quick! It's Eleanor!" she called again.

He raced through the kitchen and into the hallway where Eleanor was lying flat on her back with June hunched over her. June's face was covered in tears, and her breaths sounded quick and shallow, like she was about to hyperventilate.

Savannah burst through the front door at the same time that Evan knelt on the floor beside Eleanor, trying to assess the situation. "Aunt Eleanor!" Savannah called out, dropping her things and kneeling on the floor at Eleanor's head.

Eleanor's eyes were open, flicking between all three people gathered around her. She had a grimace on her lips, and Evan could tell she was in pain.

"Where are you hurt?" he asked.

"Mostly my pride," she said with a wince as she tried to move.

"I thought she was dead," June cried, wiping at her eyes. "I walked in and saw her on the floor and…" She sucked in a shuddery breath.

Eleanor reached for her hand. "I'm not dead, dear. Far from it. I'm so sorry that I scared you."

"We should call an ambulance," Savannah said, looking pale and worried.

"You will do no such thing," Eleanor snapped, her grimace turning into a stubborn frown. She tried to move and groaned. "I bruised my hip when I fell. I slipped on something."

"I agree with Savannah. It would be good to have a doctor check you out," Evan said.

"No. I'm not going anywhere. I'm staying right here in my own home, and I won't hear another word about it." With great effort, Eleanor shifted to her side and used her arms to bring herself to a sitting position.

"Why not?" Savannah asked. "Why are you scared to go to the hospital?"

Eleanor looked insulted. "I am not scared; of course I'm not." She looked at Evan. "Would you mind helping me stand? I'm afraid I do need a bit of help with that. I'll need an ice pack as well. And a cup of tea." She looked at June. Evan could tell she was putting on a smile to ease June's worries. "If you ask me, a cup of tea and a good book are the best kind of medicine."

After getting Eleanor settled in her reading chair with an ice pack and a cup of tea, Evan returned home to make the lunch he'd intended on making a couple hours before.

"You hungry?" he asked June, who was sitting at the kitchen table with a book in front of her. It was *Anne of Avonlea*, the second book in the Anne of Green Gables series. He'd never read that one personally. If he recalled, he'd begged his way out of it the summer it had landed on his reading list from Eleanor.

"Not really," June said. She still seemed visibly shaken after finding Eleanor on the floor.

Pulling out a chair in front of her, Evan sat down. "Want to talk about it?"

June shook her head, but she closed her book and looked at him. "What if she had been dead?"

Evan taught English literature. He'd never had to talk about death with his students. He felt ill-prepared. He'd lost his share of loved ones though. "It's part of life. I'm glad Eleanor is okay but there will come a day when she might not be."

"Like Mom. Except Mom didn't get to live as long as Eleanor." Tears sprang to June's eyes. "How is that fair?"

"It's not," Evan said simply, wishing he had something better to say. "Death definitely doesn't play fair." He'd felt so angry after his own mom had died. Even after his dad died last year. Not angry at them but angry at whatever force had snatched them from him.

"What if Grandma Margie dies? What if you die?" June asked.

Evan was surprised by the questions. Were these the fears running through his daughter's mind this summer? "I want to promise you that won't happen, but I can't. I never want to lie to you, June. All I know is that death is part of life and what-ever happens and when, we'll get through it. You have so many people who love you and who will help you get through all the things that come."

June pressed her lips together, visibly working hard not to cry.

"It's okay to be sad, or angry, or confused. It's okay to cry too."

June sniffled and shook her head. "No. Mom told me not to cry. When she was sick and I was by her bed, she told me not to cry. So I don't want to."

Evan reached for June's hand. "I wasn't there so I don't know her reasons. I think she just didn't want to see you sad. A parent never wants to see their child upset but that's also part of life." He squeezed her hand. "It's okay to cry, June."

A tear slipped down her cheek. She sniffled again. "Why didn't Ms. Eleanor want to go to the hospital? She needed to see a doctor."

Evan furrowed his brow. He'd been able to navigate the preceding questions but this one stumped him just as much as it did his daughter. "I honestly don't know."

"Maybe she's scared of doctors. Or shots or something," June offered.

Evan nodded, even though he didn't think that was the case. He thought maybe Eleanor was afraid for a different reason. "I'm just glad she's okay."

"Me too." June's eyes were dry again, her tears receding. "I guess I am a little hungry. You should know though that if I'm going to be here, I need more than just cereal and milk. You need to go grocery shopping, Dad."

Evan slid back from the table and stood. "Sorry about that. I'll do better." He'd do just about anything to help June get settled in Bloom. "So, Cheerios or Lucky Charms? What'll it be?"

"Mom used to mix them. Our pantry was bare sometimes too. No one's perfect."

Evan's own eyes blurred with tears. He cleared his throat and walked to the pantry. "A mix of Cheerios and Lucky Charms it is. We'll call it Lucky Cheerios."

"I like it," June said, smiling just enough to make him feel like a lucky dad.

Chapter Six

Eleanor

*Because for some of us, books are as important as
almost anything else on earth.*

Anne Lamott, American novelist

Eleanor balanced her laptop on her thighs, suppressing a
small groan when her hip began to throb at the sudden movement. She smiled at her screen. "Hello, everyone!" she said
cheerfully.

The members of her Books and Blooms Club were all seated
together at Jessie's home this week.

Eleanor had the blackest thumb there ever was but she still
enjoyed listening to discussions about the best time to plant
your dahlia seeds. And she never passed up an opportunity to
discuss a book, even if she'd hated it. Sometimes those were the
best discussions.

"Are you still there, Ellie?" Charlie lowered a pair of reading glasses on his nose and leaned into the screen. He was neither a reader nor a gardener. Eleanor guessed he had originally joined the club because of the yard art he made, which sometimes landed itself in someone's garden. Or he was here for the company. More likely that.

Charlie was a social guy. Everyone loved him. Until his death, Aaron had also loved Charlie. He used to jokingly tell Eleanor that he was glad she'd met him first, because otherwise Charlie might have stolen her heart.

It was a silly thing to say, of course. Eleanor had always been madly in love with Aaron. They were soulmates. She did think the world of Charlie too though.

"I'm here. Is my screen frozen again?" Eleanor adjusted the ice pack wedged between her hip and the armrest of the chair. What happened yesterday was just further proof that she wasn't ready to leave home for things like these Books and Blooms Club meetings. "I've never been tech savvy."

"You could always just join us in person." Ruby Evers drew out the syllables of her words almost in a lyrical manner.

Eleanor suppressed another groan, because this wasn't the first time the group had suggested it. "Zoom is fine."

"Eleanor, you're missing out on these lemon tarts that Dill's wife made," Danida commented. She was sitting next to Charlie on the couch, which ruffled Eleanor's feathers just a little bit. Danida was always flirting with him. Charlie swore her feelings weren't reciprocated but Eleanor wasn't sure why not. Danida was a pretty woman. She didn't have a single gray hair, and she only had half the wrinkles Eleanor had.

Eleanor smiled into her laptop's camera. "Oh, I've had Ruth's tarts before. They're delicious." She raised a finger in the air, as she often did when summoning a quote from one of the thousands stored in the library of her mind. "If more of us valued food and cheer and song above hoarded gold, it would be a merrier world." She didn't bother waiting for one of the club members to identify her bookish quotes. While most loved books, they enjoyed more of the modern variety over classics. "*The Hobbit*. J. R. R. Tolkien," she said.

Charlie was the only one in the group who seemed to appreciate what she called her literary language. "Bravo, Ellie. How about I pack one of the tarts up and drop it by to you when I leave here?"

Eleanor tried not to smile too hard, especially when she caught the little flicker of disappointment in Danida's eyes. "I'd appreciate that. If it isn't too much trouble."

"You know it's not," he said with a low chuckle.

Eleanor listened as the group made chitchat, piping up when she felt like it. Figaro, Savannah's kitten, curled into a ball on Eleanor's lap right in front of the laptop. Eleanor slid a finger over the top of the kitten's head, petting it gently as its purr grew louder.

"I heard about all the storm damage to your garden," Ruby said next. "A lot of folks had damage but I hear that your place got it the worst. Will you still be hosting Madison's wedding?"

The other group members looked concerned.

"It's only two weeks away," Ruby said. "What awful timing. Perhaps Danida can host it at her house. She has a beautiful garden too."

Eleanor shook her head quickly. "Don't you all worry. Charlie's granddaughter will have the wedding of her dreams in *my* backyard. My niece has offered to help me get the garden back in tip-top condition."

"Savannah is in town?" Danida asked. "I didn't know that."

"She is." Eleanor gently scratched below Figaro's chin. The kitten seemed to enjoy it for a moment and then playfully swatted a paw against Eleanor's hand.

"How wonderful for you, and how sweet of her to help," Ruby said.

Jeanne, another member of the group, fanned herself. "I hear Evan is also helping you repair the Finders Keepers Library. Very handsome, that one."

Charlie bit into one of the treats they were eating. "I was thinking about trying to set him up with Mallory," he said between chews.

Eleanor leaned toward her screen and pointed her finger. "Don't you dare, Charlie Blue! Evan is taken."

Charlie's forehead wrinkled as his bushy silver-colored brows drew upward toward his receding hairline. "Evan is seeing someone?"

"Well, no." Eleanor looked around to make sure no one in the house could overhear her. It was just her and Savannah's tiny kitten right now. "But I have my own matchmaking plans for him."

"Your niece?" he asked.

Eleanor adjusted the ice pack on her hip and leaned back in her recliner, absently massaging the top of Figaro's head. She'd never had a cat before but she rather liked the company of this little creature. It was equal parts calm and playful, just like herself. After her fall yesterday, the kitten had stayed by her side nonstop. "That's right."

"But how long is Savannah staying with you?" Ruby asked.

"Long enough to read at least three or four novels." Eleanor loved to measure time by how many books a person could read. "And if my matchmaking plans work out, maybe she'll stay longer than that."

Chapter Seven

Savannah

Anyone who ever gave you confidence, you owe them a lot.

Breakfast at Tiffany's, Truman Capote

On Thursday morning, the sun beat down on Savannah, penetrating through her thin sundress as she wheeled a small cart of gardening tools out of the garage toward the backyard. The cart had belonged to her uncle Aaron. It held a variety of tools, including a pair of nippers and a tiny trowel. There were also bags of soil on the bottom tier. The bags were probably a few years old.

Savannah stopped long enough to pull out her cell phone and make a short video of her uncle's old cart, landing lastly on the bags of dirt. She captioned the video "Does dirt expire? Anyone know?" It was asked half in jest because she knew the answer. Potting soil had a shelf life that her uncle's dirt had long surpassed. She just wanted to ask the question and engage her followers on TikTok. Later, she'd include the short video snippet in a new gardening vlog. When she was finished with the quick video, she shoved her phone back into her back pocket.

Today's goal was just to trim back the unruly roses. It was no wonder the storm had ravaged the garden and torn down the arbor that the roses had been trained to climb. Savannah couldn't believe the frame was even able to support the weight of the flowers prior to the storm. They likely hadn't been trimmed since her uncle had passed away. If any bride attempted to marry in the garden's current state, her dress would be ripped to shreds by the roses' thorns.

Savannah glanced around and tried to figure out where to start. *Don't get overwhelmed, Savannah.* She loved a good project and so did her social media audience. Pulling out her cell phone again, she tapped the camera app so that she could document progress with a "before" shot. Hopefully, the "after" pictures would show a dramatic difference. Knowing her followers, they'd get a kick out of Eleanor's garden transformation.

After taking several pictures of the unruly roses, Savannah decided to do a live stream to garner some excitement about her new project. She tapped her iPhone's screen and adjusted her hat as she inspected her reflection. When the green recording dot started blinking, she waved to the camera.

"Hi, everyone! I know this isn't my usual type of thing. I also know that I've been mostly MIA for the last couple months. That's a story for another day." She grimaced softly. "It would probably bore you because, if you're following me, it's because you want to discuss plants, right? Well, I have a huge undertaking planned for this summer." She turned her phone's screen toward the flowers. "My aunt's rose garden has been devastated by a recent storm. We get those a lot during North Carolina summers. Anyway, she has enlisted me to get these beauties in shape because there is going to be a wedding happening here in just a few short weeks. What do y'all think? Hopeless cause or doable?"

"Hey. Who are you talking to?" Evan asked.

Savannah nearly dropped her phone as she turned her screen toward his voice. "Oh. Hi." She let out an embarrassed giggle, feeling foolish.

"Talking to the roses?" he asked with a growing grin. He had a really nice smile, she realized. "Just like old times."

For a moment, Savannah couldn't take her eyes off him. Her heart sputtered with uneven beats. Then she realized she was still filming. "Oh, sorry. Hi, everyone. This is Evan. He's a neighbor who will be working on rebuilding the garden's library. Yes, this garden has an adorable little library at its center that we call the Finders Keepers Library. I'll drop a video of that project later. But for now, wish me luck." She turned the camera back to herself, smiled, and waved. "Bye, guys!" Then she tapped her screen to stop filming and lowered her phone to face Evan. "Not talking to the flowers. I was just talking to my followers. I was live streaming to document the before-and-after for the rose garden. My followers are mostly gardeners."

"Your followers?" Evan lifted his brows. "You're not one of those TikTok celebrities, are you?"

She shook her head, feeling a blast of heat through her cheeks. She was equally hot and embarrassed. "No. It's part of what I do for work. I'm a writer-slash-vlogger-slash-gardener extraordinaire." At least that's what she'd been so far in her adult life. What kind of gardener had to avoid the sun though? Would her life be one big before-and-after now? Before and after Randall. Before and after her diagnosis. Before and after returning to Bloom.

At least the assistant professor job would be indoors. She loved teaching people about plants online through her vlog and social media accounts. Teaching in person in an academic setting might be just as enjoyable, although the thought of standing at the front of a large auditorium intimidated her.

The other job she'd interviewed for was working at an aviary. The birds' habitat was full of exotic plants, and they had been looking for someone to manage it. That job was only two hours from Bloom, and it sounded exciting. An added bonus was that it was indoors so she was safe from the sun. The interview had gone well—better than well—but it had been crickets since the call.

Savannah shoved her phone back into her pocket and glanced at Evan. "What are you doing out here anyway?"

"I'm about to head to the home-improvement store. Hollis and a few other guys are helping me with the library's roof tomorrow. I need to purchase lumber, nails, and some sheets of tin. I saw you over here and thought I'd see if you needed anything." He seemed to inspect the contents of her cart. "Looks like you already have a few necessities."

Savannah pressed her hands together in a little prayer gesture. "I know it's a lot to ask but I would love it if you could bring me a few sheets of lattice. The old ones are pretty much ruined. I'm also going to need a new rose arbor. I'd like to use as much of the original one as I can but I'll need a new structure to attach the old pieces to. A little old, a little new." Eleanor had already okayed the money needed to repair and replace what was lost. "I want to return the arch to its glory days. Imagine Madison walking through a path of roses before coming out where all the chairs for the guests are set up."

Evan looked at her thoughtfully. "I never pegged you as a romantic."

"You had the same reading lists I did every summer. There was usually a romantic storyline in one or two of them." Savannah tilted her head. "Why wouldn't you think I was a romantic?"

"If I recall, you weren't one to date a lot when you came down for the summers," Evan said. "Guys were always interested but you never seemed to return the attention."

Savannah didn't remember it that way. "Anything romantic would have been a lost cause. I was only ever in Bloom for a few short months."

Evan looked like he wanted to say something. Instead, he turned his attention back to the flowers. "It's no problem for me to get you some lattices and an arbor. You're going to need help putting it all up."

Savannah tugged her lower lip between her teeth. "Do you, um, happen to know anyone who might be able to give me a hand?"

Evan chuckled. "You really are your aunt's niece, that's for sure."

Savannah's jaw dropped in mock offense. "What do you mean by that?"

"Just that you have a way of asking for a favor that's hard to say no to."

She smiled. "I didn't ask you to do it, you know."

"You didn't have to." He cleared his throat and looked down for a moment. Then he lifted only his eyes. "Anything else?"

"I'll probably need more supplies in the long run but not today." She let her gaze sweep over the ground. "These garden stones are broken. If Madison catches a heel in one of these cracks as she's walking down the aisle, she'll fall. Her beautiful gown will be ruined."

"I don't think that's very likely, considering Madison's situation."

"Situation?" Savannah wondered at the sudden sadness in Evan's eyes. She hadn't heard anything about Madison except that she was getting married in Aunt Eleanor's backyard, and everyone was thrilled on her behalf. "Care to share what you mean by that?"

He furrowed his brows. "You're on social media. Don't you at least look at Facebook?"

Savannah shook her head. "I'm only on social media to discuss gardening tips. I don't know most of my followers in real life."

"I see. Well, I'm sure you remember that Madison has always loved riding that ATV of hers through the woods."

Savannah's stomach immediately dropped.

There was a pained look on Evan's face as he continued. "Last summer, she hit a log in the path, and her ATV rolled. She was out in the woods by herself when it happened."

Savannah covered her mouth with one hand. "That's horrible." She was afraid to ask how Madison was doing now.

"Madison was trapped underneath the ATV for hours before Sam found her."

"Sam. Isn't that the name of the guy she's marrying?" Savannah asked.

"One and the same. Sam saved Madison's life. He's her real-life hero," Evan said.

"Was she…badly injured?" Savannah held her breath. She didn't know Madison well but she was Mallory's sister, and Savannah had always thought of her fondly.

Evan looked at the ground, which told Savannah the news wasn't going to be good. "She's paralyzed from the waist down. That's why Eleanor offered her the backyard for the occasion. Madison and Sam don't have much money due to all the medical expenses. That's a consideration when you're working on this path. It needs to be wheelchair accessible. Madison won't be catching her heel in the cracks of the stepping stones but she might catch a wheel."

"I see." That made Savannah even more determined to make this garden as beautiful as ever and give Madison the wedding of her dreams.

Evan blew out a breath. "So, I'll bring you the lattice and the arbor you asked for. You know, there's a lot of good shopping to be done at the farmers market, if you don't mind getting up early on the weekends. You can find gardening supplies, stepping stones, fountains, all kinds of stuff. A few of the Books and Blooms Club members also have tables out there."

"I haven't been to a farmers market in ages." The thought brought back so many memories of going with Aunt Eleanor and Uncle Aaron.

"Trust me. Eleanor will fix that. She loves to shop there. Or she used to," Evan said.

"Used to?" Savannah got that gut feeling she'd been having since arriving in town earlier that week. There was something going on with her aunt that she couldn't quite put her finger on.

Evan shook his head and shrugged simultaneously. "Last winter's fall made her a bit of a shut-in. Understandably so, but I've been trying to get her back out in the community."

Savannah's aunt had always been on the go. Staying home for an entire day was a rarity and usually meant Eleanor wasn't feeling well. Staying in for longer than twenty-four hours was suspicious. "If it makes her feel better, she could use a mobility aid, like a cane. She seems to be getting around just fine."

"I agree. Maybe you can lure her out this Saturday for the farmers market," Evan suggested.

Savannah liked that idea. Perhaps a little farmers market shopping this weekend would be good for both of them.

After Evan had left to go to town, Savannah finished trimming the roses and headed back toward the house, her gaze sticking on her uncle's greenhouse as she walked. Her uncle's man cave wasn't where he drank or watched TV. Instead, it was the place where he sprouted various types of rare and exotic flowers.

Curious what the greenhouse was used for now, Savannah headed in that direction. She unlatched the rusty lock on the door and peeked inside. The building was completely empty, which made Savannah's chest ache. Uncle Aaron had always filled his man cave to the brim. Maybe she'd use this space to store her own plants while she was here this summer—her own little Savannah Cave.

On a whim, Savannah pulled out her cell phone one more time and made another video to post.

"Look at this adorable, completely empty greenhouse in my aunt's yard. Over the next couple weeks, I'll be spending a lot of time bringing her rose garden back to life but I think I'll spend some time in here too. This gardener has never had a greenhouse of her own. Even if it's just for a short while, I'm going to enjoy this tiny gardening haven." She moved her phone's screen to scan the space. After she stopped recording, she tapped in a quick caption and posted. Within minutes, her first comment popped up.

@LiveLoveGardener: *Awesome! But where's the cute guy from earlier? Maybe you need his help fixing that greenhouse up.*

The comment was followed with a winking-face emoji. There were more comments.

@JazzySocks: *Where's the guy? We need updates!*

@LibbyKnowsGardening: *Who is that hottie? Details please!*

Who knew her love life would be such a hot topic? Actually, she didn't have a love life anymore, and maybe that was for the best.

Before putting her phone back in her pocket, a text came through from Mallory: *I just switched shifts with a coworker so I'm unexpectedly free to help in the garden on Friday if you need me.*

Savannah: *Help would be much appreciated! Thank you!*

Even though a few people from the community had stopped by to pick up fallen tree branches and debris, there was still a lot of work to do on the garden itself. Savannah wasn't sure she was up to the challenge alone.

Another text came through.

Mallory: *BTW, this doesn't count as our girls' day. We still need to catch up—soon!*

Savannah: *We can plan our girls' day on Friday while we work.*

Mallory: *Perfect—See you early!*

Chapter Eight

Evan

I have been bent and broken, but—I hope—into
a better shape.

Great Expectations, Charles Dickens

Evan had breakfast on the table when June headed into the kitchen on Friday morning.

"What's this?" she asked, blinking heavily as if the lights were hurting her eyes. There was a deep pillow crease along her cheek. He didn't have to ask if she'd slept well.

"Toast and scrambled eggs. It's basic but it's better than cereal and milk. Have a seat."

She stood there for a moment longer, as if debating whether to comply or head back to her bedroom. Then she pulled out a chair, sat down, and reached for a slice of toast. "Thanks."

"You're welcome." He looked back to the stove. "Hey, I was thinking that later this evening we might catch a movie or something. To reward ourselves for all the outdoor work today. I was hoping you could help me and the guys with the library's roof. Maybe pass the nails for us to hammer into the boards." He'd already torn out the wet and rotted wood. Then he'd measured out several new boards that needed to be nailed into place to fix the gaping hole in the roof.

June bit into her toast with a loud crunch. "No, thanks," she said as she chewed.

Evan carried his own plate of food to the table, pulled out a chair, and sat down. "You'd rather help Savannah with the roses then? You'll need gloves. Those thorns are vicious."

June brushed the crumbs from her mouth left behind by the toast. "I'd prefer to read actually. I'm not finished with my book yet."

Evan reached for his glass of juice and sipped, trying to decide how to go forward with this conversation. She'd allowed herself to be vulnerable with him yesterday, but her guard was back up. There was a fine line between giving her space to heal and still being a parent. Kids needed chores to learn responsibility. "You have a choice of working with me or Savannah but no choice in whether you work at all. There's a lot to be done out there and it's all-hands-on-deck today."

"I don't want to," June said flatly, picking up her fork and stabbing at a mound of eggs.

"Well, I love you, but you're working out there regardless of what you would rather do," Evan shot back. When he was a kid, he'd never dared argue with his dad about doing yard work.

"Mom never made me work outside." June's lower lip poked outward. "I could get hurt out there, you know. I could fall off a ladder or step on a nail. I could get scratched by thorns. Forcing me to work could be considered child endangerment."

This kid. "The only thing you're in danger of is being asked to do more work," Evan said.

June dropped her fork and pushed back from the table. "I'm done eating. I lost my appetite."

"Maybe you'll find it after working a few hours outside," Evan called to her back as she stomped off. He flinched as she slammed her door behind her.

That had gone horribly. Every time he made a tiny advance with June, he got bumped three steps back.

"Knock, knock."

Evan looked up as Savannah pushed his screen door open and peeked inside.

"Sorry to intrude," she said, "but I've been knocking for a while. I guess you didn't hear me over your, um, conversation."

Evan sighed. "I'm sorry you heard that."

Savannah grimaced. "I didn't mean to eavesdrop."

"It's okay. If you have any good parenting advice, please let me know."

She shook her head. "I'm not a parent."

"Did your parents make you do yard work?" he asked.

Savannah laughed. "No. They don't even do their own yard work. They hire out for those jobs. But Uncle Aaron made me work outside." She lifted a shoulder. "He didn't really have to make me. I enjoyed it. Some of my favorite memories are working in the garden with him." Savannah stood in the doorway. "Give her time."

"I need to stand my ground though, right? In my classroom, if you ask a student to do something, you don't back down. Once you back down, that's when they learn to walk all over you."

Savannah smiled. "I bet you're a fantastic teacher."

"The most loved and the most hated. My popularity vote is fifty-fifty," he said, which was something he was proud of. It meant he was teaching, which some students loved and some were bound to hate.

Savannah held up a plastic container. "Aunt Eleanor asked me to bring these over for you and June. They're biscuits, fresh from her oven." She set the container on the table.

Evan peeked under the lid. "Ah. These look great." And normally this would be enough to make his day.

"I told Aunt Eleanor she should bring them over herself, or at least come with me. Half the enjoyment of giving is seeing that look of pure joy on your face."

"What can I say? I've always loved Eleanor's biscuits."

Savannah grinned but he could see the tiny hint of worry in her eyes. "Does Aunt Eleanor ever come over here?"

Evan thought about the question. "Not lately. Not for a while at least. Why?"

Savannah shrugged. "It's just, Aunt Eleanor has always been a social butterfly. I'm starting to worry about her reluctance to leave home."

"Give her time. She's still healing. She'll be out and about doing all the things she used to do again."

Savannah nodded but she didn't look convinced. Evan had to admit he'd had concerns as well. On several occasions, he'd invited Eleanor out and about. He'd offered to take her to the farmers market, which was one of her favorite places, and she'd turned him down every time.

"Anyway, I'd better head back," Savannah said.

"Hey," he called after her, waiting for her to face him again. "I want June to help out today. I'm guessing she'd rather hang out with you and Mallory over me. Do you mind keeping an eye on her and putting her to work?"

"You want me to put your daughter to work?" Savannah gave him a sideways grin. "You're making me the bad guy?"

Evan blew out a breath. "No, I'll still be the bad guy for some reason. I'll owe you if you say yes."

Savannah tilted her head to one side. "Oh? That's appealing. What would you owe me?"

A thought came to mind. "How about I take you out?"

Her lips parted.

He waved a hand in front of him. "Let me rephrase. You've been gone awhile so you've never been to the Moonflower Festival. It's happening next Friday night. Eleanor loves it. I've taken her for the last couple of years."

"Aww, that's sweet of you. Have you asked her to go with you this year?"

"I did, and she said no." He could see in Savannah's eyes that she took that as further proof that something was amiss with her aunt. "I plan to take June there. I'm not sure it's the kind of thing a twelve-year-old enjoys but I think you'd love it."

"I would. There's something so magical about moonflowers. I've always thought so."

Evan watched her face brighten. She was hard to take his eyes off of. Maybe inviting her out for a Friday night festival wasn't his best idea. His priority needed to be on June this summer, not romancing the girl next door.

"Okay, you have yourself a deal." Savannah held out her

hand. "It's a win-win for me, really. I get help with the yard work today and an escort to the hottest ticket in town."

Evan shook her hand. Her skin was soft and smooth. Velvet to the touch.

"Any advice on how to make June like me while we're working outside?" Savannah pulled her hand away from his.

He offered a low, humorless laugh. "How about you spend the day with her and then *you* tell me? If you figure that out, I'll not only take you to the festival, I'll buy you one of Darcy Ellis's homemade doughnuts."

"Mm." Savannah's eyes twinkled. "You have yourself a double deal."

"Work goes a lot faster with help," Evan told Hollis later that day. He swiped his forearm across his forehead, pulling the sweat from his brow. He'd been intimidated by the thought of repairing a roof but he was catching on with the help of Hollis and the crew he'd brought with him. "We might just finish patching up this structure today," Evan said. "Thanks for doing this. I appreciate the help."

Hollis popped a stick of gum into his mouth and chewed thoughtfully while watching his crew measure and cut the next boards for patching the roof. "To be completely truthful, I'm doing this for Mallory. It's her sister getting married."

"I thought you said you didn't have a thing for Mal anymore," Evan said.

Hollis gave his head a hard shake. "I don't. But I used to. And I was too chicken to ask her out. The way I see it, I owe her.

76

She could be getting married before her younger sister, if only I had been braver."

Evan stared at his friend, trying to decipher how serious Hollis was right now. "That logic makes me wonder if you're having a heat stroke out here. Do I need to take you to the hospital?"

"Only if Mallory is my nurse." Hollis bounced his eyebrows. Then he pulled the bottom of his T-shirt up to wipe his own face. "I'm just teasing, man. I'm out here for you. I missed you while I was in Delaware with my grandma."

"Aww. That's sweet," Evan teased back.

Since they were taking a small break from working, Evan reached for a couple packages of crackers and offered one to Hollis. "Want a Nab?"

Hollis took the package of crackers and ripped it open, eying Evan.

"You want the truth?" Evan asked.

Hollis chuckled as he lifted a cracker to his mouth. "I'm not sure but tell me anyway."

Evan had always been able to confide in his best friend. "My crush on Savannah never left. I think it just went into hibernation."

"You should ask her out then," Hollis said while he chewed.

Evan kind of already had but taking Savannah to the festival wasn't a date. "I have June now."

"That means you can't be in a romantic relationship?" Hollis asked.

Evan was sure his logic was misguided but he was equally sure that dating Savannah was a bad idea. "All I know is, as a father, I need to put June first."

"But as a man..." Hollis said, trailing off.

Evan bit into one of his crackers. "As a man who hasn't had a serious relationship in years, it does feel kind of nice to feel that spark with someone again," he admitted. "I thought maybe I had grown out of sparks."

Hollis patted Evan's back. "We're only in our thirties, buddy. We're in our prime."

Evan eyed him. "If that's the case, maybe you should try your hand again with Mallory. I have a daughter to consider. What's your excuse?"

Hollis held his next cracker suspended in front of his mouth. "The truth is, Mallory kind of scares me. She's smart. Beautiful. She has her act together."

"So do you," Evan said.

Hollis continued to inspect his cracker. "I actually did ask Mallory out once, you know?" He slid his gaze over to Evan.

"You never told me that."

"Yep. She turned me down. She didn't even blink or think twice about it. She just said, and I quote, 'I don't think that's a good idea.'"

Evan pretended to drive a stake through his heart. "Ouch. I'm sorry, buddy," he said as he lowered his hand back to his side. "I had no idea."

Hollis finally popped the cracker into his mouth and stood. "Well, now you do." He gave Evan a thoughtful look. "Did you and Savannah ever try to date back in the old days?"

Evan nodded. "Once."

"I suspected as much but you never told me. What happened?"

"The same thing that always happened. She left town at the end of the summer. Then I joined the military." That was another reason Evan didn't need to explore anything romantic with Savannah. She never stayed in Bloom for long. In fact, experience told him that, like the bumblebees and swallowtails, Savannah usually disappeared when summer ended.

There was no reason to think this time would be any different.

Chapter Nine

Eleanor

That's the thing about books. They let you travel without moving your feet.

The Namesake, Jhumpa Lahiri

Eleanor's hip throbbed as she forced herself down the deck steps and along the stone path. She still felt a bit unsteady on her feet but she loved being out here. There were at least a dozen shades of color blending in the melting pot of her late husband's garden. The air was rich with an intoxicating floral scent as she continued forward. She wanted to see how far Evan and the others had gotten with repairs on her beloved library. She couldn't bear the thought that it might have been lost in the storm. Even the loss of the books felt about as painful as her hip at this moment.

Figaro scurried at her feet, bounding forward and then waiting for Eleanor to catch up. Eleanor had never really considered herself a cat person. She'd always had dogs, ever since she was a young child. Her mom had been allergic to cats, or so she'd said, and that was that.

Figaro made Eleanor wonder if she'd been missing out all these years though. She enjoyed the curious nature of a cat, and she was pleasantly surprised at how smart they were. Figaro didn't fetch balls but she did chase butterflies when she was outside. The other day, she'd also caught one unlucky lizard in her mouth and had dropped it at Eleanor's feet as a sort of gift. The equivalent of someone bringing her flowers.

As Eleanor chuckled at the memory, her shoe caught on a crack in one of the stepping stones. Her arms flew out to balance herself, and she stopped breathing for a moment. *Not again.* Once she was certain she would win out over gravity, she inhaled deeply and pressed a hand to her chest.

"Eleanor?"

Eleanor nearly stumbled again at the unexpected voice. It wasn't unusual for someone to be wandering in her garden. Visitors came and went to her library all the time. It was more the voice itself that made her heart jump just as forcefully as it had with the near fall. Turning, she faced Charlie. "Well, hello. I didn't know you were stopping by today."

"I wanted to check on you. An added excuse is that my granddaughter is working out here today."

"She is, yes. Somewhere. You never need an excuse to drop by though, you know that. I always enjoy seeing you." Eleanor sidestepped the kitten as she took a few steps toward Charlie. "So many volunteered to come over and work today. I feel bad making everyone else do the hard work. Staying indoors is more my speed these days."

"You might enjoy going out with the right person. If you'd like, I can pick you up in my Oldsmobile and drive you to the beach sometime soon. We could take a stroll and look for shells."

"People don't seem to understand that I don't feel like I'm missing out on anything by staying home. I can go anywhere, in any time period, just by opening a book," she told him. "But thank you for offering. You are such a good friend." Eleanor noticed the subtle way his mouth tightened at the word *friend*. She always managed to work it into their conversations. It was a reminder both to him and to herself.

Shoving his hands in his pockets, Charlie tipped his head forward. "Mind if I walk with you?"

Eleanor loved to walk out here alone, but if she were honest, spending time with Charlie was the highlight of her days. He was a good bit older than her, maybe by five years, but he was young at heart. And like most men, he only got more handsome with age. "I was just going to check on the progress of the library."

"I can't wait to see it myself. I've said it before, but I appreciate you allowing Madison and Sam to get married here in the garden. It means a lot to me, Ellie. And since you were the brains behind that match, it feels fitting that they're marrying on your property."

Sam had rescued Madison after her ATV accident but Eleanor and Charlie had come up with ways to encourage Sam to visit Madison in the hospital and after her release. Eleanor had sent books through him, and Charlie had asked Sam for favors in modifying Madison's living situation to make it more accessible for her wheelchair. There were other people to ask, of course, but Eleanor had an instinct about Sam. And her instincts were always on point.

Eleanor glanced over at Charlie. "We were both the brains. You're the right brain, and I'm the left. I think we make a good team."

"So do I," he said, quietly.

Eleanor could feel his gaze on her, making her heart race even more. She stumbled again, too distracted by Charlie.

He reached out and caught her this time, holding on tighter and a little bit longer than he probably needed to. "You all right, Ellie?" he asked in a low voice that stirred the untouched and cobwebbed places inside her.

Her heart raced so much that she felt dizzy in the most pleasant way. "Oh, I'm just getting clumsy in my old age."

His voice dipped impossibly lower. "No less beautiful though."

"You didn't argue that I'm getting old," she teased.

His eyes twinkled. "Let's see, how does it go?" He tapped his index finger to his temple as he seemed to pull words from the air: "She looked much younger than her age, indeed, which is almost always the case with women who retain serenity of spirit, sensitiveness and pure sincere warmth of heart to old age."

If it were possible, Eleanor's heart would have tumbled right out of her chest and fallen at his feet. "I do love a man who can quote Dostoevsky's *Crime and Punishment*."

Charlie held her gaze for a long moment. "And I love a woman who can appreciate my efforts. I highlighted that line in the book and reread it for a week on end. Then I waited for the perfect moment to recite it to you."

Eleanor laughed. "Am I really worth all that effort?"

"You're worth more. Let me tell you, *Crime and Punishment*

is an even tougher read than *The Time Traveler's Wife*. But I read it for you."

Her cheeks felt hot. "I'd be just as impressed if you quoted Dr. Seuss," she said, still trying to catch the breath he'd just stolen straight out of her lungs.

"Now you tell me," Charlie quipped, chuckling quietly.

She took another step, feeling even less steady on her feet. Charlie had been there for her after Aaron died. He'd helped her around the house, helped with things that Aaron had always taken care of. And somewhere along the way, he had started doing more than was expected of a family friend. He brought her food and small trinkets that he said reminded him of her. He invited her out for meals—just as friends, of course—and she'd accepted until her fall last winter.

She couldn't deny that she felt a little spark whenever she looked at him. More than a little one. She wasn't sure she could ever be romantically involved with another person though. *What would Aaron think?*

"The library is a little farther ahead," she told him, even though he'd been to her library a thousand times. She focused her attention forward and took slow, deliberate steps. She didn't want to trip again, although some part of her did want to feel herself in Charlie's embrace. "I'm glad you're here to see it with me."

"Me too, Ellie."

Figaro meowed and scurried between them.

"Her too, apparently." Charlie bent low and picked the kitten up, holding her against his chest.

Something about seeing him holding that tiny creature warmed Eleanor's heart. What was she doing? She was too old for romance, wasn't she? Her gaze flicked up to meet Charlie's. The thing was, her heart still felt young, and her heart was telling her that one was never too old to fall in love again, if she could just step outside her fear.

That was easier said than done. When Aaron had been alive, she'd always felt invincible. Part of it was his influence but it had been her too. Now, after one little fall, she felt like a frightened animal.

"What are you thinking about?" Charlie asked, squeezing her hand.

"So many things all at once." It was an honest answer. "What are you thinking about?" she asked, already anticipating his response. He was an open book that she loved to read lately.

"You, Ellie. These days, I'm always thinking about you."

Chapter Ten
Savannah

He thought only about each step, and not the impossible task that lay before him.

Holes, Louis Sachar

Savannah tugged her hat lower on her head, trying to shield her face. The day was hot, pushing ninety degrees and rising. Savannah was wearing long sleeves and pants to protect her skin and sweating buckets even though she'd only been out here for an hour.

June eyed her with a curious look on her face. "Are you cold or something?"

Savannah breathed a laugh. "No."

"Then take off some of those clothes," the girl half suggested, half demanded. It was June's way. She was quiet, with relatively few words for the adults around her, but her body language was loud. June was usually holding a book in a way that made it appear more like a shield. She often had her arms crossed over her chest and angled her body away from others. But sometimes June seemed to forget that she was keeping herself closed off. That's when Savannah saw sparks of interest and excitement in the young girl. Savannah suspected that June didn't want to be left alone. She just didn't want to be hurt.

"I think I'll keep my clothes on but thanks for the suggestion," Savannah said, changing the subject back to the task at hand. "We have to be careful with the roses, okay? They're old and very important to Eleanor and me."

"Because your uncle planted them?" June asked.

"Yep." If Savannah didn't know better, she would think June was enjoying herself today. For the last hour, they had carefully removed the roses that were still clinging to the original lattice and arbor. The original posts were still standing, and all they needed to do was attach the new sheets of lattice.

"Can I use the stapling gun?" June reached for it before Savannah had even responded.

"No way." Savannah grabbed the staple gun from June's hand. "Your dad would kill me."

"That's because he's overprotective," she huffed.

Savannah remembered that she was supposed to be the "bad guy" today and not Evan. "I'm overprotective too. In fact, you stand back while I do the honors with this thing. Just in case."

June put her hands on her hips. "Why am I still out here if you won't let me use the power tools?"

"Believe me, there's more work to be done today," Mallory said, walking up to them. Mallory was wearing a ball cap today with a pair of short denim overalls. Her thick hair was pulled into a ponytail. She lifted a sheet of lattice as if it were nothing and lined it up with the first post. Then she nodded for Savannah to do the stapling.

"This thing is a lot heavier than I expected," Savannah said, lifting the stapling gun.

Mallory hooked a brow. "You want me to do it? Nurses are surprisingly strong, you know. We have to be. We lift people for a living."

Savannah didn't want to appear weak. "I got it." She lined the staple gun up to the top of the lattice and pressed the trigger with Herculean effort. After four staples, which covered the first two posts, she relented. "Okay, we can take turns."

"Or I could do it," June volunteered, raising her hand.

"Not a chance, kid," Mallory said.

They got the lattice attached to the posts that led to the new arbor. Once they were done, they started to slowly attach the roses, one by one, using gardening string. It was a tedious process that involved tying the string around the stems and connecting them to the new structures to train them in the direction they needed to go.

"I remember helping my uncle Aaron do this when I was younger," Savannah said, trying to make more conversation with June.

June looked over with interest and then she screeched. "Ouch!" She held up her finger with a dark red spot of blood.

Savannah stood quickly to go help and then stopped as her own blood rushed away from her head. The world seemed to spin out of control and all she could do for that moment was brace herself.

Mallory was on her way to help June but headed over to Savannah instead. "Hey, are you okay?" She grabbed both of

Savannah's arms, nearly holding her up. Mallory was right. Nurses were surprisingly strong.

"I think I just stood up too fast." Savannah kept her eyes closed and tried not to pass out.

"Hello? I'm the one bleeding out over here," June said sarcastically, but she was suddenly standing near Savannah as well. "Are you okay, Savannah?" There was a tinge of worry in her small voice.

"June, go inside and ask Ms. Eleanor for a Band-Aid for your finger," Mallory instructed. "Get a bottle of water for Savannah too." Once June was gone, Mallory led Savannah over to the cement garden bench that sat under the new arbor. "Have a seat."

"I'm okay. Really," Savannah objected, hating that she was calling attention to herself.

Mallory pushed down on Savannah's shoulders, forcing her to comply. Then she took a seat beside her. "I'm a medical professional, you know. I can tell that you're not feeling 100 percent. I'm a good listener when you're ready to talk about what's going on with you."

Savannah pressed her hands down on the bench beside her, still keeping her eyes closed and waiting for the world to slow down. "Thank you. Noted," she said. No part of Savannah wanted to get into that discussion right now. But maybe she'd confide in Mallory soon.

A couple minutes later, June ran up to stand in front of them. "Here's the water!"

"Did you get a Band-Aid too?" Mallory asked.

"I will. I just thought I'd bring Savannah's water first. She looks like she needs urgent care," June said.

"I think we have ourselves a future nurse on our hands." Mallory gently nudged Savannah.

Savannah opened her eyes just in time to see June grin.

"Maybe. Or maybe a gardener like Savannah," June said. "Today hasn't been all bad, even though I nearly sliced my finger off."

"Dramatic much?" Mallory teased.

Savannah exhaled softly, relieved that her world was slowing down. She took the water that June offered, twisted off the cap, and drank gratefully. "I agree," she finally said. "Today hasn't been all bad." But they were only a quarter of the way through the job at hand. And if she was already feeling like passing out, she wasn't sure how she'd get through the rest of the work.

It was late afternoon when Savannah, Mallory, and June finally called it a day.

Mallory made a show of wiping off her hands as she seemed to visually assess Savannah from head to toe. "You go on inside. I'll finish putting away the yard equipment."

Savannah had worked hard not to sound any additional alarms about her health, especially with June watching. She imagined that, after losing her mother, health scares might be triggering for June.

Savannah wanted to insist on cleaning up with Mal but she really was on her last leg. "Thanks. I'll owe you."

"Perfect," Mallory said. "I'll collect at some point while you're here."

Savannah noticed the soreness in her muscles as she headed

toward the back deck. The ground was flat but it felt like she was climbing a mountain. Her skin felt hot but a chill ran through her body. She also had a tiny headache thrumming at the center of her forehead.

I'm fine. Everything is fine.

"We don't have to cook if you're not up for it," Mallory called, making Savannah aware that she was still being closely watched. She'd felt Mallory's gaze on her all day, and Mallory had forced water breaks on the hour after Savannah's near collapse. "We could order takeout."

"It's fine," Savannah called back. "I'll be up for cooking. I just…need some water." And a chance to sit. Savannah's head felt unnaturally heavy on her shoulders. She could already tell that tomorrow she was going to pay for all the work she'd done today.

"Are we inviting my dad to eat with us too?" June asked, coming up beside Savannah as she entered the house.

Savannah glanced over. "He's been working hard today too. He deserves to eat, don't you think?"

June offered a tiny shrug. "I mean, I guess it's not fair if we cook an awesome meal and he doesn't get to join in."

"I agree. Thanks for helping, by the way."

"Not like I had a choice." The words held attitude, but the tone didn't. In fact, June was almost smiling. "Maybe Uncle Hollis will join us for dinner too. You'd be shocked at how much Uncle Hollis eats. He can eat like five hot dogs in one sitting and an entire bag of chips."

Savannah laughed, already feeling better now that she was in the air-conditioning. "We'll cook plenty. It's a date." Savannah wasn't sure why she said those words, but they visibly affected June.

"A date?" June asked. "What do you mean? With Dad or Uncle Hollis?"

"Oh. No." Savannah shook her head, which she immediately regretted. The spinning came back along with a wave of nausea. "I didn't mean *date* date. I meant *plan*. It's a plan. Not a date."

"Oh." June seemed to relax. "That's good. Because I don't think my dad is ready for dating anyone."

"Oh?" Savannah grabbed a bottle of water from the fridge and faced the girl as she started to drink. "Why is that?" she asked between gulps.

"Because he has me. That's another reason that I think I should return to California. It's not easy to date with a kid around, you know," June said matter-of-factly. "My mom always told me that. So, if you *did* want to date my dad, I think the best thing you could do is tell him to send me home. Immediately."

Savannah stammered for a moment. "Bloom is your home," she finally said.

June tipped her chin to her chest and looked up at Savannah through her lashes. "No. It's. Not. My home is in California."

After showering and getting dressed, Savannah lingered a moment in front of the bathroom mirror assessing just how much sun she'd gotten. Her shoulders were red, along with the tops of her hands and forearms. She'd layered on thick sunscreen while she was outdoors but the rays had still penetrated in some places. Hopefully, Eleanor had a bottle of aloe floating around somewhere.

She stepped out of the bathroom, eager to escape the steam

from the shower. Then she walked over to the bed and sat down. Mallory had gone home to freshen up as well. After that, she'd return to help make dinner with Savannah, Eleanor, and June. The evening promised to be fun—even if Savannah was nearly exhausted enough to skip dinner altogether.

Pulling out her cell phone, she tapped on the TikTok app and blinked heavily, wondering if the heat had contorted her vision.

One hundred and twelve new followers? What is going on?

She pulled up her latest post, surprised to see that her followers were still talking about Evan.

@GreenThumbsandHam: *Girl, he is so HOT! If you don't snatch him up, I will.*

@ApothecaryMary: *I like the roses but I really want to see more of the guy.*

There were dozens of similar comments. Savannah would be so mortified if Evan ever saw her post. There were also a couple more comments from people asking about her hat.

@DarlingDaisy123: *Love that hat! Tell us where to get it!*

To reach more followers, Savannah decided to pull one of the comments and make a video response. She tapped the RECORD button, looked into her phone's camera, and waved.

"Hi everyone, it's me. I'm just coming on quickly to address your questions about the guy." Savannah shook her head. "Sorry to break some of your hearts, but I am freshly out of a relationship and romance is the last thing on my mind. The hot guy," Savannah said, making air quotes around the description, "is just a friend. That's all." She nibbled her lower lip and leaned in as if telling a secret. "But yes, I agree, he is pretty cute." *Gah*, she hoped Evan never found her TikTok page. "And for everyone asking about the hat, it's from the Sun Shade Company. I was recently diagnosed with lupus so it's important for me to avoid getting too much UV light."

She wasn't sure why she was sharing this detail with her followers. Her diagnosis wasn't even something she'd shared with her own friends and family. Just her ex, who'd promptly opted out of their relationship as if it were a timeshare that he'd gotten bored with. "So, the hat is a fashion statement, *and* it's good for my health. Romance, however, is not. At least not anytime soon."

She tapped the red square icon and stopped the video. Then she posted it and stood, her legs feeling wobbly. In her research on lupus, she'd read that patients' skin didn't just burn more easily in the sun. The sun also tended to wipe people out. It could cause long-lasting fatigue and body aches in some cases, sending some people into a full-on flare—just from having a little fun in the sun.

Everybody was different though. Savannah was still navigating how her own body would react to various triggers.

That was where her focus needed to be. She'd already thought Evan was handsome, but after seeing how her followers reacted, she realized he really was a catch. Maybe at another time, she would have considered dating him.

Just like when they were nineteen, the timing was all wrong this summer. The only job on her horizon was in South Carolina. Far, far away from Bloom. Which meant, as always, Evan was off-limits.

Chapter Eleven

Evan

You never really understand a person until you consider things from his point of view... until you climb inside of his skin and walk around in it.

To Kill a Mockingbird, Harper Lee

Evan turned as Hollis walked into Evan's bedroom.

"Well?" Hollis held out his arms. He was wearing one of Evan's shirts and a pair of Evan's trousers. When they'd gotten the dinner invitation from next door, they had just come inside from working all day. They were sweaty, dirty, and not presentable for a proper meal. Hollis made it clear that, if he went home, he probably wouldn't come back, and Evan knew his friend well enough to know that was the truth. So Hollis showered at Evan's place and borrowed some of his clothes.

"It looks nice on you," Evan said.

"It's a little small." Hollis tugged at the hem of the shirt. "I'll try not to split your pants when I bend over."

The clothes that Evan loaned Hollis had belonged to Evan's dad, which is why he'd kept them around. He was a little sentimental in that regard. His dad's favorite chair still sat in the corner of the living room, and it was off-limits for sitting, as if his dad would come back home one day.

"You clean up nicely," Evan told Hollis.

"You as well, buddy. Savannah won't be able to look away."

Evan turned from the mirror. "June will be there tonight, okay? Keep those comments at bay. I probably forgot to mention that Mallory will also be there."

Hollis's whole demeanor changed in the blink of an eye. "You didn't tell me that."

"Oops." Evan patted a hand along his friend's back as he walked past. "Come on, buddy. I know how much you love a home-cooked meal."

Hollis caught up to him as they walked out the front door. "Why is Mallory going to be there?"

"She worked all day too. Plus, she's one of the cooks. A really good one, I hear."

"I guess I just thought she would have gone home by now." Hollis rubbed a hand behind his neck.

"Nope." Evan stepped out his front door and turned to his friend, who seemed more than a little nervous. "I thought you said you were over that crush on Mallory."

Hollis tugged on his clothing again. "I am."

"Great. So having dinner with her is no big deal." Evan started walking again. "I've never known you to pass up free food. Don't start now."

They crossed onto Eleanor's front lawn. The line between their yards was obvious. It was as if he'd stepped from the ordinary into something unworldly. Evan breathed in the fragrant air, catching the floral scent of roses and other flowers that he couldn't name. Eleanor had made sure he knew his literature growing up but he wished he'd spent more time with Aaron learning a thing or two about gardening.

He climbed the steps of Eleanor's front porch and rang the doorbell. "I wonder what they're cooking."

Hollis batted his hand away from the door. "What are you doing? The sign says to walk right in."

"I know but that's not safe," Evan said. And he hadn't been able to make himself do so after he knew that Eleanor was getting around well enough.

"I'm pretty sure that if someone barged in this place with ill intentions, Eleanor would scare them off with a cast-iron frying pan." Hollis let out a hearty laugh.

"Careful not to split those pants with that laugh," Evan joked. Then he turned the knob and pushed the door open. "Hello?" he called, just in case Eleanor did have a frying pan. She was tough, that was for sure.

"In the kitchen!" Savannah's voice sounded clear and happy. That was a good sign that today had gone well. Some part of him had worried that June would give her a hard time.

Following the sound of laughter, Evan and Hollis headed down the hall into the kitchen, where June was sitting on the counter. She had a large mixing bowl in her lap that she was circling a wooden spoon through. Eleanor sat on a stool next to her as Mallory poured tea over glasses of ice cubes. Savannah stood at the stove with her back turned to them still.

"And now," Eleanor said enthusiastically, lifting a finger in the air.

Evan knew what that meant. She was about to pull a bookish quote from her brain.

"Let the wild rumpus start!" Eleanor said, her eyes sparkling as she looked around.

"*Where the Wild Things Are*," Evan supplied. "It's a book," he told Hollis.

"I know that," Hollis said.

Eleanor beamed. "But can you name the author? One should always remember the person behind the masterpiece."

Savannah turned from the stove and faced them finally. "Maurice Sendak."

Eleanor clapped her hands but Evan paused for a moment, noticing a deep flush on Savannah's cheeks. He guessed it was a sunburn but Mallory and June weren't nearly as red.

Even though Savannah was smiling, Evan thought she looked like she'd fought the day and the day had won. He hoped it wasn't June's fault. She could be a handful when she wanted to be.

"Can I help?" Evan asked Savannah.

She wiped her hands on the sunflower-print apron that was tied around her waist. Evan had always thought Savannah was like a sunflower. Tall, slender, golden hair, and brown eyes. "Actually, can you tend the stove for a minute?" she asked. "I need to freshen up."

"Of course. Need anything else?" he whispered when he was standing right beside her.

"No. The food's nearly ready. I just need to splash some cool water on my face, that's all." Her eyes fluttered up to meet his. "I feel a little sunburned."

98

"There's some aloe in the bathroom, bottom cabinet," Eleanor said loudly. The woman had always had canine-like hearing.

"Thanks," Savannah said as she walked away.

Evan watched her for a moment and then turned his attention to what was cooking. Rice was boiling to a finish, the sweet aroma telling him it was jasmine. On another burner, there was a saucepan filled with mushrooms and green beans. He pulled open the oven door and found a golden-brown rotisserie chicken. *Yum.* "What are you stirring over there, June?" he called over his shoulder.

"The salad dressing. It's homemade. Mallory's recipe," she told him.

"And it's the best you'll ever have," Mallory announced with a small laugh.

"I'm sure it is." Picking up a large metal spoon from the counter, Evan stirred the rice. When he felt like he'd done a sufficient job, he picked up a wooden spatula and moved the mushrooms and beans around. Evan wasn't the greatest cook, and he didn't exactly know what he was supposed to be doing right now. Hopefully, Savannah would be back soon so that dinner wasn't ruined.

"Hollis, do you mind helping me get these glasses to Eleanor's dining room table?" Mallory asked.

"I don't mind at all," Hollis said.

"And what should I do?" Evan asked.

Mallory grinned. "How about grabbing the plates?"

"Yes, I can do that." Evan opened the cabinet and pulled down a set of Eleanor's favorite china. He didn't need to ask. Eleanor had always used her best dinnerware whenever friends or family were over, even when he'd been a child and it was only him stopping in for an afternoon snack. He pulled out the matching bowls and silverware as well.

Savannah still wasn't back, which had him more than a little worried. She hadn't looked quite herself. June seemed to be on her best behavior this evening though. Maybe whatever was going on with Savannah had nothing to do with his daughter.

Eleanor stepped over to him and lowered her voice. "I'll serve. Do you mind checking on Savannah for me?"

"Sure." Evan knew this was one of Eleanor's subtle matchmaker tactics. He was taking the bait though, because checking on Savannah was exactly what he wanted to do right now. He left the stove and headed down the hall. Before he reached the bathroom, the door opened, and Savannah stepped out.

She wrinkled her forehead. "What are you doing?"

"Coming to make sure you're okay."

"Just sunburned and tired." She forced a smile that Evan wanted to call her bluff on.

"The food is ready. That should make you feel better," he said, analyzing her every move.

"Much." She started to walk past him. Then she turned midstep, nearly making him run into her. Evan's arms reflexively caught her, holding her in place. "Oh, um. Thank you," she said in a quiet voice.

Evan didn't want to let go but he did. "For what?"

"For coming to check on me. It's kind of, I don't know, refreshing."

He took that to mean that others in her life had ignored the subtle hints of a rough day. Some part of him wished he could pull her back in for just a moment. They'd been so close when they were growing up, and while it had been many years, she still felt as familiar to him as his own reflection. Over the years, he'd thought about her, and he'd wondered what might have been if she hadn't gone off to college that last summer and if he hadn't joined the Marines. His life would look different, that was for sure. Not necessarily better, because those choices would have meant that June was never born. For that reason, there was no room for regrets.

"You're staring," Savannah said.

"So are you," Evan pointed out.

This made her smile. "Are we having one of our stare-down competitions? Because you know I always win."

"Not true," Evan said.

"So true." She wasn't blinking and neither was he. If it meant staying in this dark hallway with her, he'd stare all night.

"Come on, you two lovebirds," Eleanor called. "Dinner is served."

Evan looked past Savannah to his neighbor.

"You blinked!" Savannah said, giving his shoulder a playful shove. "I win!" Then she turned and headed toward the kitchen.

"I want a rematch later," he called. But really, he just wanted another excuse to look into her eyes.

When the meal was finished, Evan slid back from the table. "Okay. The women cooked, so the men will clean."

"What?" Hollis was clearly pretending to be opposed to the suggestion. "No one mentioned anything to me about cleaning dishes."

Evan gestured for Hollis to get up. "Fair is fair."

June looked across the table at Savannah. "Want to play a game of cards? Or Scrabble? My grandma Margie always plays those games after a big meal."

Evan found this interesting. June really did like Savannah. Maybe they'd bonded even more today while working in the garden. He was a little jealous, because his daughter wasn't being that easy on him this summer, but he was mostly happy the two of them were getting along so well.

"I'm sorry, June, but I think I'm going to turn in early." Savannah had been quiet during dinner. She'd only nibbled at the food on her plate. She stretched her arms overhead and made a show of yawning. "I'm really tired."

"Yard work has a way of exhausting people," Mallory agreed. "I'm beat too. And since the men are pulling their weight, I'm heading home."

"Or you could stay and help," Hollis suggested.

"I could." Mallory grinned as she pushed back from the table. "But I'm not going to. My bed is calling my name."

"I'll walk you out." Savannah got up and followed Mallory down the hall.

"Come on, buddy." Evan waved Hollis over to where he was standing. "We have a pile of dirty dishes in our future."

"No, no, no. You boys worked all day long." Eleanor made a shooing motion from where she was still sitting at the table. "Go on home. I'll take care of the mess here. Evan, maybe you can play those card games with June."

Evan expected June to shoot that idea down but instead she shrugged.

"We can if you want to," she said.

Evan couldn't believe his ears. Maybe yard work had been better for June than he'd hoped. "Really?"

"Lose the goofy dad grin or I'll change my mind," she threatened, but she was smiling.

Hollis started gathering the dirty dishes in his arms. "I'll help you clean, Ms. Eleanor. It's been too long since we've gotten a chance to talk anyway. You go, Ev. I've got this."

Eleanor looked pleased. "It's settled then. Hollis and I are on cleanup duty. And Evan and June are going home to play cards."

June shot up from the table. "See you at home, Dad."

"It might take a few minutes," he called after her as she beelined toward the back door.

Evan wanted to wait and talk to Savannah before he left. When she returned from walking Mallory to the door, he motioned for her to step onto the back deck with him. "Can I talk to you for a minute?"

She gave him a wary look but followed him outside. The summer air had cooled considerably now that the sun had gone down. It was also louder outside, the sounds of the cicadas forcing him to speak up.

"So?" Savannah hugged her arms around her body and looked at him expectantly. "What's on your mind?"

"You."

Her eyes subtly narrowed, and he realized that hadn't come out the way he'd meant it to. "Is everything okay?"

Savannah tilted her head. "As I've already told you, I'm just tired. No need to worry about me."

"I know. You can take care of yourself. There's nothing wrong with letting someone else help, though—if needed." His gaze lingered on her face. In the moonlight, her skin seemed to glow. For the millionth time since she'd returned to Bloom, he got the impulse to pull her in and hold her. These weren't feelings he typically had. There was something about Savannah that attracted him. She was beautiful, yeah, but it was more than that.

"I appreciate your concern," she said, with a small smile. "All I need is my bed tonight though."

"Understood. I'm beat as well." He ran a hand through his hair and felt the soreness in his arms from repairing the roof all day.

"You say you're beat, and yet you still plan to stay up playing cards." Savannah's grin spread wider through her rosy cheeks. "You are a good dad, Evan Sanders."

He didn't expect those words to hit him so forcefully. He looked away and took a breath, pushing his emotions down, where he preferred they stay. "I try," he said, swallowing hard.

She laid a hand on his shoulder. He wasn't expecting that either. She seemed to wait until he met her gaze, and when he did, it felt like she could see right into his soul. "You don't have to try. You just are."

"How would you know?" He didn't mean it in a smart way. "I just, I really want to believe you. I need to." He shrugged. "So how do you know I'm a good dad?"

Savannah pulled her hand away from his shoulder. "Because if you weren't, you wouldn't care so much. It's easy to see. I'm sure June can see it too. Just don't give up on her." Savannah rolled her lips together, looking thoughtful. "Something tells me that's what she wants."

"For me to give up on her?" Evan shook his head. "That makes no sense."

Savannah sighed as she glanced up at the stars. "I think sometimes, when we've been wounded, we humans like to push people away, to prove our greatest fears." She looked at him again.

"What fear?"

She shrugged. "That we're unlovable. That we don't deserve love. That the person we love doesn't love us enough. Take your pick. You just have to dig your feet in the sand and stay consistent. Whatever her fear is, prove her wrong."

"I had no idea you were so good at giving advice. I should have been calling you all these years instead of letting Eleanor hand me a different book for every problem I've ever had." Calling Savannah might have been the cure for everything that had ever ailed him.

"I should really get to bed," she said quietly.

"And I should get to that card game with June. You know where I am." He pointed at his house next door. "Text or call. Anytime."

"And vice versa," she said. "If you need anything from me, I'm right here." She took a retreating step toward the door. "Good night, Evan."

"Night." He watched her disappear back inside the house. Then, reluctantly, he cut across the lawn and dipped through the missing panel in the fence. June was waiting for him, and he didn't want to pass up a rare opportunity to connect.

Was Savannah right? Was June afraid that he might let her down somehow?

He walked through the back door where June was seated at the table. "Where are the cards?" he asked, noticing that the table was empty. Then he noted June's pensive expression.

Uh-oh. He pulled out a chair and sat down. "What's up? You don't want to beat your old man at a game of cards after all?"

"Dad, something is wrong with Savannah," she said.

"What do you mean?"

June looked at her interwoven fingers. "I remember when Mom got sick. She wasn't saying anything at first but there were little things I noticed. She got tired all the time. She would say she was fine but she wasn't. I'm not stupid. Grandma Margie is twice Mom's age and Mom was the one needing to go to bed early and still sleeping in late."

"You're worried Savannah is sick the way your mom was?"

June's brow line pinched. "I don't know. Savannah got tired today. Like, really tired. Mallory is the same age as her and Mallory wasn't exhausted. And Savannah's face was pale but also red at the same time. Something is wrong with her, Dad. Can't you see it?"

Evan had noticed that Savannah seemed abnormally tired too. Almost too tired to carry on a conversation at some points tonight.

"If you know something," June pressed, "it's only fair that you tell me. After all I've been through this year, I deserve to know if a person I'm becoming friends with is dying."

"Whoa." Evan held up his hands. "Hold on there. No one is dying." Just like after Eleanor's fall, June seemed to be overly upset.

"Do you know that for sure?" June's voice cracked.

Evan's heart felt like it was breaking. "She's just tired. That's what she said so we have to trust that's all there is." Evan covered June's hand with his. "Are *you* okay?"

June sniffled softly as she looked down at the table. "It's just, it's not easy for me since losing Mom."

Evan remembered what Savannah had said after dinner. "I want you to know that I'm not going anywhere, not if I can help it."

June took a moment, seeming to process what he'd said. "Great." She swiped a finger below her eye. "So I'm stuck with you then?"

This kid. "I'm afraid so. Still want to play a game?"

"No." June pushed back from the table and stood. "I just want to go to my room and read. If that's okay."

"You sure?" he asked, worried about her. He was also worried about Savannah. June was right. There was something going on that he couldn't quite put his finger on.

"I'm okay." June dipped and kissed his cheek. It was quick and then she turned her back to him and shuffled down the hall with her stocking feet. "Love you, Dad," she called behind her.

"Love you back." Evan sat there, wondering if he'd handled that conversation okay. What would June's mother have said or done to ease June's mind? Or Margie?

An idea popped into Evan's head. There was no way to call Juliana but he could pick Margie's brain. He didn't want to give her any reason to contact her lawyer like she'd threatened but he was desperate. If Margie knew of anything that might help June, he needed to hear it.

Grabbing his phone, he walked onto the back porch for some privacy. Then he tapped on Margie's contact, already regretting this decision as the phone rang in his ear.

"Is June okay?" Margie asked, skipping formalities.

"She's fine." He cleared his throat. "Physically. Emotionally, she's still having a hard go." Evan tipped his head back to look up at the stars. "I was just wondering…" He sighed. Was calling Margie a good idea? His instinct was to handle things on his own but that wasn't working all that well for him this summer. "Margie, do you know something that I can do for June? I know I can't just snap my fingers and take the hurt of losing her mother away. I remember the pain of losing my mom. And my dad last year. It's not something that ever goes away. Not completely." It hurt to breathe for a moment. Just discussing the death of his parents made his emotions feel raw.

"I was an adult when I lost both of my parents," Margie finally said, "and it still shook me. I can only imagine how June feels. How you felt as well," she added.

Evan was surprised that Margie was empathizing with him. Maybe there was hope for their relationship after all. Margie was so bitter about him taking June, even though he was June's father. He'd assumed she'd hold that against him for the rest of her life. Maybe not though. Maybe her threat about contacting a lawyer was just her way of ensuring he knew someone would be holding him accountable and doing right by June.

"There's only so much a young girl can take," Margie continued. "She needs protection right now. She needs calm, and in my opinion, she needs the familiar."

Evan closed his eyes momentarily. Here it came. Margie was about to use his moment of vulnerability to make her case for June to live with her. "Margie, I love my daughter," Evan said. "I love her so much that it hurts to breathe sometimes. Seeing her in so much pain this summer is just…" He pressed his hand to his chest, clutching the area over his heart. "It's unbearable.

I am her father. I should be able to fix anything in her life but I can't. And I feel so helpless. I would do anything for that little girl. Anything at all, if I thought that it would make her feel better for even a moment."

Evan inhaled and braced himself for Margie's response, because he was certain she was going to turn that claim around on him. If he would do *anything*, then he should send June to California.

Margie cleared her throat. "Whenever June had a bad day, I always took her shopping." She chuckled softly. "I know that material things don't buy you happiness but it is fun. Then I always took her out for ice cream afterward. That's familiar for her. It's like a Band-Aid. It doesn't fix the problems but it covers them up for a little while. There is no right or wrong answer, Evan. You just take each moment as it comes."

It was exactly what Evan was looking for. Something immediate that he could do to help his daughter. He was a fixer by nature, and while he knew he couldn't fix the fact that June's mother had died, he wanted to give her an hour or two where she remembered how it felt to smile and have fun. "Thank you."

"Anytime. And I do mean that. I would do anything for my granddaughter."

Evan might regret what he was about to say next. "You know, there's a guest room at my house. You're more than welcome to visit us anytime."

"In North Carolina?" Margie asked.

"This is where your granddaughter lives now," Evan reminded her. "If you would really do anything for her, come and show your support. My home is always open to you." He was surprised that he felt that way but it was true.

Margie was quiet for a moment. "I'll think about it."

"Good. Margie?"

"Yes?"

"Thanks."

"You're welcome. Good night, Evan."

"Night." When Evan disconnected the call, he sat down on one of the outdoor chairs and laid his phone on the armrest before looking up at the stars. He felt good about that conversation. Having Margie as a houseguest would be trying but the one thing he and Margie had in common was June.

Shopping and ice cream, huh? Who would have thought the key to a young girl's heart was something so simple? It was almost too simple but he was willing to give it a try.

Chapter Twelve

Savannah

Memories need to be shared.

The Giver, Lois Lowry

Savannah held her breath as she flipped through the pages of *Little Women*. This book was magic. This was the exact copy she'd read the summer after tenth grade. *Please be salvageable.* Throwing away this book would break off a piece of her heart.

The pages flipped freely. All of them.

There'd been a few books that had been so damaged by the storm that the pages had practically melted together. Those were sitting in the trash can next to her. Not this one though. *Little Women* had survived. Of course it had. With the likes of Jo March within its pages, there was no way this book would find its way into the dump.

Savannah released a sigh of relief. She'd been slowly working on drying out the damaged books over the weekend but she hadn't gotten as far along in the project as she had wanted. The workday in the garden on Friday had taken its toll on her body, and she'd spent a lot of the weekend lying in bed. Even Aunt Eleanor had seemed to notice, although Eleanor hadn't questioned Savannah. That was good, because Savannah wasn't ready to discuss her health with her aunt. Not when Aunt Eleanor was having issues of her own.

"Aunt Eleanor, you'll be glad to hear this news!" Savannah called out, eager to share that *Little Women* had survived the storm.

She waited for Eleanor to respond, but instead, Figaro pounced into the room and meowed loudly.

"Aunt Eleanor?" Alarm bells sounded in Savannah's head. Had Aunt Eleanor fallen again? Was she hurt? Reaching for her phone, Savannah tapped out a quick text: *Just checking on you. Are you okay?*

The dots on Savannah's screen started bouncing as Eleanor replied.

Eleanor: *Just in the garden, enjoying the sunshine and my flowers.*

Savannah relaxed. Thank goodness Aunt Eleanor was okay.

Savannah: *Do you want me to keep you company?*

Eleanor: *The roses keep me company, dear. You stay inside and rest. Aunt's orders.*

That statement was further proof that Savannah's fatigue over the weekend hadn't gone unnoticed. Savannah was feeling better this morning though. Well enough to start boxing up books to return to the Finders Keepers Library. She'd been able to salvage half of the ones that had gotten water damage in the storm. They'd dried out with the help of a fan, and now that the roof was patched, they were going back where they belonged.

Savannah: *Let me know if you change your mind.*

Savannah was about to set her phone down when it vibrated again. This time the message was from Mallory.

Mallory: *I've been spying on you!*

Savannah laughed as a GIF of a person peeking out from behind some bushes came through. Then she looked out the window, wondering if Mallory was actually here.

Savannah: *Oh?*

Mallory: *On TikTok. You're famous!*

Savannah laughed to herself.

Savannah: *Hardly. Why would you follow me? You hate gardening.*

Mallory: *Maybe gardening is not one of my favorite hobbies but you are one of my favorite people.*

This made Savannah smile.

Mallory: *Why didn't you tell me?*

Savannah: *About my TikTok profile?*

There were so many other things she'd want to tell Mallory before getting to that.

Mallory: *You tell your TikTok followers that you have lupus but not your friend who happens to be a nurse?*

Oh. Right. Savannah had forgotten that she'd mentioned that in her last video. It was easier to share some things with an audience of people she didn't see in her everyday life. It wasn't that she was ashamed or embarrassed of her illness. It was all just so new, and she didn't want anyone to treat her differently.

Mallory: *If I had known, I would never have allowed you to spend all day working in the garden.*

Case in point.

Savannah: *That is the exact reason I didn't tell you. I can take care of myself.*

Mallory: *You felt horrible at dinner on Friday night. That's because you pushed yourself too hard. I wish you had told me.*

Savannah made the comparison in her mind to herself and Aunt Eleanor. Aunt Eleanor didn't share her health issues with Savannah either, probably for similar reasons.

Savannah: *I didn't want to worry you.*

Mallory: *How about this? I promise not to worry if you promise to let me know when you need something. Deal?*

There was some element of relief in having a friend who knew about her illness. It felt like a small weight had been lifted, which was refreshing. She had someone she could go to now. Someone to talk to if she was struggling.

Savannah: *Deal. Thank you.*

Mallory: *You're welcome. I watched ALL your TikToks, BTW. I saw the Hot Gardener Guy stuff.*

Savannah slapped a hand over her mouth. Then she tapped out a reply text.

Savannah: *I might need to block you.*

Mallory: *I happen to side with your followers. You need more content with Evan.*

Mallory followed that message with a winking-face emoji. Then she sent an emoji of a hand waving goodbye.

Mallory: *I have to head to work now. TTYL!*

Savannah sent an emoji of a hand waving as well. Then she set her phone to the side and returned to organizing the books by genre. Romance. Nonfiction. Mystery. Classics. Horror.

Since when did Eleanor read horror?

The next book she picked up was a hardcover copy of *Along Came a Spider* by James Patterson. She could already see the pages curled and bent together. As she tried to flip the pages, some clung to each other, refusing to let go.

"Sorry that I have to do this, James," Savannah said to the book's author somewhere out in the big world beyond this small town. Then she chucked the book into the bin beside her.

"Hello?" Evan called from the foyer.

"Hey." Savannah craned her neck over her shoulder to see him holding several grocery bags in his arms. "What do you have there?"

"Just a few things for you. I'll bring them into the kitchen." He started walking in that direction.

Curious, Savannah got up and followed. "For me? It's not my birthday. What did you bring? And why?" She watched as he laid the bags on the counter and pulled items out one by one. "Electrolyte drinks. These are good to have if you spend any time outside. Keeps you from getting dehydrated."

Savannah furrowed her brow.

"Some protein bars. I don't know if you like these. Then I have some bananas and berries. A salad from the deli part of the grocery store. To keep up your energy. And chocolate. Three different types because I wasn't sure if you preferred dark, milk, or white chocolate."

"Dark." Savannah folded her arms across her chest. "Are you for real?"

He gave her a questioning look. "What do you mean?"

She gestured at the bounty of gifts. "Why did you feel the need to do all this?"

He shrugged. "June and I went shopping this morning. Her grandmother informed me that shopping and a trip to get ice cream have always been a good stress reliever for June."

"For most women, I'd say," Savannah agreed. She hadn't done much of either lately. Without a job, her stress relievers needed to be more of the free type, like reading.

"We stopped at the grocery store because June needed a few things and, I don't know, I wanted to get some things for you too. I could tell you were wiped out the other night, and I felt partly responsible since I asked you to watch June."

"I really didn't mind. June was a big help, actually."

"Glad to hear it. I still wanted to do something for you. So here are some nutritious and delicious treats."

She couldn't help but smile. Had Evan always been this thoughtful and generous? This handsome. She knew the answer was yes because she'd always been charmed by him. "That's very sweet of you."

He watched her for a long moment. "How are you feeling this morning? Better?"

She pulled in a slow breath. It had felt good to share what was going on with her health with Mallory, although she'd found out on her own. Maybe it was time for Savannah to tell others in her life. She couldn't hide her lupus forever, and she didn't want to.

"Evan, I need to tell you something." Her body started trembling. Why was it so hard to share this information?

Evan seemed to understand that the conversation was taking a turn for the serious. "You can tell me anything. Do you want to sit down?"

She shook her head quickly. "No." How was he going to

react? When she'd told Randall, he'd gotten quiet, and an unmistakable look of disappointment had crinkled his brow. She'd convinced herself that he'd just been worried about her when really, he'd been more worried about himself. "I don't want to sit. I just want you to know that earlier this year, I was diagnosed with an autoimmune disease. Lupus," she said. Then she sucked in a breath, because she'd spilled all that out without breathing. It was like she'd plunged into the ocean and now she was finally coming up for air.

"Lupus," he repeated. "I knew someone who had that once."

Savannah studied his face, looking for some trace of emotion. "Knew?"

"Well, it was a coworker's mother. She walked with a cane, and I think she was on dialysis because of kidney disease. She was pretty sick." The worry lines on his face seemed to deepen.

"Some people do get very sick. Some don't."

"I knew something was wrong, I just didn't know what. I definitely didn't realize it was something so serious."

"Lupus is what one might call an invisible illness. You wouldn't look at me and know I'm sick. Unless I have the red cheeks." She pointed at her face. "It's called a malar rash. Or some say butterfly rash, which sounds a lot more fanciful than it actually is."

Evan quietly looked at her, as if seeing her differently. She could only imagine what was going through his mind. He was probably wondering how fast he could leave without hurting her feelings. Or maybe he was regretting allowing himself to get so close to her.

Was she being paranoid?

"That's why my ex called off our engagement."

Evan's brows lifted. She watched a sequence of emotions pass over Evan's expression. Surprise. Concern. Anger.

Savannah still felt all those same emotions. "I guess my circumstances no longer lined up with his idea of a happily-ever-after. According to him, I'm broken."

Evan reached for her hand again, holding it tightly. "Not broken. You're beautiful, Sav."

His blue eyes were a steely gray right now, and they were laser focused on her. He didn't look disappointed or like a man who wanted to run away. Instead, he seemed to look like he wanted to stay.

No, that was definitely her imagination. All the comments on her TikTok profile about the Hot Garden Guy were starting to go to her head. "Anyway, I thought you should know. Thank you for these supplies," she said, looking away. It was foolish of her to fantasize that anything would happen with Evan. He was just a crush from a long time ago, and she was on the rebound after her broken engagement. There were a million reasons to not even consider anything romantic with him. "These nutritious and delicious treats will keep me fueled today as I work on getting the books back to the Finders Keepers Library for Eleanor."

"You sure you're up for such a huge undertaking?"

"I didn't tell you about my illness to worry you. You were already worried so I guess I told you so that you would know that I'm taking care of myself."

"Good. In my opinion, chocolate is part of self-care. If you want to share with me though, I won't complain." His voice dipped low, luring her to look at him.

"Share chocolate? After what I just told you, I think it's clear that I need all the chocolate."

"I've done some chocolate-worthy things myself lately though." He cleared his throat. "I invited June's grandmother down for a visit and she's actually considering taking me up on the offer."

Savannah widened her eyes. "In-laws can be difficult."

"Yeah, especially this one. June's grandmother has been trying to take custody of June for the last six months. It's going to be hard to coexist under the same roof while she's judging my every action. At least that's the way it feels. If that's what June needs though, then that's what will happen."

"That is chocolate-worthy of you."

His gaze held hers. "There's another reason I need chocolate."

She lifted her brows in question. "Oh?"

"You see, there's this woman from my past who has suddenly shown up in my present. We've been skirting around our attraction since we were teenagers, and it's driving me a little nuts this summer."

Was Evan really going to go there with her? There'd always been an unspoken agreement that the two of them would stay friends, regardless of the undeniable attraction that had been brewing for ages. There was only one time that they'd ever given in. They were nineteen. They'd kissed and then they'd said goodbye. Savannah had gone to college, and Evan had joined the Marine Corps. "Sounds complicated."

"It is. This woman is just getting out of a relationship, and her ex was apparently a moron. She probably thinks all guys are lousy jerks."

Savannah's lips parted. "Evan, what are you doing? You're supposed to back away after what I told you."

He scrunched his brow. "Are you doing exactly what you suggested June might be doing? Pushing me away because of a fear?" His eyes searched hers. "Are you afraid I'll treat you the way he did?"

She swallowed hard. "No, because I'm not staying long enough to let that happen." She shook her head, unwilling to admit out loud that she was incredibly, undeniably attracted to the man in front of her. "So there's no way for you to hurt me like he did."

"If I was given the chance, I would never treat you like that, Sav."

Her gaze flicked to his, which was a mistake because she found it hard to look away.

Evan was looking at her right now like she was the most beautiful, unbroken woman he'd ever seen, and after the way her ex had treated her, that felt nice.

"I don't know how it's possible, but you're more beautiful than you were back then. And I am more attracted to you every time we're in the same room," he said in a near whisper. "Not just on the outside. On the inside too."

The air around them was charged. It felt like there was an electric current running through her body, and the only way to release it would be to press her lips to Evan's. "Even if a day in the sun is all it takes to completely ruin me for an entire weekend?"

"A day in the sun for the sake of helping Eleanor? And Madison. A day in the sun where you also look after my daughter? Yeah, even if." He lifted a hand and slowly swiped a lock of her hair away from her face. "Call me selfish, but I didn't want you to leave for college when we were nineteen," he said quietly. "We'd finally crossed that forbidden line between friends and more, and I just didn't want the summer to end."

Savannah's lips parted. "What?"

"But I couldn't ask you to stay," he continued. "I mean, you had bigger and better things to do with your life. When I kissed you that night, that was as close as I could get to asking, begging, you to stay."

Her eyes suddenly burned with tears. She couldn't believe what she was hearing. "I wished you'd asked me."

"You needed to go. The day after you left, I went down to the recruiter's office and signed up for the Marine Corps. I wanted to make something of myself. Be someone that a girl like you would be proud of."

She reached for his hand again. "I am proud of you, Evan. You've done so much. You're a good man." And she'd been searching for someone exactly like him since she was nineteen.

They stared at one another, saying nothing with their mouths but everything with their eyes. Then, slowly, they both leaned in simultaneously until their lips connected in a kiss that felt like an explosion of emotion inside of Savannah.

"Savannah?" Eleanor asked.

"Dad?" June squeaked out almost simultaneously.

As if they'd been jabbed with a hot poker, both Savannah and Evan jumped back, pushing away from one another.

"This isn't how it looks," Evan immediately said.

Eleanor chuckled. "Of course it is."

Savannah looked at June, who seemed horrified.

"Take this advice from someone who is older and wiser,"

Eleanor told the girl. "When your dad is happy, you get your way much more often."

June's deeply furrowed brows relaxed a touch. She looked between Evan and Savannah. Then she huffed. "Great. Then that means soon I'll be going back to California to live with my grandma Margie."

Chapter Thirteen

Evan

*Some old wounds never truly heal, and bleed
again at the slightest word.*

A Game of Thrones, George R. R. Martin

Evan could hear noises coming from June's bedroom. She'd been
in there for over an hour now, ever since they had gotten home
from Eleanor's house. June had come straight in and slammed
her bedroom door, making it clear that she wasn't happy about
the kiss she'd witnessed between Savannah and him.

Evan prepared a cup of coffee and sat down, his gaze drifting down the hall to June's bedroom door. His focus needed to
stay on her. She needed him, and for the life of him, he couldn't
seem to help her. Hopefully she would calm down enough for
them to have a rational conversation. At least he hoped so. That
or she would go to sleep and he'd be out here waiting until
morning.

His coffee cup was nearly drained when he started to hear increasingly noisy movement coming from June's room.

What is she doing in there?

He drank his last sip and then stared down into the depths of his empty mug, wondering if he should make himself a second cup or go knock on June's door. A third option was just heading to bed early. Being a dad wasn't easy, especially to a preteen girl. It felt like everything he did was wrong, at least in June's eyes.

With a weary sigh, he stood. The best thing he could do was make sure June understood that he was here for her, even if it ruffled her feathers. Knowing that someone loved you enough to bother you when you wanted to be alone was always better than leaving that person alone and letting them believe that no one cared.

Decision made, he headed down the hall and knocked on her bedroom door.

The rattling and shuffling sounds stopped but June didn't respond. He knocked again. "June? You okay in there?"

"I'm fine." The soft sniffles he heard after she spoke revealed she wasn't.

"You want to talk about what happened?" He cleared his throat. "I'm a good listener."

"There's nothing to discuss." He heard feet dragging along the floor. Finally, she opened the door a crack and peered back at him, her eyes puffy and underscored with dark circles. "You kissed my friend and now you two are going to spend all your time together."

There was so much to unpack in that statement. "Savannah is your friend but she is a twenty-nine-year-old woman." That was a very important fact. "And Savannah was my friend first.

Regardless of what Savannah and I do when we're together, she'll still be your friend, and I'm still your dad. We're not going to stop paying attention to you just because we, uh, we…" A father should never have to discuss his love life with his children. Not that he had a love life. This kiss was the closest he'd gotten to a woman in over a year. "We…"

"Kissed," June supplied. "It's fine. Mom had boyfriends all the time. She always shoved me off on Grandma Margie so that she could go on her dates."

"She did?" This was news to Evan.

"But at least I had someone to be pushed off on. I don't have anyone here. No one. That's why I want to go back to California and live with Grandma Margie."

June's words were like a sucker punch to his stomach.

"Bloom sucks and so do the people here," June continued.

Was he part of that group? Evan knew June was going through a difficult time but she wasn't acting like herself at all. "You've always loved coming to Bloom. What's changed?"

"Everything," June said quietly, her gaze falling to the floor. It took Evan's heart right along with it.

"June, sweetheart, I want you to be happy. I know it's a lot to ask right now, but I'm willing to do whatever it takes to get you there. I'm here for you." He reached out to squeeze her shoulder. When he did, she pulled back, bumping her bedroom door and causing it to swing wider. Evan peered inside. Her suitcase was on the bed, and it was full. "Wait. You're packing?"

"I know that I can't leave unless you let me. Not without being marked as a runaway, at least. I also know that you want what's best for me. Let's face it, Dad, being here is not what's best."

Evan looked between June and her packed bags. "Have you already contacted your grandmother?"

Guilt flashed in her eyes. "She said I'm always welcome."

So much for him and Margie making any kind of progress on a truce. Evan didn't know what to say right now. Anything he said would likely be a strike against him. "You do have people in Bloom who love you. You haven't even given this town half a chance."

"I don't have any friends here." June's eyes welled with tears.

He'd always hated to see her cry. When she was young, he'd gone to great lengths to stop her tears in their tracks. He didn't think lollipops or a ride on his shoulders would do the trick this time.

"I've been coming to visit you every summer for my entire life, and I still don't have friends here."

"Because you've never stayed more than a couple weeks at a time. You haven't tried to make friends, June. You don't leave the house unless you're forced to."

June put her hands on her hips. "I made friends with Savannah. And now you're lip locking with her so I don't even have her."

"Friends your own age," he emphasized. "There's a youth center. The kids get together every Friday night." Evan knew this because he had several students who attended. It was a safe place for middle and high schoolers to hang out, play games, and eat free pizza. What kid didn't want a slice of greasy pizza?

June folded her arms over her chest. "I don't want to go anywhere like that," she said stubbornly.

Evan wasn't sure what the right move was with his daughter. "I need to see you give Bloom half a chance. If you do and you're still unhappy next month, then we'll discuss California." There was no way he was letting June move back without him. Whether she thought so or not, she needed her father. He'd always wanted to be there for her, and now he could be.

"So if I go to this youth center, you'll let me move back to California?" she asked.

Evan looked at her packed suitcase again. "I didn't say that. I said if you genuinely try to like it here, I'll consider. That involves more than one trip to the youth center but that's a start."

"Fine. I'll go. But just so you know, it'll probably make me hate it here even more."

"We'll never know unless you try."

"Tomorrow?" she asked.

"That's right." He'd planned to bring June with him to the Moonflower Festival but this was more important for her. If she could only meet other kids her age, she might find that she wanted to stay.

"Are we done?" she asked with red, swollen eyes.

Evan wanted to pull her in for a hug but he suspected she'd just push him away. "For now."

"Good." Taking another step backward, she shut the door on him, practically slamming his big toe in the process.

Evan had spent the entire day dreading this very moment, and June had spent the day making sure he knew just how awful he was for keeping her in town any longer than she wanted to be here.

His stomach tied itself in knots as he pulled up to the youth center. He parked and glanced over at June. Her arms were tightly crossed at her chest, and she hadn't spoken a word since they'd gotten in his truck. "I'll walk you inside. I'm sure I know a lot of the kids in there. I can introduce you."

He reached for his door handle but June grabbed his other arm. "No!"

He turned back to her. "What's wrong?"

"Having my dad walk inside with me is not going to help me make friends," she said, her eyes pleading with him.

"My students love me. Most of them, at least."

June gazed out the passenger window, not moving to get out. "I don't want to be Mr. Sanders's daughter. I just want to be me, okay? At least at first."

Evan released the door handle. "Okay. Well, I'll have my phone on me. Call or text if you need anything. I'll be right around the corner at the festival."

"With Savannah," June said, looking at him now.

"We're just friends."

"Friends who kiss," she replied. Then she tapped a finger to her chin. "I'm confused. Is that the kind of friend I'm supposed to be looking for tonight?"

Evan's mouth fell open.

For a brief second, June smiled. It was just a flicker. "Kidding," she said before pushing the door open and stepping out. "I'm twelve. I don't really like boys yet."

"Good to know," he said, still stunned. He really wished he could walk her inside. That would ease his worry about leaving her here. If he could, he'd stay and watch over her all night.

"I'll come get you in a couple hours. By the time I return, you'll probably beg to stay a little longer." He offered a smile that she didn't return. Then she slammed the door and walked toward the building without looking back.

Everything would be okay tonight, he told himself. It had to be, because otherwise, June would sit at home with her nose in a book for the rest of the summer.

With a heavy sigh, he put his truck in drive and went toward Eleanor's, distracting himself by thinking about Savannah. There was something magical about the Moonflower Festival, and he knew Savannah was going to enjoy it. It had only started a couple years ago so it wasn't a thing during the summers when Savannah had come to Bloom as a teen. The youth center hadn't been a thing either. They hadn't needed such a place back then. Kids had just gathered, and it didn't matter where.

The front porch lights were on at Eleanor's house as Evan pulled up ten minutes later. He got out and walked up the steps. Then he rang the doorbell and listened to the sound of rustling behind the door, nerves wrapping around his chest like a vise. He was the good kind of nervous. The kind akin to sitting on a roller-coaster ride, waiting for it to launch him at high speeds and toss him around on its bends and loops.

Finally, Savannah appeared in the doorway wearing a light purple sundress that hit just above her knees.

She smiled shyly at him. "Hi."

"Hey." Evan rocked back on his heels and shoved his hands in his pockets to keep from fidgeting. "You look great." He immediately wished he had a more descriptive word. One that would convey exactly what he saw when he looked at her.

Savannah glanced down at her dress as if that was what he was referring to. The dress was nice but she was what had his pulse jumping. "Thanks. Is June okay?"

A woman who cared about his daughter was a woman after his own heart. "She'll be fine. Right about now she's creating lifelong friends." *Hopefully.* "Ready?"

"Ready." Savannah turned to call over her shoulder. "Bye, Aunt Eleanor!"

Evan heard Eleanor call back. "Have fun, you two! Don't do anything I wouldn't do!"

Savannah slid Evan a look before closing the door behind her and walking alongside him toward his truck.

Evan stepped ahead and opened the passenger door for her.

She hesitated. "This feels weird. You've never opened a car door for me before."

He wasn't sure how to respond. "We've never been on a date before."

"True." She dipped into his truck and settled into the seat.

Closing the door, Evan walked around to the driver's side and got in. "If I seem nervous, it's because I am. I think I'm partly worried about June. And partly because of you." He put the truck in reverse without looking over at her.

"I feel the same. We can be nervous together." She angled her body toward him. "Is this going to make things weird for us? I mean, after I leave Bloom and return to visit. I don't want to not be friends anymore."

Evan shook his head. "We muddied those waters when we were nineteen, remember? There's no going back but I'll always be your friend. Even when I was mad at you for not visiting Eleanor, I still cared about you."

Savannah nodded. "Okay," she said, seemingly satisfied by his answer.

Things had been weird for them for a while. A good weird but he understood her concern. Dating sometimes turned friends to enemies, and he never wanted that.

"Thanks for taking me to the festival this evening," she said.

Evan's palms were slick against the steering wheel as he backed out of the driveway. "Of course. This'll be fun."

"And it'll be good material for my vlog and social media. My followers love anything that has stems and petals."

"I think it's cool that you have a following," he said, directing the truck toward the end of the road.

"Small as it is. It's fun. My followers feel like friends."

Evan smirked. "I tell June that friends online don't count."

"They totally count when you're an adult," Savannah argued. "I feel like I know some of my followers the way I know you. Like we've always known each other."

"Yeah, it does feel like you and I have known each other forever." His feelings for her when they were nineteen had been intense. He would have thought after such a long time, they would have dulled.

By the time Evan parked for the Moonflower Festival, he felt more relaxed. He and Savannah had laughed and enjoyed each other's company. He pulled the keys from his ignition and got out, noticing that Savannah remained seated in the truck. Something told him she was waiting for him to open the truck door for her.

He walked around and pulled the door's handle, trying not to notice the hem of her dress slipping up her thigh as she swung her legs across the seat to place her feet on the ground.

"Thank you." She stepped out, pushing her hands down along the dress's fabric to iron out the wrinkles. When she looked up, her brown eyes were sparkling. "Is that a live band I hear?"

Evan tuned in as well. "I believe that's the Cherry Blossom Quartet. Everyone will be out here tonight."

"Everyone except Aunt Eleanor." Savannah's enthusiasm visibly faded, the sparkle in her eyes burning out. The corners of her lips dropped along with her shoulders.

Reflexively, Evan reached for her hand. Savannah looked slightly caught off guard but she didn't pull away. Instead, she held on tight as they approached the lights and music, walking across a small wooden bridge that traversed a stream.

The festival was held on Bloom Acres Farm, which specialized in growing strawberries that were used for the town's famous strawberry wine.

Savannah squeezed Evan's hand. "Oh, I love the fairy lights! They look like fireflies. We should add fairy lights to the arbor in Eleanor's garden. Madison's wedding is in the evening. We'll need some sort of lighting. Fairy lights would be perfect," she said, talking quickly.

Evan enjoyed watching Savannah get excited. She'd been through some rough patches before arriving in Bloom this summer, and it was nice to see her feeling better. "There's already solar outdoor lights in the garden."

"But fairy lights are so romantic." There was a wistful tone in her voice.

Evan found it impossible to say no. "I can make that happen."

Savannah grinned and then she seemed to sniff the air, her eyes rounding. "Mm. I do believe I smell powdered sugar."

Evan recalled that Savannah always had a thing for powdered sugar. "I'm sure you're right. Every food vendor imaginable will be out here tonight. I'm guessing you're smelling Darcy Ellis's homemade doughnuts."

Savannah pulled her hand from his to press her palms together in a prayer position at her chest. "Doughnuts for dinner? That sounds like a recipe for the best night ever."

"What are we, thirteen again?" he asked with a laugh.

"If only." She caught his eye as she giggled. It felt like the air between them was alive with some sort of magic. Like there were invisible fairy lights sparkling in the space that separated them.

"I think doughnuts for dinner is a great idea. Do you want to get one and eat as we walk the Moonflower Maze?"

"The answer to that question is obviously yes." Savannah winked at him.

"Okay, but do you know the answer to the ultimate question of life, the universe, and everything?" Evan asked, referring to a book that Eleanor had put on their summer reading list when they were eighteen years old.

Savannah looked thoughtful. "I know this one. Hmm. What is it?" She pressed her lips together, squinting her eyes as if searching through a catalog of bookish quotes in her mind. Then, looking a lot like Eleanor, she raised a finger in the air. "Forty-two! The answer to the ultimate question of life, the universe and everything is forty-two. *The Hitchhiker's Guide to the Galaxy*," she said, beaming. "By Douglas Adams. You loved that book, if I recall."

"And you did not," Evan said, enjoying himself so much, and the night had just barely gotten started.

Confirming that she felt the same way, Savannah said, "Best night ever."

They headed to the vending truck for Darcy Ellis's doughnuts and purchased two powdered sugar doughnuts, heavy on the powdered sugar. Then they carried their doughy treats toward the maze, which was tonight's main attraction.

"Do you know a lot about moonflowers?" Evan asked before biting into his doughnut.

She gave him a serious look. "You're talking to a botanist. I know more than anyone could possibly want to learn about most flowers." She stood a little straighter. "For instance, as you know, moonflowers only bloom at night when the moon is out. During the day, they are no larger than an inch or so." She moved the tip of her tongue to get a powdery crumb at the corner of her mouth. "But, when the sun sets, their blooms can reach up to seven inches."

"I did not know that," Evan said, chewing his bite of doughnut. "I'm impressed."

Savannah shrugged. "Also, not scientific fact, but like the fairy lights, moonflowers are extremely romantic."

"Is that so?" There was another spot of powdered sugar on her lips that some part of him wanted to brush off with a kiss.

"It's probably a result of their sweet aroma combined with the fact that they only open for the moon." Her tongue flicked to the spot of sugar, retrieving it. "I guess the fact that they attract bats and moths isn't so romantic though."

"Bats?" Evan glanced around, pretending to look worried. "Should I be afraid?"

A laugh tumbled off her lips. "Only if you smell as sweet as a moonflower." She leaned toward him and inhaled. "You smell good but not sweet," she said, pulling back. "I think you're safe from the bats."

Evan leaned in to her as well and sniffed the air. Her hair was fragrant. "I think you're the one who needs protecting. You smell about as good as these flowers." In fact, she smelled better, in his opinion.

"Well, thank you," Savannah said.

"You're welcome." Evan resisted the urge to reach for her hand again. He just longed to touch her in any way he could. Being out with her tonight felt good. He almost forgot his worries about June and how miserable she seemed and how much she wanted to move back to California.

"I've never been to a Moonflower Festival. This does not disappoint." Savannah squatted to get a closer look at a section of white flowers with long, creeping vines that crawled around an old fence that appeared to be made of driftwood. Other moonflowers crawled over antique bicycles and out of old milk cans. "I may have to return every summer just for this one occasion."

"Just for this?" he asked.

She stood upright and faced him. "And for Aunt Eleanor. My friends." She shrugged slightly. "And you."

Evan found it interesting that he was in a category separate from friends. He wondered what that meant. At the same time, he reprimanded himself for wondering. It couldn't mean anything.

As they left the maze, Evan led Savannah toward a section of vendors. It was mostly the same people who sold down at the farmers market on the weekends but Leanne Murphy was here tonight.

Evan led Savannah toward the table with dozens of houseplants and stopped.

Leanne had shoulder-length silver hair. She smiled from behind her plants as they approached. "Evan! It's so nice to see you out here tonight." Her gaze moved to Savannah, and she pointed excitedly. "Hey, I know you!"

Savannah pulled back, looking wide-eyed and uncertain. "Um…"

"Eleanor told me about you, and I've been following you online for years. Late Bloomer, right?"

Savannah nodded. "That's me."

"I can't believe you're here. I love your content," Leanne went on.

"Leanne owns the local plant nursery in town," Evan told Savannah.

Now Savannah's jaw dropped. "I didn't realize there was a nursery in Bloom."

"Well, I only opened it about seven years ago," Leanne said. "I needed something to do after my husband passed away. So I bought the old hobby shop and turned it into my passion."

"The hobby shop. I remember that store." Savannah nodded. "Beside the ice cream shop, right?"

"That's correct," Leanne said.

"Wow. That's wonderful. Every town needs a plant nursery. I've always thought so."

"I watch your vlog," Leanne said. "I'm subscribed so that I never miss a video. I've told some of my customers about you too."

Savannah looked shy. "That's so nice of you."

"Well, we gardeners have to stick together right? Your aunt and I go way back. We're both part of the Books and Blooms Club. Oh, Eleanor speaks about you all the time. She's so proud of you." Leanne reached across the table and patted Savannah's arm. "You'll have to come to my nursery while you're in town. I'd love to show you my babies." She waved a hand in the air. "My babies are my plants, of course."

"Right. Mine too." Savannah had such a huge smile on her face. This was her element. Plants and gardeners. She was like her late uncle in that respect. "I would love to come visit your nursery while I'm here. I'll be sure to do that."

"And if you're ever in need of a job, come find me," Leanne said.

Evan was certain that Leanne was just being nice, but then again, Leanne was known for being slightly impulsive. The hobby shop wasn't all that she'd purchased after her husband passed away. She'd also gotten a bright green, fully loaded Jeep. "Which one of these plants is your favorite?" he asked Savannah.

She looked down at the selection. "Oh, they're all so beautiful. How can I pick just one?" She tapped a finger to her chin. "Hmm." She seemed to admire them all but then pointed to a small potted moonflower with pale pink petals.

Moonflower. Apparently, Evan could name one plant in front of him right now.

"That one," Savannah said. "I have so many plants that I brought with me to Aunt Eleanor's, but I don't have a single moonflower."

"Well, now you do." Evan looked at Leanne. "I'll take that one."

"Oh, Evan, you don't have to," Savannah protested but he could see the joy in her eyes, making them sparkle against all the festival's lighting. That was worth any amount of money.

Was it naive of him to think anything that happened between them this summer would put those feelings of first love to rest? What if, instead, it woke them up?

"Maybe not," he said, handing Leanne a ten-dollar bill and lifting up the small pink-petaled flower. "But I want to."

Chapter Fourteen

Eleanor

I took a deep breath and listened to the old brag of my heart. I am. I am. I am.

The Bell Jar, Sylvia Plath

Eleanor was dozing off when her phone's ringer startled her. She flicked her gaze to her bedside alarm clock and checked the time. Who would be calling at this time of the evening? She didn't recognize the caller ID but everyone she knew was out tonight. Charlie had already come and gone. He was probably home sleeping by now.

She stared at her phone. She couldn't in good conscience not answer. *What if something is wrong?* Tapping her screen, she connected the call. "Hello?"

"Ms. Eleanor?"

Eleanor knew who it was with just those two words. "June?

Why are you calling me? Aren't you out at the youth center tonight?"

June sniffled on the other line. "Unfortunately. I tried to call Dad but he isn't answering his phone. I called Uncle Hollis and Mallory too. They're not picking up either. I want to go home. I can't stay here. I need to leave right now."

The vulnerability in June's voice got Eleanor's attention. "Why? Are you hurt?"

"No." She sniffled some more. "I just don't like it here. The kids at this place are mean."

"To you?" Eleanor sat up on the couch. "They're bullying you?"

June's silence spoke volumes.

"Please come get me, Ms. Eleanor." June's voice trembled. "Please."

Eleanor couldn't see a way around saying yes. "Of course. Of course, I'll help you. Just hold tight, okay? I'm coming."

"Okay. Thank you."

The crack in June's voice broke Eleanor's heart. After disconnecting the call, Eleanor sat on the couch for a moment, trying to figure out what to do. She couldn't go get June on her own. Could she? Even though June had told her Evan wasn't answering his phone, Eleanor dialed his number anyway. No answer. She brought up Savannah's number and then Mallory's. Where were they?

Eleanor's heart sank into the deep recesses of her stomach. "I guess I'll have to do this myself." Resolutely, she stood and walked to the hook by her door, retrieving her car keys. She couldn't remember the last time she'd driven anywhere. It was probably the day she'd gone shopping and had slipped and shattered her pelvis.

Hands shaking, she clutched the cool metal keys. "June needs me," she told herself. "I have to get her." She looked down at Figaro. "Don't worry about me, little one. I'll be fine." It was June she was concerned about. June had sounded so upset. Eleanor had told her that everything would be okay. She'd encouraged June to try to make friends tonight.

Opening the door, Eleanor hobbled down the driveway. She opened her car door and slid behind the steering wheel. Then she put the key in the ignition and cranked the engine. By this point, she was trembling, and her shallow breathing was causing her to feel lightheaded.

The true courage is in facing danger when you are afraid, and that kind of courage you have in plenty. Even a book quote from *The Wonderful Wizard of Oz* wasn't helping her muster the strength that she needed to push past this overwhelming, all-encompassing fear.

It felt like she might pass out. Or die. It was irrational to think those things but she couldn't seem to help it.

June needs me. Come on, Eleanor.

She placed her hand on the gear and pressed the brake. Then she moved the gear into drive. Her vision started to go gray in the periphery. She was terrified. Truly terrified. Finally, after several long minutes, tears filled her eyes. "I can't. I'm sorry, June. I just can't," she said out loud.

As if on cue, her phone rang in the passenger seat where she'd tossed it. The caller ID showed Charlie's name.

She picked up the phone quickly and tapped the screen. "Oh, Charlie. Thank goodness, you called. I need you."

"Well, it's about time you understood that," he said with a low chuckle.

"Charlie Blue, now is not the time for flirting. Let me rephrase. June needs you. She's at the youth center and needs to be picked up. Evan and Savannah aren't answering their phones. Neither is Mallory. Please, Charlie. Will you go get her for me?"

"Of course." Charlie didn't hesitate. He really was there for Eleanor whenever she needed him. He always had been. "I'm leaving my home right now. June will be with you in fifteen minutes. Hold tight," he said.

Eleanor released a breath, feeling like the weight of the world had rolled off her shoulders. "Thank you, Charlie. Thank you so much."

When the call was disconnected, she turned off her car's ignition. She'd been driving since she was sixteen years old. Backing out of her driveway should be as simple for her as categorizing books by the Dewey Decimal Classification system. It wasn't simple though. Her fear had too much power over her. She needed that power back but she had no clue how to get it. All she knew was that tonight June had needed her, and Eleanor wasn't able to be there. And that could never happen again.

Chapter Fifteen

Savannah

*If you clear out all that space in your mind...
you'll have a vacuum there, an open spot—a
doorway.*

Eat, Pray, Love, Elizabeth Gilbert

Savannah slid into the passenger seat of Evan's truck and suppressed a quiet yawn. Tonight had been wonderful but exhausting at the same time. She and Evan had stopped to speak to nearly every vendor, and they had ended up walking the Moonflower Maze a second time.

As she waited for Evan to get into the driver's seat, she pulled out her phone to check her messages. *Uh-oh.* There were half a dozen missed messages on her screen. "What is going on?" she said out loud.

Evan opened the driver's side door and got in, closing the door behind him.

"Have you checked your phone?" she asked. "I've missed several calls from Eleanor and Mallory. And from June too."

Worry deepened the faint lines on his face. He pulled out his own phone and frowned.

"I've missed calls from them too," he said, the concern evident in his voice.

Savannah tapped her screen and listened to the voice messages while Evan did the same.

"Savannah?" Eleanor's voice sounded frantic in the message. "Something is going on with June. She's been trying to reach you and Evan. Where are you?"

Savannah listened to the next message.

"Hey, Sav. It's Mallory. June needs to be picked up but Evan's not answering his phone. I got called into an emergency at the hospital. I can't leave. Where are you?"

Savannah looked at Evan. He looked as worried as she felt. They both lowered their phones at the same time. "I guess the reception out there was spotty," she said, referring to Bloom Acres Farm.

"Apparently so. We need to go," he said quietly.

She exhaled slowly. "Is everything okay with June?"

Evan put his key into the ignition and cranked the truck. "All I know is that some kids were being mean to her. Charlie has already gone to the youth center and picked her up. She's at Eleanor's house."

Savannah's heart sank. "Sounds like while we were having an amazing time, the rest of our world was having a small crisis."

"Sounds like it." Evan reached for Savannah's hand across the center console. Before putting the truck in gear, he looked over at her. "I don't want the first half of our night to be forgotten and replaced by this next part. It was a nice night. Better than nice. I enjoyed taking you to the festival." The smallest of smiles curved his lips.

Savannah didn't think it would be possible to feel flutters in this moment but she did. "Best date of my life."

He narrowed his eyes. "I just wish it was ending on a better note."

"Me too."

Facing forward, Evan put the truck into motion.

They were mostly quiet as they traveled. Savannah noticed Evan was driving over the speed limit and guessed he was probably more than a little anxious to get to June. Savannah had dealt with her share of mean girls in the past. It wasn't fun and she hated that June wasn't having the easiest of times making friends in Bloom. She was a good girl with a good heart. Savannah had seen it, and being Evan's daughter, she couldn't be anything less.

"I thought if she went tonight that she'd make friends, and that would fix everything." Evan blew out a breath as he gripped the steering wheel. "She only went because she thought I'd let her go back to California if she gave Bloom a decent shot."

Savannah put a hand on his shoulder. "You didn't know what would happen. Don't beat yourself up."

"I've worked with a lot of kids who, once their lives were hit with a tragedy, they spiraled in a direction that changed their lives forever. Drugs. Drinking. I just want June to be okay."

Savannah heard the crack in Evan's voice. "She will be. She has you."

He glanced over. "You seem to have a lot of faith in me."

"I do. I have enough for both of us."

As soon as Evan pulled into his driveway, Savannah pushed open the truck door and got out.

Evan met her around the front of his truck. "Thank you for a wonderful night."

Savannah knew he was in a hurry to reach his daughter, but even so, he wasn't moving to leave. Instead, he was staring at her with an unmistakable look in his eyes. A look that said he wanted to kiss her.

There was a possibility that he was just looking for a Band-Aid for the hurt on his heart but she wanted to kiss him too. A lot.

"I agree. The night was wonderful." She felt him lean in. She leaned in as well, their lips coming closer. And for a moment, she stopped breathing.

A soft groan came from Eleanor's yard as June headed in their direction. "*Ugh,*" she said loudly.

Evan pulled back from Savannah. "Oh. Hey, June. You okay?"

"Looks like you're *super* concerned about me." She glanced between them. "I'm going home now." She stomped past them, crossing from Eleanor's yard into Evan's without looking back.

"Good night, June!" Savannah called after her. "Things will look brighter in the morning."

June didn't respond.

Savannah could imagine all the possible reasons why. June probably hated her right now. She probably hated everything and everyone.

"I'm sorry about that," Evan said quietly. "I guess I'd better go talk to her. Thanks again for tonight."

"I should be thanking you." Savannah hugged her arms

around her body. "I need to check on Aunt Eleanor," she said. "I'll see you tomorrow?"

"Sure. Good night, Sav." Evan turned and headed toward his own house.

Savannah did the same, walking toward Eleanor's front porch. When she stepped through the front door, she laid her keys and purse down on the table right next to the door. "Aunt Eleanor?"

"In here!"

Savannah followed the direction of Eleanor's voice, finding her aunt in the front room. Savannah took a seat in the rocking chair across from her. "What a night, huh?"

Eleanor smoothed her hand over the cover of the book in her lap. "When June called to ask me to come get her tonight, I really wanted to," Eleanor said shakily. "I got into my car and cranked the engine. But I just...I couldn't do it. I am so disappointed in myself."

Savannah leaned forward to touch her aunt's arm. "Aunt Eleanor, have you thought about talking to a counselor?"

"Oh. No." She shook her head and then looked down at her hands, seeming to fixate on her wedding ring. "The day I fell and broke my pelvis was terrifying. I was just lying there on the pavement with no control over what was happening to me. I never want to feel that way again."

Savannah leaned forward and took Eleanor's hands in hers. "No one likes to feel out of control but you're not alone. You have Evan. Charlie...Me." Although Savannah wouldn't always be here. Not if she went to South Carolina.

Eleanor nodded thoughtfully. "I really did hate letting June down tonight."

"Me and Evan let her down too. Thank goodness for Charlie."

"Yes. He's a good man." Eleanor smiled softly now. "Maybe I do need to speak to a professional. I've never seen a psychologist before. I wouldn't even know what to say."

"I'm sure you could figure it out. Would you like me to set it up for you?" Savannah asked.

"Yes, I think I would. You're such a good niece. Thank you, Savannah."

A good niece would have known about Eleanor's broken pelvis last winter. A good niece would have known something was wrong long before now. "Do you need anything else tonight? I can get you a tea or some water."

"No, no. I'm fine. I'm just going to sit here with my thoughts awhile longer."

"Okay." Savannah stood back up. I'm going to my room to tuck myself in for a little reading."

"Reading is always a good way to end a night," Eleanor said.

Savannah's feet were heavy as she headed back to her bedroom. She'd been more tired since her day of yard work, and going out with Evan tonight, while wonderful, had taken its toll. She had to be careful and listen to her body's protests and demands for rest. Otherwise, she might find herself back in the hospital, which was the last thing she wanted or needed.

Savannah needed to keep herself well for a new job, whether it was the one in South Carolina or perhaps one of the others she was waiting on. She knew there'd be flares in her future but she preferred for her next boss and coworkers to see the healthy version of her first. She was hardworking and capable. She was creative too.

Savannah shut her bedroom door behind her and walked

over to the bed. Lying back on the mattress, she reached for the book on her nightstand. Savannah remembered when *Eat, Pray, Love* by Elizabeth Gilbert had been one of the number one recommendations among her friends. Savannah hadn't taken the time to read the memoir back then. She'd been too busy and too wrapped up in her own interests. But why not now?

Opening her book to the first page, she quickly disappeared into one woman's adventures of self-discovery. Even though the book's heroine, Liz, didn't have a chronic illness, Savannah related to her story. It was interesting, but after about fifteen minutes, Savannah's eyes fluttered, closed, and didn't reopen.

The next morning, the smell of freshly brewed coffee had Savannah picking up her pace as she walked down the hall. It was much earlier than she usually got up on a Saturday morning, but she was eager to explore the farmers market. She hadn't been in ages.

"Morning!" Eleanor turned as Savannah entered the kitchen. Fig lifted her head but she didn't move to greet Savannah.

Traitor.

"Morning. The coffee smells wonderful."

"Grab yourself a mug. I'll pour you some," Eleanor offered.

Savannah walked past Eleanor, dodging a sneak attack from Fig. "Perfect. We can drink it on the way to the farmers market."

"*You* certainly can," Eleanor said without skipping a beat.

Savannah grabbed an insulated to-go cup from the cupboard and turned to Eleanor. It was worth a try. Not being able to help

June last night had been rough on Eleanor. Savannah understood the feeling. On a smaller scale, she felt the same about not being able to help Eleanor. As soon as she got a chance though, she planned to find a counselor for her aunt to work with. "Are you sure?"

"Positive. Evan will be out there selling today. Charlie too. He'll have a table and be collecting book donations to replenish my library." Eleanor smiled broadly. Then she slid a piece of paper across the counter. "Please, don't forget my list. You'd best go. The early bird gets the worm, you know?" She reached for the coffeepot. "Now hold out your cup. I'll pour."

Coffee in hand, Savannah got into her car and drove the ten minutes it took to get to the farmers market. She parked, pulled her large hat over her head, and slid her sunglasses on before stepping out of the car. One might think she was trying to be incognito out here. Like a celebrity trying to blend in.

As she walked from table to table, she purchased the fresh peaches and honey on Eleanor's list. Then she stopped at a table for a variety of herbs, checking them off the list as well.

When she reached Evan's table, he was sitting with his legs kicked up on an overturned milk crate. "Hey, you."

"Hey, yourself." She glanced over the items on display. He had hand-carved wooden bowls, cutting boards, spoons, and other interesting pieces. "You made all these?"

"I picked up the skill in the Marine Corps. A roommate of mine carved and he taught me. It got me through a tough deployment and a few other rough patches."

Savannah continued to run her gaze over the carved items. "You're a man of many talents." One of which was making her heart race and her thoughts blur.

Savannah glanced around. "Is, um, June here today?" She'd woken up in the middle of the night worrying about Evan's daughter. Half her worry was because June had seemed upset with Savannah as well. Savannah was supposed to be June's friend and a friend didn't kiss another friend's dad. That was weird.

Evan's smile flattened into a thin line as he looked around at the different tables. "She's somewhere out here. Avoiding me. The kids at the youth center were rough with their words last night. A couple kids who had my class in the past took out their dislike for me on my daughter."

Savannah grimaced. "I'm sorry."

He massaged his forehead. "Me too." He pulled his legs off the crate, placing his feet on the ground. "I just want to call all of those kids' parents and give them a piece of my mind."

"You can't do that though."

"No. I've taught most of their kids, and I'll teach the ones that are coming up. I wish they'd bully me instead. I can take it but she's...she's fragile."

"Being the new kid in town isn't easy," Savannah said. "I was the new kid here every summer. Then I met you and Mallory, and Hollis too. Once you find a few true friends, it does get better."

"I hope so. I can't imagine it could get worse." He looked at her for a long moment. There was a sadness in his eyes. "I just...I want June to give Bloom half a chance. What happened at the youth center last night won't help my cause."

Savannah really didn't know what to say. "If there's anything I can do to help, just ask."

"Thanks. Just having someone to listen is helpful."

"Evan!" A tall African American man jogged toward Evan's table. "Evan!"

The sense of urgency in the man's voice had Evan rising to his feet immediately. "Everything all right, Odell?"

"No." The man shook his head. "It's June. You need to come with me now."

Evan's expression tightened. "Why? What happened?"

Odell grimaced. "June has been shoplifting. Sheriff Cruz has her in custody right now." He looked apologetic to have to share the news.

"Oh, no." Evan briefly pinched the bridge of his nose. Then he turned to Savannah. "I hate to ask, but can you watch my table for me?"

"Of course." She waved him on. "Go, take care of June. I've got this."

Evan didn't waste any time following Odell, leaving Savannah alone with all his handmade items and a chest full of worry. What was June thinking? Why would she steal?

Savannah plopped down in the seat where Evan had been sitting and looked out on the busy scene. It looked like everyone in Bloom had come to the market today. This place had always been popular on the weekends, even for the younger crowd.

A woman with a large shopping bag on her shoulder stepped up to Evan's table and began to peruse Evan's items.

"How much?" she asked, without looking up to make eye contact with Savannah.

"Oh." Savannah glanced around for some sort of price list. There was nothing that she could see. "I'm sorry, this isn't my table. I'm not really sure what my friend is charging for his stuff."

"Well, do you want to sell this bowl or not?" The woman looked at Savannah impatiently. "I like it and want to buy it but I might change my mind here in five seconds."

Would Evan rather Savannah sell his piece for too little or not sell it at all? "Um, twenty-five dollars?" Savannah said, wondering if that was too much or too little. She really had no idea what the value of a hand-carved bowl was.

The woman looked annoyed. "Is that a question or a price?"

"A price," Savannah said with a definitive nod.

"Sold." The woman dug a twenty and a five-dollar bill out of her bag and slapped them on the table. Then she picked up the bowl and held it against her midsection. When she did, Savannah saw the price tag on the table where the bowl had been sitting. *Seventy-five dollars?* The woman must have seen it too, because she walked off quickly without a bag or anything to wrap the bowl in.

Savannah stared at the money that the woman had laid down. Evan would never ask her to watch his table again. She could cover the other fifty but that wasn't in her narrow budget right now. Nothing more than the essentials was in her budget until she got a job.

Another customer walked up and perused Evan's items.

"Evan's work is just so perfect," the customer said, looking up at Savannah. She was maybe in her seventies, with graying hair and soft wrinkles around her eyes and mouth that deepened when she smiled. "I've never seen you out here before. You must be new to town."

"Oh, I'm just visiting my aunt for the summer. Eleanor Collins."

"Eleanor?" The woman's pale blue eyes lit up. "Oh, how is

she? Eleanor is a dear friend of mine. I need to get over there and visit her. And get a book from her little library."

"I'm sure she'd love that. She's well." Savannah was intrigued and amazed at how many people loved Eleanor. Bloom was a small town though. Everyone knew everyone. There was a lot to be said about that feature in a town.

"Well, I'm sure your aunt is glad to have family helping her out," the woman said. "She's taken on so much, agreeing to have Madison and Sam's wedding at her place. That's just like Eleanor. She has always been so gracious in every aspect of her life." The woman clasped her hands together at her midsection. "Well, I'm just so glad she has a family member here giving her a hand. Heaven knows, Eleanor is too stubborn to accept help from any of her town friends. Stubborn and proud."

That worried Savannah. Eleanor didn't have any true family here. She thought of Evan as family, and Savannah knew that Eleanor would lean on him if needed. Then again, Eleanor had held back from even letting him help her since her fall, choosing to become a shut-in instead.

The customer returned her attention to the things on Evan's table. "It's been a while since Evan has sold any of his stuff out here. I've been hoping he'd return. I lost the spoon I purchased from him several years back. How much are they?"

Savannah lifted the spoon in question and noted the price on the table this time. "Twenty dollars."

"Well, that's a steal." She dug into her purse and handed Savannah a twenty-dollar bill. "Please tell your aunt that Doris Haymon said hello and that I'll stop in to borrow a book sometime this week. I like mysteries. She'll know what to pick for me."

"I'll tell her." Savannah watched Doris take the spoon and slowly move on to the next table.

"Hey."

Savannah turned toward the sound of Evan's voice as he approached from the opposite side. June was standing next to him. Her face was drawn, her thin lips pulling down into a deep frown. Her gaze skittered up to meet Savannah's, and Savannah's heart immediately broke.

"Hey. Everything okay?" Savannah looked at Evan because she doubted June would answer.

"Not exactly." He looked just as miserable as his daughter. "Any sales?"

Savannah really didn't want to deliver more bad news. "Two but…" She trailed off. "I wasn't sure what the price was for the first one. I can cover the rest of the cost," she said, even though she didn't have the extra money for that. Some weeks, fifty dollars was all her small online store brought in.

"It's okay." There was a look of defeat on Evan's face. "Losing money on one of my items is the least of my problems right now."

"*I'm* his problem," June said glumly. "And that's why I need to go live with Grandma Margie." She lifted her chin a stubborn notch, folding her arms over her chest.

"I've got your number, kid." Evan glanced over. "You had a rough night. And you did this hoping I'd kick you out and send you to live with your grandma. Nice try, but you're stuck with me."

June's eyes glimmered with tears. "Mom wouldn't want me to be miserable."

"She wouldn't want you turning into a thief either," he shot back.

Savannah felt uncomfortable watching the father-daughter spat. Evan was trying so hard, and June was angry and hurting. Both of their emotions were palpable and all of them valid.

Turning back to Savannah, Evan said, "Thanks for watching my table. June and I will take over so you can continue finding the items on Eleanor's list."

"I still don't know where half the items are."

Evan ran a hand through his already disheveled hair. "I'll grab anything you aren't able to locate."

"Just make sure you pay for them," June muttered, loud enough for them to hear.

Evan glanced over. "Of course I would. I'm not a thief, and neither are you."

Her lower lip quivered even though she was selling the tough-girl act pretty hard. "You sure about that?"

Evan released an audible breath. "I'm not giving up on you, kid."

T minus five days until the wedding.

Savannah walked along the garden path with bare feet and a full heart. She would have thought she'd feel jealousy or some thread of disappointment right about now. July was supposed to be her wedding month too. She didn't harbor any of those feelings though. Instead, she was genuinely happy for her friend.

The garden was beautiful. No one would have ever known a storm had swept through, tearing everything down a couple weeks back. It was the perfect setting for a summer wedding.

Savannah took a seat on one of the garden benches, closed her eyes, and listened to the birdsong around her. It was also the perfect place to reflect on life. Savannah needed to give her answer to the chancellor at the university early next week. Was she moving to South Carolina or not? She wished there was another option, because her heart said no, whereas her mind told her that she needed that job.

The sound of sniffles got her attention. Savannah froze and listened to the quick intake of breath and subsequent sniffle. Was someone crying in the garden? She felt like she was in a scene from one of her favorite childhood books, *The Secret Garden*. For a moment, she wondered if she was imagining the sound of crying. She was about to get up and go in search of the source when June started talking.

"I hate Bloom!"

Savannah held her breath. She couldn't see Evan's daughter but she could hear her.

"Let me count the ways I hate it here," June muttered from the other side of the rose lattice before proceeding to rattle off a list of reasons why she didn't want to be in Bloom any longer. The girl obviously didn't know Savannah was here. Otherwise, she wouldn't be so open with her feelings.

Savannah should probably make herself known. Anything less felt like eavesdropping, and she was already on June's bad side these days.

"Mostly, I just miss my mom," June finally said. "She wouldn't want me to be so difficult. I know that but I can't seem to help it. I feel like I don't know or like who I am anymore. I'm mean and awful—especially to my dad. I don't even know why I treat him the way I do."

She continued rambling inaudibly with periodic sniffling. "Anyway, thanks for listening."

Savannah wished she could just give the girl a hug.

"I just..."

A bee buzzed around Savannah, flying toward her hair as if she were a flower. Savannah shooed it away, which only made it more determined.

"You were spying on me?" June stepped around the lattices and placed her hands on her hips, glaring at Savannah with a tightly pinched expression.

Savannah's jaw dropped. "N-no. I-I was already here."

"And you just let me spill my guts knowing that I would never want to tell you any of that stuff? It's none of your business."

"I know." Savannah ducked away from the buzzing bee again. "I'm so sorry. I should have left. I just didn't want to interrupt you. It's clear you needed to talk to someone, even if it's just the roses."

June crossed her arms over her chest. "And now you're going to run and tell my dad everything I just said."

"I won't. But, um..." Savannah felt like she was walking a fine line. "You should. You should tell him how you're feeling, June. The good, the bad, and the ugly."

"I'm pretty sure he's aware." June frowned. "I've been open with him about hating it here."

"What about how much you miss your mom?"

June went quiet for a moment. "I don't think that's a secret."

But Savannah doubted that June had talked about it. "I don't know exactly what you're going through, June, but we can't help you if you don't let your guard down."

June stuck up her chin. "You first. Everyone's dealing with something, right? So, what are you dealing with?"

Savannah blew out a breath, relieved that the bee had finally moved on to the flowers. "Well, my life kind of fell in on itself this year. Now I'm trying to fix it."

June narrowed her eyes. "You call that letting someone else in?"

Savannah wasn't sure if sharing about her illness was the right thing to do but she instinctively knew that June needed something deep and true to fully trust her. "Okay. I got sick this year. Really sick. And then my fiancé, who'd promised to stand by me forever, decided that forever was too long to deal with my list of symptoms. Mind you, *he's* not the one who has to deal with those symptoms."

June's eyes were wide and unblinking. "I knew something was wrong with you."

Savannah furrowed her brow.

June shook her head. "Not in a bad way. I could just sense it. Your ex sounds like a jerk. Are you … okay now?"

Savannah didn't want to lie but she wasn't sure what the truth was either. "Getting there."

June's defensive demeanor from just a few minutes ago seemed to vanish. "I guess you are kind of better than talking to the roses. You actually talk back." She stepped over and took a seat next to Savannah on the cement bench.

"I really like talking to you too," Savannah said. "I enjoyed hanging out last week when we worked in the garden together."

"Before you started kissing my dad?" June asked, but one corner of her mouth kicked up in a smirk.

"Yeah." Savannah cleared her throat. "I want us to be friends again, and I want you to feel free to talk to me anytime."

June fidgeted with her hands on her lap. "Just so you know, I do talk to someone. My grandma."

Savannah wasn't sure but she thought June looked guilty.

June blew out a breath. "I should probably stop calling her so much. I only tell her the bad stuff." June nibbled at her lower lip. "I just need to vent, you know?"

"I understand. You can vent to me," Savannah said. "I don't mind."

"But you're not staying in Bloom."

"No, but I'll come back to visit." Savannah regretted that she hadn't come nearly often enough in the last couple of years—for Eleanor's sake and her own. Bloom felt like home, and there was something so healing about being here. "And there's such a thing as a phone."

June gave her the slightest smile. "Why can't you stay? I mean, my dad likes you. And you seem to like him too. I can tell." June glanced around the garden. "I have a feeling that my dad also probably needs someone to vent to. I'm not an easy daughter to have, you know."

"I'm sure he'd say you're worth it."

June looked at Savannah again. "Your ex should have said you were worth it too."

Savannah swallowed painfully. "I guess that's how I know he wasn't the one for me."

"Well, if my dad is willing to put up with me, I'm sure he'd stick around for you, no matter what."

Savannah thought June was right. Evan was the loyal type. A

generally good guy. He was the forever kind of guy. After being dumped so harshly only a few short months ago, Savannah needed a rebound guy—not Mr. Forever.

"Well, nice talk." June studied her. "You sure you're okay now?"

Savannah was supposed to be asking June that, not vice versa. "Yeah. You're better than talking to the roses too."

Chapter Sixteen

Evan

Her stillness defeated his storm.

The Pursuit of Happyness, Chris Gardner

Evan dipped his paint roller into a pan of paint, letting it cover the applicator in a deep creamy tan color. Then he held it to the outside wall of the library and moved the roller up and down. Up and down.

It was a mindless task, which worked for and against him. He needed a distraction from thinking about Savannah too much, because the more he thought of her, the harder he was falling. He hadn't felt this way about anyone in a long time. It was nice, except the tiny voice in the back of his mind was sounding off concerns. This thing between him and Savannah was a dead end.

"Need some help with that?"

Evan turned toward Savannah's voice. "You're offering to help me paint the library?"

She was wearing her wide-brimmed hat along with a flowing yellow sundress. "I've done some painting in my time."

"I'm not sure you should do something like this, you know, considering."

Savannah folded her arms over her chest. "It's not like we're digging ditches, Evan. It's painting." She reached for a second roller that he'd carried out in case June or Hollis joined him. "I'm perfectly capable of pushing a paint roller back and forth. This is easy compared to cleaning up the garden benches like I did earlier. They look almost as good as new now."

Evan wasn't sure letting Savannah work even harder than she already had was the best idea but he certainly didn't mind her company. "Okay, but I'm counting on you to stop when you get tired."

"I'm counting on you stopping if *you* get tired," she countered.

"Deal." He tried not to let her notice him watching her closely as they worked. Even though he was sure she could take care of herself, he wasn't so sure she had figured out her limits yet. She was related to Eleanor, after all.

"I've actually never painted a building before. Am I messing this up?" Savannah asked about ten minutes into the job.

Evan set his roller down for a moment and headed in her direction. "I didn't want to say anything, but…" He trailed off.

Savannah laughed. "Really? Am I fired already?"

"No, but let me show you how it's done." He stepped behind her and wrapped his arms around her to grab hold of her roller. Then he guided her to dip the roller in the pan, modestly coating the applicator. "There we go. Now we move it to the bottom and roll up. Down. Up. Down." They worked together. It almost felt like they were dancing.

"I'm not sure how you're making this task feel so romantic." She grinned at him over her shoulder.

In this position, Evan was tempted to kiss her cheek. Maybe even her neck. They weren't there yet in their relationship though.

Relationship? He was not allowed to think that way. That's what his mind told him but his heart begged to differ. Getting reacquainted with Savannah had been so easy. It was like no time had passed in some ways, and in others it was clear that they'd matured. There wasn't as much hesitation now. When they'd been nineteen, crossing that line from friends to more had been terrifying.

Their friendship wasn't on the forefront this time though. This time, the attraction took the lead, and they were becoming friends again as they spent more time together.

Savannah glanced over her shoulder at him. "You're suddenly lost in thought. And I must say, your painting skills aren't much better than mine right now."

He lowered his arms and took a step backward. "Because you're a distraction." He moved to pick up his own roller again and they worked side by side.

"Eleanor and I had a talk last night," Savannah said, slipping out of his hold. "About her fear of leaving the house."

"Oh? She admitted that she was afraid?"

Savannah dipped her roller back into the pan. "She did. We discussed her seeing a counselor. She's open to the idea. I told her I'd try to call around and find someone for her. Any suggestions?"

"Not off the top of my head. Let me think on it. I'm sure I know of a couple people who might work well for Eleanor." He swiped his forearm over his brow, catching a bead of sweat. If he was hot, Savannah must be too. Her cheeks were already flushed. "I think I need a break."

She narrowed her eyes but lowered her paint roller. "I know what you're doing but don't stop on my behalf. You stay. I'll go inside. I want to check on Eleanor anyway. Want me to bring you an iced tea?"

Evan shook his head. "I have a bottle of water that I'm still working on for now."

"Okay." Savannah adjusted her hat. "The library is looking great. I'm almost done transferring all the books back over here too. One wagonload at a time takes forever but I'm making slow progress."

"I can do the rest for you," he offered.

Savannah tilted her head. "Are you treating me differently now that you know I have lupus? Because if you are, my answer is no."

Evan considered the question. "Maybe I'm just treating you differently since we kissed."

Her smile stretched wider. "In that case, please continue. And yes, I'd love for you to help me cart the rest of the books to the library."

After finishing up the second coat on the entire building, Evan cleaned up his mess and headed inside for the afternoon. That glass of sweet tea that Savannah had offered him earlier sounded enticing right about now but not as much as a cool shower.

Evan cut through the rose garden and dipped through the missing panel in the fence. Something felt off in his gut as he made his way home but he wasn't sure why.

"June?" he called as he opened the back door. "Hey, June?"

"In the living room, Dad!"

There was a lightness to June's tone that relieved any worry he had that something was wrong. Then Evan heard June say something in a lower voice that wasn't meant for him. Was someone else here?

Evan picked up his pace as he walked through the kitchen toward the living room. June wasn't supposed to let anyone inside when he wasn't home. He turned the corner and stopped short when he saw his unexpected guest.

"Well, hello, Evan." Margie sat on the couch alongside June. She looked as if she were going to a dinner party, wearing a fitted pink dress and a full face of makeup.

Had he missed something? "Margie. I didn't realize you were coming for a visit today."

June's grandmother smiled primly. "I didn't realize I needed to schedule visits with my granddaughter."

June eyed her dad, pleading with him to behave. "You don't need to schedule, Grandma."

The look in Margie's eyes seemed to dare him to blow up at her. That's what she wanted him to do. If he had to guess, Margie wanted him to be the bad guy here—and he wasn't going to do that. "Of course you don't need to schedule. This is a nice surprise." He would have at least cleaned the house if he'd known Margie was coming. That's probably why she hadn't forewarned him. Knowing Margie, she wanted to catch him at his worst and prove he wasn't the best choice as June's caregiver.

At least most of the work in the garden was complete for the wedding. "To what do I owe the visit?" he asked.

"I'm not sure if you knew but June here has been having a rough time lately." Margie tilted her head as she looked at him.

Don't lose your cool, Evan. That's what she wants. He really hoped Margie was only here to visit her granddaughter but something in her eyes hinted at more.

"I'm aware, yes." Evan glanced over at June, who had her head down now.

"When June called me the other night, she was so distraught over what you did."

"What I did?" he asked.

"Forcing her to go to that place just to be bullied." Margie clasped her hands together over one knee.

Evan felt like he'd been kicked in the gut. "Obviously, I didn't know that would happen. June can't just stay indoors all summer, alone in her room, Margie. It's not good for her."

"She wouldn't be alone in her room if she were still in California with me," Margie shot back, her tone sharp but her smile still plastered on her face. "She's grieving, Evan," she said.

As if he didn't already know that.

"She doesn't know anyone here," Margie continued. "Why on earth would you leave her somewhere that she has absolutely no one? What kind of parenting is that?"

Evan's lips parted but no words came out.

She pointed her manicured finger at him. "While you went out on some date. Is that the real reason you left my granddaughter with a group of mean kids? So that you could have a little one-on-one time with your new girlfriend?"

June was still looking down. She seemed to be sinking into

the couch cushion. Evan knew that the only way Margie knew any of this was because June had told her.

"The woman was not my girlfriend," Evan said through gritted teeth. "She's a friend of mine. Of June's too."

Margie folded her hands back over the knees of her crossed legs. "I also came because I missed June. When June invited me to come, I couldn't say no. She needed me, and quite frankly, I needed her."

"June invited you?" Evan asked.

"That's right. This visit isn't a surprise. June knew I was coming. She didn't tell you?" Margie asked, feigning innocence.

Evan looked at June again. Her sheepishness had now morphed into guilt. "Nope," Evan said.

"Must have slipped my mind," June said quietly. "Anyway, Grandma Margie is here for a couple of days."

A couple days? Yeah, his daughter hadn't mentioned that.

"Great." Evan had invited Margie as well but a reasonable guest would have given a heads-up. He gestured down the hall. "I'll just go wash up and then head out to town to buy a few steaks to put on the grill."

"Oh, don't go to any trouble on my account." Margie's eyes narrowed. "A bowl of cereal would be fine by me."

June looked guiltier by the second. Evan guessed she'd shared with her grandmother the few times he'd served cereal for dinner too. Apparently, Juliana could do it, but if he did, it made him a bad father. "We'll have steaks," he called behind him, heading down the hall toward the shower, leaving the conversation before he said something he might regret.

Chapter Seventeen

Eleanor

*Maybe (happiness) was about stringing together
a bunch of small pleasures.*

*The Sisterhood of the Traveling
Pants*, Ann Brashares

The wedding was only four days away. Eleanor pulled on her sneakers to take a walk in the garden. She wanted to see the progress and imagine the love story that would unfold on her property this weekend.

She took slow steps as she navigated the porch steps. Once she was on even ground, she picked up her pace and followed the garden's path. The roses were abloom, fragrant, and dripping with color. "Aaron, are you here?" Some part of her always waited as if he would respond with words. All she ever got was a warm breeze that she credited to him or a memory of his voice in her head. Truthfully, some part of her hoped he wasn't a ghost in her garden. She hoped he was somewhere in a larger, grander garden building a larger, grander library for her when she finally joined him.

Even so, what was the harm in her talking to her late husband if it made her feel closer to him? "I suppose if you are here, you know that Savannah is struggling a touch these days."

Eleanor imagined Aaron telling her in his calmest voice, "We all struggle, whether we show it or not." Aaron had always seen the bigger picture, the forest, while she sometimes focused on the trees.

"I suppose you also might have overheard Savannah telling me I should talk to someone. Someone other than a memory. Other than the roses." She dipped to smell one of the open blooms along the path. "Mm. If I could bottle that scent up, I'd be a millionaire. A lot of good it would do me without you. We never got to go on all of our adventures," she said, continuing forward. "And part of me has no desire to do them without you."

A breeze blew through, and maybe it was her imagination, but it smelled just like that flower. She inhaled deeply, wishing her late husband were here. He'd been gone for so long, and the only thing keeping her from being lonely was books. And Charlie.

"You told me to talk to a counselor one time. Do you remember?" It was after two long years of trying to have a child. Finally, Eleanor accepted what the doctors had told her. The likelihood of becoming pregnant was negligible. It was heartbreakingly hopeless, and Eleanor had felt broken in a way she thought might never be fixed. "You convinced me to get help, and it was good for me." It wasn't always easy to do the thing that you knew would help, especially when you were in a down-and-out state of mind.

Figaro darted out of the bushes, playfully launching herself at Eleanor's feet. Eleanor lost her footing and stumbled forward. Her arms flew out to her sides, attempting to steady herself. Once she was sure she wasn't in fact falling, she pressed a hand to her chest and took a few deep breaths. Her wristwatch made a beeping noise, alerting her to her increased heart rate.

Eleanor closed her eyes. "When did I become this person who can't even walk around my own backyard without being afraid? I'm growing old, Aaron, and it's not fair that you're not doing the same with me." She pointed a finger in the air. "I am quite sure that between the two of us, I would have aged more gracefully."

"Who are you talking to?"

Eleanor nearly stumbled again as she turned to face the visitor in her garden. "Oh, June. What are you doing out here?"

Today June was wearing a cute shirt with clouds printed on the front and a pair of military-green cargo shorts. Her hair was sectioned into two low-hanging pigtails. "Your yard is way cooler than ours. I've been hanging around the library too, when my dad isn't working on it."

"I see."

"Is that okay?" June asked, suddenly looking worried. "Will I get in trouble?"

Eleanor dodged another playful attack from Figaro. "Not with me. The library is for anyone."

June gave Eleanor a curious look. "There's no one out here. Who were you talking to just now?"

"The flowers." Eleanor decided it was best not to tell the

girl she was conversing with her deceased husband. "So, your grandmother is in town, hmm?"

"Yep." June started walking, leading the way down the path. "Dad isn't thrilled about it. I can tell."

"And that fact makes you happy or sad?" Eleanor asked, trying to match the girl's pace.

June glanced over. "Do you really think I want to irritate my dad?"

Eleanor laughed softly. "I think you're a young girl and he's a parent. It's part of the dynamic."

"Maybe." June sighed. "He doesn't listen to me though. Not really. I miss my grandma."

Eleanor found this interesting. "What exactly about being with her is it that you miss?"

June seemed to think on this question. "For one, her house is always stocked with food. That's very important."

"I see." They walked under the wooden arbor, enjoying the momentary shade.

"My grandma plays piano. She's kind of like a professional. She taught me a little bit."

"I didn't know that." Eleanor stopped walking for a moment to catch her breath, smiling down at Figaro as she clawed at Eleanor's shoelaces. "I have an old keyboard in my closet. Would you like me to get it out for you?"

June offered a half smile. "Cool. Yeah. Dad might not like the noise though."

"Which would be a good thing or a bad thing?" Eleanor asked. "Or just another of those things young people do to get on their parents' nerves."

June shrugged. "I don't know. My grandmother misses me too. Without me, she has no one to talk to anymore."

"I see. Well then, it's nice that she's here for a visit. Where is she right now?" Eleanor asked, continuing forward.

"At the house. She's cleaning because she said Dad is incompetent." June slid a guilty gaze to meet Eleanor's.

Eleanor paused again. "Your father is the most competent man I know."

"Yeah." June shrugged. "He and Grandma bump heads. He left the house because he said Grandma is insufferable. He went to the store for gardening supplies with Savannah." June reached down and gathered up the kitten in her arms. "Grandma is supposed to be watching me but I doubt she even realizes I left. I can get away with anything when her soap operas are on." Mischief sparkled in the girl's eyes, making Eleanor laugh as they approached the Finders Keepers Library.

Eleanor studied the library's exterior, amazed at the progress that Evan had made. "After that storm," Eleanor told June, "I was devastated. This place means the world to me."

June couldn't possibly understand but Eleanor felt like there was a lesson that couldn't be taught with any quote from a book.

"My late husband, Aaron, worked so hard to build this little place for me. It was the most romantic thing anyone has ever done for me. Then the storm swept through, tearing off pieces of the roof. Part of the building caved in on one side. I couldn't see how it would ever be the same, much less better." Tears burned Eleanor's eyes. "But look at it now! Now my library looks as if there were never a storm at all." Eleanor could draw similarities with her fall last winter. She'd shattered her pelvis and couldn't even walk. Yet here she was, strolling through the garden as if nothing had ever happened. "Your life has gone through the worst kind of storm," Eleanor told June, reaching to pet Figaro in June's arms. "With time and love, your life will be pieced back together. It'll look different but different isn't always bad."

June twisted her mouth to the side. "My life isn't some library in the middle of a garden."

Eleanor shook her head. "No, it's not. Come inside with me. I have the perfect book for you." She opened the door to the library. There were a few boxes on the floor from where Savannah had been working to reshelve some of the books that were moved after the storm. Eleanor had lost some of her favorite books from water damage after the roof caved in. Most had been salvaged though, and Eleanor had received a lot of donations from folks in town.

"How do you pick out books for people?" June spun in a slow circle to take in the space. "Do you just guess at what people like or is it more like a superpower?"

"A superpower." Eleanor chuckled. "A chef knows food. A musician knows songs. I know books." The books were categorized by genre, sectioned off with signs so that anyone looking for romance or mystery could find it easily. She stepped over to the section that she'd labeled Adventure. Then she ran her eyes over the spines facing out, humming softly under her breath.

"What book are you looking for?" June asked impatiently.

"You'll see." In Eleanor's peripheral vision, she saw June petting Figaro in her arms. An animal had never been allowed in the library but this little kitten was the exception. "Aha!"

Eleanor pulled the book face out to show June. On the cover, there was a striking picture of a pair of blue jeans.

"*The Sisterhood of the Traveling Pants*," June read.

"By?" Eleanor refused to mention a title without naming the author.

"Ann Brashares." June placed the kitten back on the floor and took the book. "What's so great about this book?"

"Friendship, for one."

"Don't you think reading this would be kind of like rubbing it in my face that I have no friends?"

Eleanor loved this girl's spunk. "No, I don't. I think this is the perfect book for you right now."

June studied the book's cover. "What else is special about this book?"

"How about you read it and tell me once you're done?"

"I could just watch the movie, you know?"

Eleanor gasped.

"Just kidding. I'll read it," June promised, hugging the book to her. "But only if I can pick out a book for you."

"I've read them all," Eleanor told her.

"All these books?" June's lips parted.

"More than once probably. But which one would you choose for me?"

June walked around momentarily, stopping at the young adult section. "This one." She pulled the book off the shelf and held it, cover out, for Eleanor to see.

Eleanor frowned. "Where did that come from? That's not one of mine." She took the book in her hand and studied it for some clue as to where it'd come from. It had likely been donated from someone in town.

June looked pleased with herself. "If I read the pants book, you have to read *The Hunger Games*. By Suzanne Collins," she added. "And you can't just watch the movie." She wagged a finger. "It's against the rules."

Eleanor had heard of this book before. Of course she had. It just wasn't something that she thought she'd likely enjoy. She looked at June, who was practically beaming. Eleanor imagined June had the same face watching her dad's irritation with her grandma Margie. "Fine," she said. "I'll read it. Then I'll get back to you on how I liked it."

June grinned. "We could have a movie night afterward. *The Sisterhood of the Traveling Pants* and *The Hunger Games*. With lots of popcorn."

"I never thought I'd say this, but watching the movie sounds like fun. With you."

Chapter Eighteen

Savannah

The memories I value most, I don't ever see them fading.

Never Let Me Go, Kazuo Ishiguro

T minus three days before the wedding.

Savannah was lying on a massage table next to Mallory, who had Madison lying on the other side of her. Tonight was a quasi–bachelorette party for Madison, just among the three of them.

"Massages first. Then we'll get smoothies and have our nails and toes done," Mallory announced cheerfully.

Savannah tried to take some deep breaths, but she couldn't force her muscles to relax. There was a hot towel draped along the arch of her lower back and hot stones placed along her upper back. In her mind, she knew it was supposed to feel good, but she was having difficulty enjoying the spa treatment. She had too much on her mind.

The deadline for when she needed to respond to the job offer in South Carolina was quickly approaching, and she was conflicted over what her response would be. She didn't have any other offers and she needed a steady income. And continued health insurance. No part of her wanted to move so far away. She'd promised to visit Aunt Eleanor often. How could she, if she lived five hours away? With her lupus, driving so many hours might be problematic.

Mallory gave Savannah's side a playful shove. "Relaxxx."

Madison giggled. "I'm the one getting married. If anyone should be tense, it's me."

Mallory turned her head to look at her sister while Savannah listened. "Are you excited?"

"I guess." Madison's tone of voice dropped a notch. "And a little scared, if I'm telling the truth."

"Scared?" Savannah propped herself up on an elbow. "From all accounts, you and Sam are perfect for each other."

"He's perfect for me, that's true," Madison said with a hint of sadness creeping into her expression.

Mallory sighed. "And you are perfect for him. You're just getting too much in your head."

"I can't walk," Madison said flatly. "Sam and I will never go on a hike together. Going anywhere will be fifty times harder for me than it would be for a spouse that has functioning legs."

Savannah couldn't help comparing herself to Madison, even though they had very different health issues. Going on a hike would be harder for her as well. Any guy she dated would have to accommodate certain activities when they were together. A day at the beach would never be a full day for her anymore.

Mallory reached out for her sister's hand. "Sam doesn't care about that stuff; you know that. Without you, he'd be sad and lonely. You make him happy, and that's all that matters."

Was that true? Savannah believed it was for Madison and Sam so why should she doubt that she could have the same?

"Sav?" Madison called across Mallory. "This celebration isn't making you feel weird, is it? Because of your broken engagement."

"Not at all," Savannah said quickly. "I honestly can't wait to see you and Sam recite your vows. He's a lucky man."

"Thanks." Madison blew out a breath. "I can't feel my legs but my feet sure are cold these days. Pun intended."

Now Mallory shoved Madison. "Bad joke, sis. You're only kidding about the cold feet, right? Because I love you, and I don't want anything to hurt you. But I also care about my future brother-in-law. You aren't going to break his heart and no-show him at the wedding, are you?"

"Not a chance," Madison said. "He's stuck with me forever."

The door to the room opened and three masseuses walked in, announcing themselves as Amy, Amber, and Lee.

"We are here to loosen you ladies up a bit," the first masseuse, Amy, said, rubbing her hands together. "Feel free to keep talking among yourselves. What is said in the masseuse room, stays in the masseuse room. That's a promise."

"And believe me," the second masseuse, Amber, said, while cracking her knuckles, "we've heard a lot of juicy stuff in here, and we've never uttered a word."

"This place is like a confessional," Lee, masseuse number three and the taller of the three women, added.

Everyone laughed, although Savannah's was more from nervousness than humor.

"Why do we only do this kind of stuff when one of us is getting married?" Madison asked a few minutes into the massage.

"We should do it more often," Mallory said. "And you should come with us," she told Savannah. "If you can make the trip down from where you're staying."

"Staying?" Madison asked.

"Sav has a new job at a university," Mallory answered for Savannah. "It's in South Carolina. She'll be an assistant professor," Mallory went on while Savannah remained quiet.

"Really? Wow, that's amazing." Madison looked so impressed.

There was a feeling of dread as Savannah listened to Mallory talk. *Dread?* This was something she was supposed to be looking forward to. So why wasn't she?

Deep down, Savannah knew the answer. She was falling for Evan. She'd promised herself she wouldn't but the feelings were there. They'd already been rooted during her teenage years and had only needed a little attention to grow. Savannah also wasn't thrilled about leaving Aunt Eleanor. Or Mallory. Or June.

"I haven't officially accepted the job yet," Savannah said quietly.

Mallory lifted her head off the massage table to look at Savannah. "What? Why not?"

Savannah looked at her friends. "I had several phone interviews last month. Two have declined but there's still one more job that I'm waiting to hear back from. It's at an aviary."

Mallory's expression twisted. "For birds? How does that have anything to do with plants?"

"Aviaries have exotic plants," Savannah said. "The habitat is amazing. I've seen pictures online. Plus, it's only two hours from here."

And even that distance felt like too much.

"So, if that job makes an offer, you'll take it instead?" Madison asked.

Deep down, Savannah knew the fact that she hadn't heard from the aviary yet was her answer. She was just using the faint possibility of a job offer as an excuse to delay accepting the assistant professor job in South Carolina. "What if I decided to stay?" Savannah asked.

"Stay?" Mallory practically shouted.

"Why on earth would you stay?" Madison added. "That job sounds perfect for you. Well, the first one does. The second one sounds cool too."

"Are you being serious, Savannah?" Mallory's gaze narrowed.

Savannah shook her head. She didn't have the financial ability to stay. She had bills and only enough money saved to pay them through the end of August. "Not really." She avoided her friend's concerned look and lowered her face back into the massage table's hole.

"Good," masseuse number one said. "Now close your eyes and let your worries melt away," she practically demanded, as her forceful hands took hold of the muscles on Savannah's back.

Savannah wasn't sure what she was thinking, pondering out loud the possibility of staying. Surely the essential oils were getting to her head. Her parents were very vocal about their disappointment over sending her to college to get a degree that she wasn't using. Yes, she had a vlog and social media following, but they considered that more of a hobby. Randall had too.

So no, she couldn't stay in Bloom. Bloom didn't have a university or an aviary. It had a farmers market and quaint shops typical of any small town. Savannah didn't quite have a plan set in stone yet but she knew that staying wasn't in the cards. Neither was falling in love with Evan.

By the time Savannah got back to Eleanor's home, she was equal parts relaxed and exhausted. It felt like someone had taken a meat tenderizer to her body, which was about right.

"Did you have fun?" Eleanor was in her reading chair with a book open about a quarter of the way through and her reading glasses perched halfway down her nose.

"I think so. Although massages have never really been my thing." Savannah thought she recognized the book's cover. "Are you reading the Hunger Games series?" Surely Savannah was mistaken.

"Indeed I am. June picked it out for me. The entire series was in my library. I assume it was a donation from someone."

Savannah raised a hand. "I added the books. They were mine. I've been driving around with them in my car for ages. I finally took them out and added them to your shelf. I hope that's okay."

"Of course it is. It's a library. You can give and take as much as you like."

Savannah was still stumped as to why Eleanor was reading that book—but Eleanor had been known to read anything and everything.

"I've never had a massage myself," Eleanor said. "Do you feel more relaxed? I do."

"I do." Savannah set her bag down on the coffee table next to the door and took a seat across from her aunt. "Maybe you should come out with us next time. It'll be fun."

Eleanor gave her an amused look. "Perhaps. It would be more appealing than being in one of the twelve districts and forced to play some bizarre game of survival."

It took a moment for Savannah to make the connection to the book in her aunt's lap. "I would hope a massage is better than that, Aunt Eleanor."

Eleanor tapped her finger on the book's cover. "There is a lesson in every book. I think this one's lesson is that nothing is as bad as poor Katniss's plight. It makes me feel so much better about my own circumstances." She narrowed her eyes. "How are you feeling about your circumstances these days?"

Eleanor always seemed to know exactly the right questions to pry into Savannah's soul.

"Truthfully, I feel lost. I should be excited, but..." She shook her head. "Maybe I'm just tired."

"You need to listen to your body. That's especially important now."

Savannah inhaled softly. "Mallory told you?" She hadn't told Mallory to keep her lupus a secret.

"June did," Eleanor said. "I suspect that if June knows about your illness, then Evan does as well. Why haven't you told me?"

"You need to focus on yourself right now. I didn't want to worry you."

"Everyone is going through something. Not one person, not even a twelve-year-old girl, is spared. The only way we survive is to band together." She got a thoughtful look on her face. "Like the kids in *The Hunger Games*. See? These books are a reflection of life. There are lessons to learn." Her eyes bored into Savannah's, looking deep. "I could tell when you arrived last month that you were dealing with something more than just a broken heart."

Savannah nodded. "I could never hide anything from you."

Eleanor smiled. "But you're doing better now. I see it in your eyes. They're full of life again. Your cheeks are rosy."

Savannah ducked her head. "Well, that might be a symptom of my lupus."

"It's not. It's because you're feeling well. You're happy. And you're falling in love."

Savannah looked at her aunt, too stunned to speak.

Eleanor held up a hand. "You could never hide anything from me but I do recall that sometimes you were good at hiding things from yourself." She lowered her hand to her lap. "You said you were tired. You'd best get some rest. Good night, dear."

Savannah stood. She'd obviously just been dismissed. Part of her wanted to refute what Eleanor had said but the other part wanted to pretend she hadn't heard it. "Night."

As she walked down the hall and into her bedroom, she knew Aunt Eleanor was right. When Randall had broken off their engagement, she'd wondered if she'd missed her last chance at love but she hadn't. She had a chance with Evan if she turned down the job in South Carolina.

Plopping onto her bed, Savannah stared up at the ceiling. She didn't want to be an assistant professor in a place where she didn't know anyone. She wanted to stay in Bloom with Aunt Eleanor and Mallory.

And Evan.

Nerves wrapped around her chest like the roses on that arbor outside. She needed a reason to justify staying that wasn't based on her feelings for Evan. She'd changed her life for Randall. She never wanted to alter her wants and needs for someone again. No, she couldn't do that.

Savannah rolled onto her side and looked out her window where the moon shone brightly. Maybe she was just scared of the unknown. Maybe she needed to go, regardless of what she wanted.

Chapter Nineteen

Evan

We stand against the small tide of those who want to make everyone unhappy with conflicting theory and thought.

Fahrenheit 451, Ray Bradbury

"Something in here smells delicious."

Evan turned toward Margie's voice as she came down the hall, already dressed for the day. He'd started cooking half an hour ago, determined to present himself as a satisfactory father. He hated that he felt like he needed to prove himself to Margie but he did.

Before she died, Juliana had made it clear that she believed in his ability to raise June but Margie didn't seem to share that opinion. Evan wasn't sure why. He'd always tried to do right by Juliana and June. The military had taken him away physically but he'd called, FaceTimed, sent gifts, and provided financially. He'd sent cards and had gone to California to visit at every opportunity. Maybe he wasn't dad of the year but he was a good father.

"You cooked?" Margie pretended to be surprised.

"Of course." He bit back any sarcastic response he wanted to counter with. "Have a seat and I'll prepare you a plate."

"Breakfast is the most important meal of the day, after all," Margie said. "June mentioned that you have a lot of cereal around here."

Evan scooped scrambled eggs onto a plate and used a pair of metal tongs to serve two slices of crispy bacon. He included a little saucer of grits as well. Then he carried the plate over to Margie and placed it in front of her. "Home-cooked meals are ideal but we all fall back on cereal every now and then."

"Rarely," Margie said under her breath, but Evan was quite sure that she'd intended for him to hear her. "Evan, I want to be transparent about my intentions here."

"Okay." Evan had a feeling he wasn't going to like whatever Margie was about to say.

"I've contacted my lawyer." Margie avoided his eyes, instead looking down at her folded hands on the table. "June is old enough now to have a say in where she wants to be. Her life has been disrupted enough, losing the only acting parent she's ever had."

"That's not fair," Evan said, raising his voice. "I have always been there for June. Always."

"So have I," Margie said, matching his tone, her pale blue eyes narrowing on him. "Except I was actually there to hug her. To hold her when she was upset. I read her bedtime stories. I held her hand. I was there the day her mother died—on the hardest day of her life."

Evan felt like he couldn't pull in a full breath. He hadn't been there on that day, although he'd wanted to be. He had gotten on a plane the following day and had gotten to June as soon as he could. "Juliana told me that she wanted June to be with me after she died. It was her wish, Margie."

"*June's* wish, however, is to be in California. With me."

Evan needed to sit down. He couldn't decide if he was angry or sad. His emotions were all over the place. "I am June's father. I will fight you and I will win," he said softening his voice.

Margie smiled but there was nothing warm in the gesture. "Don't be so sure."

Evan really had no idea if he could win or what a judge took into account when making these kinds of decisions. "Margie, please don't do this. We both love June and want what's best. Let's just…"

Before he could complete his sentence, June came shuffling down the hall in her stocking feet.

"You cooked?" she asked with nearly the same level of surprise as Margie had shown a few minutes earlier.

Evan offered a wobbly smile. "Morning. Sit and I'll make your plate."

June pulled out the chair next to her grandmother and sat down. "Can I have coffee too?" she asked. "Mom always let me have a cup when we had breakfast together."

"Did she?" Margie pulled back and narrowed her eyes at June. Her surprise was sincere this time. "At your age?"

"Yep," June said.

"But it will stunt your growth," Margie continued, shaking her head slightly.

It was interesting to see Margie's disapproval at the parenting skills of her own daughter. Evan had thought Margie was just needling him but maybe this was the way she treated everyone in her life. Did she treat June that way as well?

"A cup of coffee is no different than a can of soda," June said matter-of-factly.

Margie looked at Evan as if pleading with him to back her up.

"You can have one cup of coffee." Maybe he'd said it out of spite but he also didn't see the big deal. One cup of coffee wasn't going to halt June's growth forever. If Juliana had been okay with it, so was he. They weren't perfect parents but they did have June's best interests in mind. He was sure of that. He'd like to think the same was true for Margie, but then, why was she trying so hard to convince June to live in California?

Margie looked down at her plate, picking up her fork and stabbing at the golden mounds of eggs. She ate quietly for several long minutes.

"So, can we go shopping today?" June finally asked Margie. "You've always been my favorite shopping partner."

Margie looked at her, her thin brows lifting subtly on her forehead. "Shopping for what?"

"The wedding this weekend. It's going to be next door in the backyard. Ms. Eleanor invited me. Dad is going too."

Evan thought that June looked more excited than he'd seen her in a long time.

Margie turned to Evan. "Do you know the persons getting married?"

"Madison Blue and Sam Lewis," he said as he added creamer to June's coffee and carried the mug to place in front of her. "I grew up with them. Eleanor offered her backyard as the venue."

"She has a really cool garden." June wrapped both hands

around her mug and brought it to her mouth, seeming to inhale the steam. "And there's a library in the garden too."

"Careful. It's hot," Evan warned, as June took her first sip.

June lifted her gaze and rolled her eyes. The morning wouldn't be complete without an eye roll.

"A library in the middle of the garden? Who ever heard of such a thing?" Margie asked, shaking her head.

June shrugged. "Ms. Eleanor has lots of visitors who come to borrow books from her."

Margie's expression was one of pure disapproval. "You're telling me there are strangers in and out of your neighbor's yard all day long, and you're not concerned for June's well-being?" she asked Evan.

Evan poured Margie a cup of coffee and placed it in front of her, along with cream and sugar. "Margie, this is Bloom. There are no strangers here. If there are, they won't be strangers long."

"You're telling me you know every single person who comes and goes to visit your neighbor?" Margie asked, disbelief evident in her voice.

Evan chuckled out of frustration. If he didn't laugh, he might find himself picking up the leftover eggs and tossing them on the ground. "I probably do. I might not know their family histories but I know their faces."

Margie pushed her plate of food away as if she'd completely lost her appetite. She reached for her mug of coffee, keeping it black. Then she brought it to her mouth, frowning as June did the same.

"So, shopping?" June asked, bobbing around in her seat. "I need a dress."

A small smile flickered on Margie's lips. "I'm not sure the shopping will be as good in a place like this."

A place like this?

"But we'll do our best," Margie added.

"Great. I need to find something to wear as well," Evan said. "We'll all go." He couldn't believe he'd just said that because no part of him wanted to shop, especially with Margie. He didn't want June to have too much alone time with her grandmother though. Margie would use every opportunity to convince June of how unhappy she was here. June was only twelve. It would be easy to sway her already fragile feelings toward hating this town for all the reasons that Evan loved it.

Bloom was small. It revolved around community and things like books, gardening, and delicious food. Maybe the shopping wasn't fancy but Evan counted that as a perk, not a con. The best shopping here happened at the farmers market on Saturday mornings.

June tipped her chin to her chest and looked at him through disbelieving eyes. "You're going shopping with us? You despise shopping."

He shrugged. "I want to look nice for the occasion as well."

"Why is that? Is there someone there you're interested in?" Margie asked. "Romantically."

Evan had to hold back from groaning out loud. Margie was just looking for things to hold against him and reasons why June should be with her instead. She'd only been here for a day but the internal struggle between them was exhausting.

"Dad is interested in Savannah," June volunteered. "She lives next door too."

"Is that right?" Margie looked delighted by this information, but Evan knew it wasn't because he was possibly falling in love. Margie wasn't happy for him by any means. "I'm guessing that is the woman you were with the other night when my June was bullied at that awful youth center."

"And if it was?" Evan asked.

Margie shrugged, looking gleeful. "Well, let's just say I'm seeing things a little more clearly now."

"What does that mean?" he asked.

"I think you know. It gives me insight into why you might insist on staying in this nowhere town instead of acting in June's best interest and moving to the West Coast where her friends and family are."

Before Evan could retort, June whipped her head to the side to look at Margie. "Grandma, that's not fair!"

Now Evan was surprised. Was his daughter sticking up for him?

"Dad has only just started talking to Savannah. And she's really nice. You'd like her if you got to know her. Mom would have liked her too," June added.

Evan wondered if that was true. Juliana and Savannah were completely different people but Juliana had liked everyone. She always saw the best in people, and she believed in true love. That's why she'd never wanted to stay with Evan. She'd told him once that he wasn't her soulmate. Evan guessed Juliana had never found that person before she died. Or maybe her soulmate had been her daughter.

"So, it's settled," June said. "We're all going shopping this morning." She put on a smile that was wider and more forced than Evan had seen from her all summer. It made him realize that even June tried hard to impress Margie.

"Yes, I guess it is." Margie looked at Evan.

"You didn't finish your breakfast." Evan gestured at her plate. "Was it good?"

"Considering. I just like to watch my girlish figure." Margie twisted at her waist to rest her elbow on the back of the chair.

June set her fork down quickly as well, obviously taking her cues from her grandmother.

Evan tipped his head down at June's plate. "You might want to finish your breakfast. Shopping takes a lot of energy." He gestured down the hall. "I'll just go get dressed for our outing. This should be fun," he said. At the very least, it would be interesting.

Two hours later, Evan was seated on a comfy chair outside the women's dressing rooms. June had come out at least a half dozen times wearing a different possibility for this weekend's wedding.

Margie was sitting in an armchair opposite him. "You know you didn't have to come with us today. I could've handled this."

"I wanted to come," Evan said. "Why wouldn't I?"

She shrugged a bare shoulder. She was wearing a sleeveless business-style dress and a pair of two-inch heels. She stuck out like a sore thumb in Bloom. Even the businesspeople in town were casual, wearing slacks and sundresses. "You didn't seem so interested in things like this when my daughter was alive," Margie pointed out. "I don't know why that would have changed now."

Evan was tired of participating in this battle of who could do better by June. "I didn't live in California. When I was in the Marines, I went where they sent me. I missed out on things like dress shopping but that doesn't mean I didn't want to be there for my kid. I did."

"You've been out of the military for years," Margie said pointedly.

Evan didn't have to explain himself, but he did anyway, because he wanted to believe that Margie was truly just concerned about her granddaughter. He wanted to think she was ensuring that June was with a responsible parent who truly did care about her best interests. "I got out when my dad got sick. He lived in Bloom all his life. That's why I came here."

"All I know is that people prioritize what's important to them. When it comes to your own child, nothing should be more important." Margie crossed her legs and looked away. Her jaw was stiff, much like the rest of her.

Evan watched her for a long moment. "Did Juliana tell you that she wanted me to raise June? That she asked me to?"

Margie looked at him. "My daughter was sick. She wasn't thinking clearly. She may have mentioned wanting June to be with a parent, and obviously that is typically what a person wants. I can be that for June though. And I want to. I don't know why you're being so stubborn about this. Selfish, really."

"Selfish? Really, Margie? You haven't given June a second to breathe and think for herself without doing your best to convince her of how miserable she is here. All I've done is for June but you aren't doing this for her or even for Juliana. From where I'm sitting, you're doing this for yourself."

Margie leaned toward him, her gaze unwavering. "I told Juliana you wouldn't add up to much when she dated you."

"Oh, I bet you did," Evan shot back, unable to hold his tongue another second. If she was going to be nasty to him, he was at least going to defend himself. He started to lean forward as well but then June stepped between them.

"Stop it!" June was wearing a silvery blue dress that fell a couple inches above her ankles. "Both of you just stop!" Her voice trembled. "I can decide for myself if I'm miserable, Dad." She looked at Margie. "And Mom could decide for herself if she liked my father or not. He's not as bad as you make him out to be, you know?"

Margie leaned back in her chair. She ignored June's statement and instead focused on the dress, pressing one hand to the center of her chest. "That looks lovely on you, sweetheart. Doesn't it, Evan?"

Evan still had adrenaline coursing through his veins. It was hard to flip the switch and pretend like all was well. "I'm sorry, June. You shouldn't be caught in the middle. Just know that we both love you and we show it in our own ways." He looked at the dress she was wearing. "I think that's the one. I like the color."

June looked down at herself. "I think so too. And I just want to be done shopping and get out of here. Okay?"

"Of course." He avoided looking at Margie, not wanting to see the judgment or indignation on her face. "We can get take-out on the way home. Burgers and fries?" He forced a smile that thankfully June returned. That's one thing that had never changed about his daughter. She loved a good cheeseburger and an order of curly fries.

"Sounds great, Dad."

After purchasing the dress that Margie insisted on paying for, they left the store and walked through the parking lot. Evan wasn't looking forward to being cramped in a tiny truck with Margie but he was ready to get home.

"Mr. Sanders?"

Evan looked up and noticed familiar faces heading toward him. It was a group of several students from last year's English class. "Hey, everyone." His mood immediately lifted. He loved the summer break but it did his heart good to see his students. Unlike the ones who'd bullied June at the youth center, these were students who enjoyed English and seemed to enjoy having him as a teacher.

Malik Brown raised a hand as he drew close to Evan, offering a high five.

Evan obliged and then high-fived the others. "Hanging out at the mall?"

"The bookstore," Julie Matthews said. "We're going through the reading list you gave us on the last day of school."

"Optional reading list," Evan said with a grin. He did that every year in honor of Eleanor. He wasn't sure he'd be the person he was today if not for Eleanor's summer reading lists. He glanced over at June. "I'm not so mean that I give my students mandatory homework during the summer; I promise."

June looked intrigued by the group of kids, who were just a few years older. She also looked a bit nervous.

"This is my daughter, June," Evan told the students.

"Oh, cool!" Malik said.

"Hi, I'm Kinley," a third teen said with a wave.

Evan had always liked Kinley. She was polite and had a creative streak a mile long. "Your dad is my favorite teacher of all time. You're so lucky."

June's gaze flicked to Evan. "Yeah? Why?"

Kinley shrugged. "Because he makes us read the required stuff, of course, but he also assigns us cool books. No other teacher would ever do that."

"And he gives us Starbursts when we raise our hands in class," Joey Tibbs said.

Evan waved a hand in the air. "Sto-o-op. You all are making me blush," he teased.

"Are you moving here to live with your dad?" Kinley asked June.

Evan noticed that June's gaze flicked to Margie now, a guilty look passing over her expression. It felt like time stopped as a puzzle piece that Evan had been missing slipped into place. It was what some might call an aha moment, and suddenly Evan understood.

June felt guilty leaving Margie behind. Margie was grieving the loss of her daughter, and June didn't want Margie to lose her too. It wasn't that June didn't want to be in Bloom with Evan. June had always loved being in Bloom with him during the summers. She was Daddy's girl. June was acting differently this summer, however, because she felt like she was betraying her grandmother if she stayed.

Evan swallowed past the lump in his throat.

"I, um, I guess so," June told Kinley with a small shrug.

"Oh, cool. I go to your dad's church. You should come sometime. We have a teen class, and you'd meet a lot of really nice people, me included."

June's smile broke Evan's heart in the best kind of way. She needed this so much. She needed a friend. Every kid June's age longed for acceptance, and June was so afraid of not getting it that she'd rather lock herself in a room with a book.

"These guys are pretty nice too, I guess." Kinley flashed a teasing glance at her other friends. "You should come."

"Maybe I will," June said.

Evan felt obligated to also introduce Margie to the kids. "Margie, these are former students of mine."

"So I gathered." Margie nodded. "I'm June's grandmother. It's nice to see a group of youngsters going to the bookstore instead of finding themselves in some kind of trouble. June loves to read as well."

"Of course she does," Malik said. "She's Mr. Sanders's daughter." He offered Evan another high five. "Stay cool, Mr. Sanders."

"I'll do my best," Evan said. "Enjoy the rest of your summer," he told the kids.

After saying goodbye, they continued walking toward Evan's truck.

"Do you really go to that girl's church?" June asked as he was driving home.

Evan's gaze flicked to the rearview mirror. "Not as often as I should." He'd gone regularly when Eleanor had ridden with him. She hadn't wanted to leave her home since her fall though so the motivation to get out of bed versus sleeping in on a Sunday morning had disappeared.

June focused her attention out the passenger window. "She seemed nice. Kinley."

"She is. She's about a year older than you." But Kinley wasn't the type of kid who minded hanging out with younger students.

Evan pulled up to a stoplight and waited for it to turn green, thinking about his realization that June felt conflicted about leaving Margie. Margie certainly didn't ease that worry for her. Instead, she seemed to play into it.

Margie had lost her daughter, and her granddaughter no longer lived on the same side of the country. That couldn't be easy for her. She was a tough woman to host but Evan needed to remind himself that she was struggling too. For that reason, he would show her nothing but compassion—regardless of how she was treating him. Right now, that meant buying her a burger, a large order of curly fries, and a milkshake to boot.

Later, he'd figure out how to relieve June's guilt. She shouldn't have felt like she needed to choose between him and Margie. She could have them both, even if they lived on opposite coasts.

Chapter Twenty

Eleanor

There is no friend as loyal as a book.

Ernest Hemingway, American novelist

The kettle was boiling, and Eleanor had three teacups in front of her. One for her, of course, and one for each of the visitors that she was expecting.

The doorbell rang, and Eleanor waited a moment. She knew the sign on her door would eventually lead people inside.

"Hello?" someone called from the front of the house.

"In the kitchen! Come on back!" Eleanor recognized the voice as Mallory Blue's. Charlie's two granddaughters were the sweetest. Mallory was bringing her younger sister, Madison, over today to look at the garden and get a feel for her upcoming wedding. Madison couldn't drive on her own now that she was in a wheelchair—not until she had a wheelchair-accessible van at least. Those cost a small fortune. When Eleanor had offered up her home for Madison's wedding, she'd hired Evan to construct a makeshift ramp on both the front and the back of the house. Being the hardworking man he was, he'd made the ramps in a day, and he'd refused payment.

Eleanor waited for her visitors to come into sight and then smiled delightedly. "I halfway expect two little girls when you come to visit, and here you are, two beautiful, grown women." She walked over and hugged them both. "The bride-to-be and her maid of honor," Eleanor added.

Mallory palmed her face playfully. "Always a bridesmaid. I know, I know."

Madison laughed. "You took the words right out of my mouth." She looked at Eleanor. "I read the book you lent me."

"And?" Eleanor pulled her hands to her chest, waiting with bated breath. She was nearly as invested with the reviews of the books that she loaned out as she imagined the actual author would be. *The Five Love Languages* by Gary Chapman was always the book she recommended to new brides. It was a wealth of information but also so simple. If a person just understood how to communicate their love, their marriage would survive. Eleanor truly believed that.

"I might need to read the book again," Madison said. "It's a lot to digest. And I want Sam to read it too."

Reading a book for a second time was the highest form of compliment. "You keep that book. Consider it a gift. Read it yearly," Eleanor suggested. Then she looked at Mallory. "And lend it to your sister afterward because her person is coming. I know it. Always a bridesmaid is not your truth."

Mallory redirected her gaze to look outside. "We're excited to see your backyard garden this morning. I told Madison how hard we all worked the other day. It looks amazing."

"Yes, it does," Eleanor agreed. "I'd like to say it looks even better than before but the garden and that library are sentimental to me."

Mallory stepped over to Eleanor and placed a hand on her shoulder. "Well, I'm glad we could salvage so much."

"I really can't wait to see it," Madison said. "I've been in your backyard before, of course, but it's been a while. I want to visualize exactly where Sam and I will be when we say our vows. I've always dreamed of having an outdoor wedding with lots of flowers." Madison's enthusiasm seemed to grow as she spoke. "When you offered your garden, it was like my dream was coming true. I was a little worried that Sam and I would have to just go to the courthouse. Not that there's anything wrong with that," Madison said quickly.

"It depends on what the bride and groom want. It's your day," Eleanor said. "I'm just honored that I get to be a part of it."

Madison glanced toward the window. "I can't wait to go outside and visualize exactly where I'll be this weekend when I recite my vows."

"Well, let's skip the tea and get straight to the good stuff, shall we?" Eleanor turned the kettle off and led the women out the back door. She was a little nervous that Madison would have difficulty navigating with her chair but that didn't seem to be a problem. "Your chair really handles itself well out here, doesn't it?" Eleanor asked as they went down the ramp and strolled along the garden's path.

"This is my outdoor chair. The community was so great to

raise money to purchase it. I am just really thankful for everyone's help. My only complaint is that, compared to my ATV, this chair is slow."

Mallory laughed. "Everyone knows how you love to speed."

"I have a new pace these days," Madison said with a grin, "one I didn't choose. But everything that has happened to me led me to Sam, and I do choose him. In fact, because of him, I wouldn't change a thing."

"Aw." Eleanor's heart swelled. "How I adore a good love story."

Madison smiled politely as she looked around at the garden. The roses were tied to the lattices now. Beyond the posts and lattices, Savannah and Mallory had put up a brand-new arbor with Evan's help. It arched over the stone path and had roses attached, climbing from one end to the other. Eleanor, Mallory, and Madison were just at the right distance to peer through the arch and beyond where the Finders Keepers Library could be seen a few hundred feet away. It had a fresh coat of tan paint and a new cobalt-blue tin roof.

"As you probably know, my husband, Aaron, built me that library nearly two decades ago. His favorite place to be was always in his garden and mine was with my books. He blended the two together. It was perhaps the most romantic thing he ever did for me."

"Your library is like one of those Little Free Libraries people have in their front yards. Only on a much grander scale," Madison said.

Eleanor laughed quietly. "So, Madison, do you see a good place for you and Sam to say I do?" She pointed at the arch. "I think it would be lovely if you came through this rose arbor on the way to your groom. Perhaps start on the far side of the yard and walk this way toward my house. You and Sam could get married on my back deck if you'd like."

Madison had a thoughtful look on her face. "Or, what if Sam and I exchanged vows in front of your library? I could roll my chair through the arch," she said. "The guests' chairs could face your library."

"Madison, it's a library, not a church," Mallory said.

"If I wanted a church wedding, that's what I'd be having. I want an outdoor wedding. And I think I want to promise forever to Sam in front of that library. I actually think that would be perfect."

Eleanor thought the library was the most romantic place on earth but she knew others didn't see it the way she did. To others, it might be compared to a dolled-up shack full of printed books that were quickly going the way of the dinosaur. "I love that idea."

Madison gestured ahead. "I'll wheel through the arch and come out on the other side. There'll be chairs set up on each side, facing the Finders Keepers Library. And Sam and I will say 'I do' right in front. Sam found me that day in the woods. That's kind of symbolic." She looked up with tears in her eyes. "Sam found me out in the woods, and despite being what some might call broken, he decided to keep me."

Eleanor had tears in her eyes too. "And you decided to keep him too. That's what two people do when they're in love. They keep one another."

"You're not broken," Mallory said, resting a hand on the back of her sister's wheelchair.

Madison grinned. "I think the truth was, I was a little broken before Sam, maybe even before the ATV accident. Loving him put me back together." She sniffled softly and then maneuvered her chair to the left. "Grandpa Charlie said we can use his big tent. We can put it up over there for the reception."

"Your grandfather arranged for the Cherry Blossom Quartet to play at your reception too. He said that was at your request?" Eleanor asked.

"They're my favorite local band," Madison said. "Sam's too."

Eleanor pressed her hands together. "How wonderful. This will be a night to remember always."

Madison reached for her hand. "Thanks to you."

"And Aaron," Eleanor said. "It's his garden and his handiwork. He would be delighted to know it's going to good use." As she said it, she caught a floral scent on the breeze and something inside her suspected it was a wink from her late husband. "In fact, I know for sure that he'd be thrilled."

Chapter Twenty-One

Savannah

*(I)n a hundred lifetimes, in a hundred worlds,
in any version of reality, I'd find you and I'd
choose you.*

The Chaos of Stars, Kiersten White

T minus one day until the wedding.

Savannah watched out Eleanor's front window as a car pulled into the driveway. "They're here!" She turned toward Mallory. "It's not a prewedding party until the bride and groom arrive."

"Bride and groom-to-be," Mallory clarified. "Who knows? One of them might walk away before tomorrow's nuptials."

Savannah's mouth fell open. "Your sister seems solid."

"She is." Mallory shrugged. "But what about Sam? I like the guy but it's my worst fear that he'll panic and run off before the vows."

"Like Randall did to me?" Savannah asked quietly.

"On the bright side, your jerk of an ex gave you some notice before backing out. Madison already has the dress. She's less than twenty-four hours from—"

Savannah interrupted Mallory midthought. "Stop. I don't know him well but from what I do know, there is no way that Sam would ever do that to your sister."

Mallory sighed. "We never really know what a person will do when they get scared though. Marriage is a little terrifying, if you ask me."

"Madison and Sam belong together. And tomorrow will go off without a hitch. I'm really happy for Madison."

Mallory grinned as she headed toward the door. "Me too. I'm also happy for you."

Savannah looked at Mallory. "Me?"

"You and Evan. Love has given you back that spark you always used to have when we were kids." She tilted her head, letting her dark hair spill over one shoulder. "So, are you staying?"

The doorbell rang. Savannah was grateful for the interruption because she didn't know the answer to that question yet.

"Hold that thought," Mallory said. "We'll chat later." Mallory opened the front door, revealing her sister and soon-to-be brother-in-law on the porch. "Hey, you two! Oh, my! What is that?" Mallory leaned in toward Sam's face and then looked at Madison dramatically. "Have you seen that thing on his cheek?"

Worry flashed in Sam's dark eyes. "What thing?"

Madison didn't miss a beat. She twisted around in her wheelchair and narrowed her eyes on Sam's face. "It's just a little zit. We can probably cover it up with some makeup."

"Makeup?" Sam looked horrified. He stepped past Savannah

and Mallory and then headed toward Eleanor's bathroom to see for himself.

Savannah giggled under her breath. "I had forgotten that you two are awful."

"He should get used to it," Mallory said. "He's marrying into the Blue family, after all. This is what he has to look forward to. Right, Mad?"

"I've already warned him and he's still here." Madison shrugged. "If he hasn't left me yet, he isn't going to."

Savannah envied Madison's confidence. Would Savannah ever feel that way in a relationship again? Was Mallory right? Did Savannah have her spark back, thanks to Evan? Was she falling in love with him?

Mallory elbowed Savannah. "Snap out of whatever fantasy you're entertaining. We have a prewedding dinner party to throw."

Sam walked back down the hall, looking at all three women one at a time. "There was no zit," he said dramatically.

Mallory cackled and pointed a finger in his direction. "But if one pops up, Madison will let you use her makeup. It'll be fine." She winked at him.

Sam chuckled good-naturedly. "What am I getting myself into?" Then he answered the question himself. "I guess probably a lifetime of feeling like the luckiest man on earth."

"Aww." Madison tilted her head to the side. "You are so right. You *are* the luckiest man. And I am the luckiest gal."

Savannah felt like a fly on the wall to their relationship. Sam really didn't seem to feel like loving someone with a disability was an imposition. Randall's reaction had painted Savannah's viewpoint all wrong. Seeing things through Sam's eyes, she saw how fortunate he was to have found the person he wanted to promise forever to. Randall would have been lucky too but he didn't deserve Savannah. Being here this summer made her realize that she deserved a whole lot better than Randall.

The front door opened again, and Evan poked his head inside. Savannah immediately felt settled and excited. He was the one she wanted to be with.

"The Sanderses are here." Evan's gaze landed on her, and her heart kicked forcefully. "Can we come in?" he asked.

"Of course." She was glad June had decided to come tonight as well. "Is Margie with you too?"

Eleanor had extended an invitation to June's grandmother since she was in town. It was the polite thing to do, and Savannah suspected that Eleanor had a list of book suggestions that would change Margie's life.

"Actually, Margie left to go back to California just before lunch today," Evan said.

Savannah tried to read Evan's face but he maintained a neutral expression.

"But she'll be back sometime soon," June added. "And she told me I could come see her before school starts."

Evan looked visibly uncomfortable now.

Savannah wondered if he and Margie had gotten into another altercation. She couldn't ask him in front of June though. "Well, Eleanor is in the kitchen with the food."

Mallory looked at her sister and Sam. "Your last meal," she told them solemnly.

"We're not dying." Madison rolled her eyes again. Then she gave her sister a *checkmate* look. "We're not all here yet though.

I invited Grandpa Charlie." She cleared her throat and offered her sister a mischievous grin. "And someone else."

"Who?" Mallory asked, glancing over at Savannah.

Savannah shook her head. "No clue."

As if on cue, the front door opened and Charlie stepped in, followed by Hollis.

Madison flashed a victorious smile at Mallory before casting off with her arms and propelling her wheelchair forward. "*Now* we're all here."

Savannah had assumed she would be sitting next to Mallory at the dinner table but Mallory and Hollis had sandwiched Madison and Sam on one side of the table. Eleanor sat at the head of the table, with Charlie at the other end. That left Savannah, Evan, and June sitting together on the fourth side of the table.

"Well? How is the food?" Eleanor asked halfway through the meal. She glanced around at each guest expectantly.

"Ms. Collins, you are an amazing cook," Sam said. "Maybe you can teach Madison here a thing or two."

Madison didn't look offended in the slightest. "I can't cook," she admitted but then held up a finger. "I have an excuse not to learn though. I don't have a wheelchair-accessible kitchen."

Hollis had been focused on his food but now he looked up from his plate. "Well, Evan and I can make that happen for you." He looked at Evan. "Right, Ev?"

Evan laughed lightly. "I have no idea how to create a wheelchair-accessible kitchen."

"Oh, come on, Dad. You can build pretty much anything," June said. "You can totally make one for Madison."

June's vote of confidence for her dad surprised Savannah just as much as it appeared to surprise Evan.

"Well, if Hollis is in, I'm in," Evan said, reaching to swipe a dinner roll from the center of the table. "We can probably come up with something."

Madison's whole face lit up. "Wow. I have the best friends there are. Thank you." She looked at Eleanor. "And thank you again for offering your yard to hold our wedding. Tomorrow is going to be an amazing day." She looked at Savannah next. "I know you did a lot of work on the garden to bring it back to tip-top condition. I really appreciate it. Thank you."

"It was my pleasure. Really," Savannah said. She hadn't done all that much. The roses had just needed cutting back and training on new sheets of lattice and on the new arbor. Savannah had also polished up the stepping stones and the garden benches to make them look almost like new.

Eleanor turned to Savannah and then looked at the bride-to-be. "I need to thank *you*, Madison. If you and Sam weren't getting married, my favorite niece might not have stayed in town as long. It's so nice to have her home. I know Bloom isn't Savannah's real home but she spent a quarter of her years here when she was growing up so I say it counts."

"And I would agree." Savannah hadn't felt that way when she'd arrived but now, after being here, she felt more comfortable in this town than she did her actual hometown. So comfortable and happy that she didn't want to leave, even though she didn't have a backup plan for work and finances.

Evan raised his glass in the air. "Let's toast to our bride and groom."

Everyone else raised their glass as well.

"To my sister, Madison," Mallory said. "And my brother-in-law-to-be, Sam. May you have the happiest of ever-afters."

"To Madison and Sam," Hollis echoed, lifting his glass.

"To my dearest Madison," Eleanor said. "May you have a love story that Jane Austin would have wished she wrote."

Evan looked at Savannah as if offering her a chance to speak.

Savannah lifted her own glass and hoped she'd find something meaningful to say. "To Madison and Sam. Both of you are the lucky ones." Her eyes immediately welled with tears. She tried to keep them at bay. She wasn't even sure why she suddenly felt like crying but her emotions flooded to the surface. She flicked her gaze to Evan, hoping he couldn't tell, but he was watching intently. "Sorry. Weddings always make me cry," she said, waving off her sudden feelings. "Just wait until tomorrow."

Evan turned to his daughter. "June, do you have anything to say?"

"You didn't put real wine in my glass," June complained, "so I don't think my toast counts." She looked at Madison and Sam anyway. "But you two deserve to be happy. I hope tomorrow is great and that your marriage will be amazing."

"I couldn't have said it better." Evan tapped his glass to June's and then Savannah's.

Everyone else tapped their glass to the person sitting next to them. Then they drank.

When the meal was over, Eleanor insisted on making hot tea for Madison and Sam to have with her and Charlie in the front sitting room. Before she led them down the hall, she made Savannah and Mallory promise not to clean up.

"You are guests in my house tonight. No cleaning," she scolded with a serious expression.

"I'm going home," June announced to Evan. "It's past my bedtime."

"It's 9:00 p.m.," he said, furrowing his brow.

"Yes, it is." She looked at Savannah. "It's not like you'll miss me anyway. You have Savannah to keep you company." There was no trace of resentment in her tone. She didn't even sound sad. She was just being matter-of-fact. "Besides, Kinley DMed me on Instagram. She wants to chat."

"Kinley? My student, Kinley?" Evan asked.

June gave him a shy look. "I doubt there are that many Kinleys. Anyway, good night."

When June left, Evan turned to Savannah. "I'm not sure what to make of anything she says or does."

"I think she seems okay. It's great that she's making friends here. I think it's a positive sign."

"I'm afraid to be too hopeful but yeah."

Savannah tucked a strand of hair behind her ear, feeling suddenly nervous for a reason she didn't understand. Those pesky emotions of hers were still at the surface. She usually tried to keep them at bay but it was harder these days. She wasn't sure if it was because her body was fatigued from her recent flare or if it was because of all the change and uncertainty in her life.

"What about you? Are you okay?" he asked.

Savannah sucked in a shallow breath. "Yeah."

He reached for her hand. "Great. How about a walk through

the garden then? We can get some fresh air and ensure that the path is perfect for tomorrow's occasion."

"That sounds nice." Savannah was comforted by the feel of his hand holding hers. His skin was warm, his fingers hugging her palm gently. "I'm always up for a walk through the garden."

Evan pushed back from the table and stood. "I love that you got your uncle's green thumb. You were into gardening before it was ever cool. You were never afraid to stand out."

Savannah considered Evan's words as she stepped outside. When she first got her diagnosis, she had kind of been afraid that she might eventually stand out. What if she needed a mobility device? Or special glasses? What if she had to go on dialysis one day or needed a transplant? She already felt paranoid wearing the huge hat and dark sunglasses when she was outdoors.

She wasn't as worried about those things anymore though—not with friends and family who showed their unwavering acceptance. If she had people surrounding her that loved and supported her, she didn't need to worry about anything. In South Carolina, she wouldn't know anyone at first. What if she were to get sick? Who would help her?

They stepped off the back deck and Savannah instinctively sucked in a deeper breath, pulling the fresh air into her lungs. Then she and Evan walked quietly for a moment. It was the kind of quiet that felt natural.

"I love this arbor," Savannah said as they approached the wooden frame Evan had helped her put up for the roses. It was new but they'd stapled lots of fragments of the old trellis to it. "In my humble opinion, we did an amazing job."

"Yes, we did. So, tell me. What do your social media followers think of your summer project?"

"Well, I've doubled my follows and likes but I think that's more about you than the rose garden," Savannah told him, feeling slightly foolish.

Evan stopped walking. "Yeah?" He tipped his head down at the phone in her pocket. "How about I say hello and thank your followers for giving your profile a boost?"

"You want to say hello on my TikTok account?" she asked.

He shrugged. "Why not?"

"Well, what are you going to say?" she asked nervously.

"No idea. What, you don't trust me?" he teased.

She pulled her phone out and tapped the icon for the Tik-Tok app. "Actually, I do trust you." She flicked her gaze up at him. "But don't make me regret it. Ready?"

He gave a brisk nod. "Ready."

She tapped the screen to begin recording. "Evan, I would like you to meet my followers. Followers, I formally introduce you to Evan—aka the hot garden guy."

Evan waved. "Hello, Savannah's followers. Hot Garden Guy here." He grimaced. "That feels awkward to say. I just wanted to come on and say that you guys must be really smart because you're following Savannah. In case you haven't figured it out yet, she has a green thumb and she's also pretty amazing. And fairly hot herself. If I'm Hot Garden Guy, she should definitely be titled Hot Garden Gal." His gaze jumped to Savannah's behind the phone. "I'm a huge fan of her, um, plants. And her."

If Savannah wasn't mistaken, he was blushing.

"And here's a selfish plug for her store. You should visit her website and adopt a plant. Because who doesn't need more plants in their lives? I hear they're pretty good listeners."

Savannah laughed, shaking her phone's camera in the process. "You're too much," she said. Then she turned her camera's screen to face herself. She lifted a brow at her followers. "Happy now? I gave you an up-close-and-personal look. The wedding that I've been preparing the garden for is tomorrow, by the way. Stay tuned." She tapped her screen and stopped the video.

"Did you post it?" he asked.

"Not yet. I will tonight. I need to add a caption and hashtags. That kind of stuff."

"Wow. Hashtags. I'm impressed." He stepped closer.

Savannah's heart bubbled up into her throat. She leaned slightly forward, finding this Hot Garden Guy irresistible.

"Are you thinking about kissing me?" he asked.

She laughed at the unexpected question. "Nope. Why? Are you thinking about kissing me?"

"Most definitely. It's romantic out here. Roses. Stars. Moonlight. I am 100 percent thinking about kissing you."

Her gaze dropped to his lips. "Okay, I admit it. I might be thinking about kissing you too."

"Well then. We probably should. Just to make sure this arbor is safe for tomorrow."

"To make sure it's safe?" she asked, not following his meaning. "Why wouldn't it be?"

He scratched below his jaw, looking like he was deliberating over what he was about to say. "Because my world shook during our last kiss."

Savannah gave his chest a gentle shove. "We're not in high

school anymore. I would have thought you'd have better lines than that, Evan Sanders."

"I do." He leaned toward her. "You just have to stick around to hear them."

An unmistakable hope flickered in his eyes. She'd seen it that night when they were nineteen and they had shared their first kiss. She just hadn't known what it meant. Before she could respond, he shook his head. "I'm sorry. I know you can't. Once again, something bigger and better is calling you away."

"I've drafted my acceptance letter to the university. I just need to hit SEND," she said, wishing he'd tell her not to.

Evan nodded. "I guess congratulations are in order."

"Thanks." She was almost disappointed that he wasn't more upset.

"And while I'm hopeful that June will want to stay in Bloom, she might not. In which case, I'll be moving to the West Coast."

"Right." Another reason that her decision couldn't be based around Evan. It had to be solely based on what she thought was best for herself.

"You'll still be my date to the wedding tomorrow?" he asked.

"Of course." Her heart felt like there was a slow-forming crack running through it, ready to shatter it at any moment. She didn't want to say goodbye to Evan.

He ran his hands up and down the length of her arms. Then he tugged her gently, pulling her toward him and bringing her mouth closer to his. Their lips brushed together, and Savannah found herself sighing into the kiss.

When Evan pulled back to look at her, he was smiling. "Yeah. I think this arbor passes the test." He didn't release his hold on her. "Regardless of what happens after this weekend, I'm glad you're here now, Savannah."

She met his blue eyes. She loved how the exact shade of blue changed depending on where they were. Eleanor's kitchen. The library. The Moonflower Festival with all its fairy lights. The garden. "I'm glad I'm here too," she said, meaning it. "The worst summer turned out to be one of my best," she said, on the verge of tears. She had no idea how she'd say goodbye to him. She didn't want to think about it. All she wanted to do was soak up every minute she had left in Bloom with Evan.

Chapter Twenty-Two

Evan

Wounds heal. Love lasts. We remain.

The Nightingale, Kristin Hannah

Evan turned as June stepped into his room. She was wearing the pale blue dress they'd purchased the other day with silver shoes and earrings. She had on a splash of lip gloss that made her look older somehow. For a moment, Evan's life flashed before his eyes. Soon, boys would be knocking on the door and Evan would have to shoo them away because he knew how teen boys' minds worked. He'd been one once, and during those years, he'd had such a crush on Savannah. The only thing that had ever come close was what he'd had with June's mother, Juliana.

June lifted a suspicious brow. "Why are you staring at me like that?"

"Sorry." Evan looked down and away. "You just look so much like your mom."

Now June looked away. "She used to say I looked like her on a pretty day."

Evan chuckled. "Your mom had no idea. Every day was a pretty day for her. And for you too."

June looked at him again. Then she seemed to assess his wardrobe for today's occasion. He'd considered shopping for himself when they'd gone out with Margie but then the conversation had gotten heated. So instead of wearing something new, he'd dressed in the same suit he'd been wearing to weddings and funerals for the past decade. "You clean up nicely too, Dad."

He tugged at the opening of his jacket. "You think so?"

"I'm sure Savannah will think so." June grinned, looking once again like his little girl.

Evan wondered if June, like him, was hoping Savannah would change her mind and stay. He didn't want to break it to her that Savannah was still planning to leave town after the wedding. That might sway her own decision about what she wanted to do.

"Grandma Margie called this morning," June said, getting his attention.

Evan hadn't heard the phone. "Your cell?"

"Yep." June leaned against his bedroom dresser.

"What did she say? Did she get back home okay?" Now that Margie had seen where June was living, Evan really hoped Margie would stop trying to convince June of how unhappy she was here in Bloom. He also hoped she would drop the idea of hiring a lawyer.

June gave him a sheepish look, nibbling softly on her bottom lip. "I told Grandma that I miss her."

Evan could see the guilt on her face. "It's okay to miss your grandmother. Of course you do."

"I told her that I made a friend here though. Kinley. We've been texting."

Evan worked hard to temper his level of hopefulness. "That's great, June."

"Grandma Margie was happy for me too. I was kind of surprised. I thought she didn't want me to be happy here," June said quietly.

"Of course she does. We all want you to be happy, no matter where you are. Whether it's here or in California." Evan placed a hand on June's shoulder. "I just want you to know that you can always tell me how you feel."

"I do. Just so you know, I'll probably be the only kid at this wedding tonight. So even though I'll be surrounded by people, I might feel a little bit lonely. I've kind of felt alone since Mom died."

Evan sucked in a breath. "You haven't been alone. I've been here."

She looked down momentarily. "But Grandma Margie really is alone. She doesn't have anyone now, Dad."

Evan had already suspected that was weighing heavily on June's mind. "She has us."

"Us?" June asked. "I thought you hated her."

Evan lowered his arm back to his side. "I don't hate your grandmother. She's important to you so she's important to me. We should make sure she knows that."

June nibbled at her lower lip. "I know that she's threatening to hire a lawyer. How can you be nice to her when she's planning to fight you for me?"

Evan wondered how June knew about the lawyer. *Did Margie tell her?* "If she's fighting me, it's because she thinks that's the right thing to do for you. I want you to know I'll always do the same." Evan stepped toward her, opening his arms wide and pulling her in for a hug. "I'm always here for you. I want you to be happy." He pulled back and searched her face. "Are you...happy?"

"Happy-ish?" she said with a grimace. "I mean, I miss my mom and my grandma. I miss my friends in California. But I have you here. And Ms. Eleanor. And I'm making new friends, slowly but surely. And," June said, a smile curling at the corners of her lips, "I'm going to get a piece of cake at the reception tonight. Who can be unhappy when there's cake?"

That statement was proof that June had inherited some things from him. "Way to see the bright side of things."

June grinned. Then, turning, she headed out of the room. "Hurry up, Dad," she called behind her, "we have to go next door soon."

"I'm almost ready. Meet you in the kitchen. Don't leave without me. You're my date."

"Savannah is your date," June said, talking over her shoulder. Evan listened for any hint of resentment. There was none.

Turning back toward the mirror, he adjusted his tie as he tried to interpret his conversation with June. Unless he was completely misreading things, it sounded like June possibly wanted to stay in Bloom. That didn't mean Margie would drop her attempts to fight for his daughter but it did mean she wouldn't win. Not if June chose her life here in Bloom.

An alarm sounded on his cell phone. It was time to go next door for the wedding. People would be arriving soon, and he'd offered to direct folks to their seats in Eleanor's backyard. Savannah was doing the same.

He headed down the hall, and June was waiting for him in the kitchen.

She looked up from the open book she was reading. Evan read the title. *The Sisterhood of the Traveling Pants*. That was an interesting choice. "Ready?" he asked.

June placed a bookmark to save her spot and then slid the book against the far end of the counter. "Ready. Maybe I can say hi to Fig before the ceremony."

"Don't let that cat snag your dress." He held out his elbow for her to loop her arm into. Then they stepped outside and crossed the lawn toward Eleanor's front porch.

"Oh, darling June," Eleanor exclaimed when she answered the door. "You look gorgeous." She pulled June in for a hug as they stepped inside.

"Thank you. Can I go see Fig?" June asked, not wasting any time in her request. Although she was growing fast, there was a still a little girl inside her, and Evan planned to cherish all the time he had watching that girl grow up.

Eleanor gestured down the hallway. "Of course. She's locked away in my room to avoid the guests. You can go on in. Don't let her out."

"I won't," June promised, darting off.

Eleanor pulled Evan in for a hug next. "Everything all right?" she asked as she pulled back to look at him.

"Everything is good."

"Happy to hear that. So then, let's put on a wedding, shall we?"

Evan chuckled. Then his breath literally stopped as Savannah entered the room. He had to remind his lungs to pull in air.

"She's giving the bride a run for her money, isn't she?" Eleanor asked. "All the single guys will have their eyes on her this evening. But I suspect you have nothing to worry about," she told Evan.

Savannah stepped over to where they were standing. "Talking about me?" She looked at Evan, her smile growing wider. "Hi."

Evan thought Savannah had never looked more beautiful than she did this afternoon. "Hi."

"I guess we should help the arriving guests," she told him. "But save me a seat for the ceremony?"

"And a dance later," he promised.

Eleanor hummed softly beneath her breath as Savannah left the room. "Love is in the air all around today. It's such a lovely thing."

The weather was perfect that evening, and the setting sun was blending into a melting pot of colors in the sky above Eleanor's garden. The roses were in full bloom, vibrant and radiant with color. It was as if nature understood that today was an important day, and it was giving Madison and Sam its own sort of wedding gift.

The guests were all seated comfortably in chairs that Evan and Hollis had set out last night just before dinner. The Cherry Blossom Quartet had volunteered their time to play for today's event. They were set off to the side, playing soft music fitting for the occasion.

Evan's gaze jumped to where June was sitting by herself. As

he watched, two boys around June's age slid into the same row with her. A girl as well. Evan recognized them from the school where he taught but they'd never been in any of his classes. The kids started chatting among themselves, ignoring June completely.

His heart dropped a notch. He would go sit with her if he could but he was helping to make sure things went smoothly prior to the ceremony.

"It's time!" someone whisper-yelled. "It's time!"

Evan glanced at his watch. Six o'clock on the dot.

The music shifted to the "Wedding March," and everyone sat up straighter in their seat, turning to watch the bride come down the garden path. Madison's father had passed away several years ago, and even though Charlie had offered to escort her down the aisle, she had insisted that she approach the wedding platform on her own, because no one could replace him.

The group collectively gasped as Madison appeared just beyond the rose lattices. Her wheelchair was wrapped in white lace and stringed pearls, and Madison was wearing a classic white gown and a short veil that trailed behind her. Her rich, black hair and makeup were done perfectly. Smiling widely, she used her arms to steer her chair along the stepping stone aisle.

Evan momentarily worried that he hadn't smoothed out the path enough. What if Madison's chair got stuck? What if there was a bump that he didn't know about that flipped her chair over? What if...?

He held his breath as she navigated through the rose arbor and came out on the other side, making her way past the guests as she navigated to the front of the Finders Keepers Library. There, at the library's entrance, Sam was waiting with his two brothers by his side. The pastor was waiting too. Madison slowly wheeled herself toward them, taking her time and beaming all the way.

Evan exhaled as she came to a stop in front of Sam.

"I was holding my breath too," Savannah whispered, coming up to stand beside him.

He glanced in her direction. "Hey, you."

She looped her arm with his. "Hi."

Then they redirected their focus to the bride and groom.

"They deserve to be happy. They're a great couple," Savannah said wistfully.

"Agreed. It took a tragedy to bring them together. I guess sometimes there's a bigger plan that we don't always see."

"I guess so." Savannah's words were barely audible.

Sensing she was thinking about her own life, Evan reached for her hand and squeezed. He had fallen so hard for this woman. He had no idea what he was going to do when she left.

She met his gaze and squeezed his hand back.

The vows took all of ten minutes, and then Madison and Sam were officially married. They kissed, and, surprising his new bride, Sam lifted Madison out of her chair, scooping her up in his arms. She laughed excitedly as one of the groomsmen took control of her chair and pushed it behind them while they retreated down the garden path.

"Looks like true love to me," Savannah said.

"That's the only kind there is." Evan looked over at her again and his heart thumped against his ribs. He realized he was still holding her hand and he didn't want to let go. Unable to stop himself, he leaned in and brushed his lips to hers in a soft kiss that made him wish the crowd around them would just disappear. He wanted to hold Savannah close and not let go until morning. Truthfully, he never wanted to let go. "Sorry. I guess the romance of the wedding got to me."

"Save those romantic feelings for the reception. Right now, I need to make sure the guests are taken care of. And that they don't mess up my garden." She gave him a wink.

Evan raised his brows. "Your garden, huh?"

Savannah grinned as she headed off. "You know what I mean."

Turning, Evan glanced around and saw June veering off toward the fence that bordered his property. *Why is she leaving?*

"June? Hey!" He followed, trying to get her attention without making a spectacle of himself. "Hey, June! Wait up."

She didn't stop walking. Instead, she seemed to pick up her pace which told him she heard him loud and clear and didn't want to talk.

"June?" He caught up to her and grabbed her shoulder just before she dipped through the missing fence panel.

Turning back to him, her expression was long and her eyes sad. "I don't feel well. Can I go home?"

"You don't want to stick around for the reception? There'll be cake," he reminded her.

She shook her head. "I'm not all that hungry. Can I go? Please."

June had seemed fine earlier. She'd seemed happy. Was that all this was? "Did something happen? I saw you sitting with those other kids your age. Did you meet them?"

Tears rushed June's eyes. "I already knew them. From the youth center."

Evan let that information sink in, along with the fact that

June suddenly looked upset. "Were those the kids who hurt your feelings?"

"Hurt my feelings?" June rolled her eyes, folding her arms tightly over my chest. "Dad, they were awful to me, and they sat beside me today on purpose. They whispered about me non-stop as if I weren't even there, knowing I could hear every word. They hate me here, and I don't know why." June's voice cracked.

"Why didn't you get up and leave? Why didn't you come find me?" Fury surged through his veins on June's behalf. He wanted to go find those teens and give them a piece of his mind.

"I did find you but I didn't want to interrupt. You were with Savannah." June's face dissolved into more tears.

Guilt roiled in his belly. Had he been kissing Savannah when June needed to talk to him? "I'm your dad. I want you to interrupt me if there's something wrong. You come first." He lowered his head to look her directly in the eyes. "Got it?"

June rolled her lips together, looking as if she was working hard not to cry. Seeing her like this broke his heart. "Can I please go home, Dad? Please? At least until those kids leave."

Evan didn't want to force his daughter to stay in an environment where she felt uncomfortable. "I should be over there to support Madison and Sam," he said.

"And for Savannah," June said. "It's okay. I'll go back to the reception in a little bit. For the cake." The smallest smile formed on her lips. "I just need some space. And maybe I want to vent to Kinley. I wish she had come here tonight."

Evan nodded. "Me too. Okay. Call or text me if you need to. I can go home."

June's eyes were shiny with tears. "Just so you know, you're doing a good job, Dad."

Evan fought back his own tears. "Just so *you* know, you're doing a good job too."

She gave him a confused look. "Of being a needy twelve-year-old girl?"

"Of being my daughter. You've been through so much and you are so strong. You amaze me."

June wiped at a tear. "Sto-o-op. I'm trying not to cry, Dad. I'm wearing mascara, you know? Raccoon eyes are the worst."

"Not even going to pretend to understand that one."

She rolled her eyes, making him laugh. "Go on. Savannah is waiting for you over there. You promised her a dance."

"Okay. I'll dance with you too, once you come back over," he promised.

"Don't threaten me like that." She was only teasing. He could see it in her eyes. He could also see that she was going to be okay.

"See you in a bit," she said.

Evan watched her turn and disappear through the fence's missing panel. Then he turned and headed back toward the reception, eager to find Savannah and wrap his arms around her. Eager to kiss her under the stars. It felt like tonight was their last night together. After tonight, everything would change. The brief summer romance they'd shared would come to an end—unless he asked her to make an impossible choice and stay.

He couldn't do that. There were so many reasons he shouldn't. Her job. Her financial stability. He needed to be 100 percent focused on June.

But maybe June was a reason he needed to ask Savannah to stay. June loved Savannah too.

Too? Did he love Savannah? Wasn't it too soon?

The L-word hit him with such a blow that he stopped walking for a moment, needing to catch his breath. The answer to the ultimate question of life, the universe and everything wasn't forty-two like Douglas Adams's book had proclaimed. It was love, and if Savannah loved him back, then they could figure the rest out.

The question was, did she feel the same way? Picking up his pace, Evan went to find out.

Chapter Twenty-Three

Eleanor

I am not afraid of storms, for I am learning how to sail my ship.

Little Women, Louisa May Alcott

Eleanor sat on the bench along her garden path and scanned the crowd for tonight's reception. She'd known Evan and Savannah had transformed her backyard but she hadn't realized until now just how magical it was. The lights. The flowers. The music. It all came together, and it was...

"Perfection." Charlie stepped over to where Eleanor was sitting. "The wedding was magnificent, Ellie. Thank you for making my granddaughter's special day as perfect as it could be."

"It wasn't really me." Eleanor shook her head, even though a thread of pride ran through her. "I wish I could take credit."

"You brought your niece back. You got your neighbor to

pitch in. It was you, Ellie." He hesitated, dropping his voice a notch. "It's always been you."

Her heart bubbled up into her throat. She scooted over on the bench to allow some space for Charlie to sit beside her. "Madison and Sam looked so in love. I hope they'll always have one another."

Charlie reached for her hand. "No one knows how long we have on this earth. I know you wish you'd had longer with Aaron. I feel the same way about my Maria. I'm just glad I had her in my life at all. It wasn't enough time but I'm grateful for every second."

Eleanor released a breath as she studied his face. "Me too." She looked down at Charlie's hand on hers. His skin was tan and leathery, the hands of a man who had worked hard during his life and who had made the world a better place. He made *her* world better. "I'm also grateful for you. I'm glad you're not so easy to push away."

"No, I'm not. Have you been pushing me away?" he asked, pretending to be clueless. "I didn't notice."

"Maybe I thought you'd get tired of waiting on me," she confessed.

He chuckled softly. "I'm a patient man, Ellie. When are you going to learn that about me?"

Everything inside her warmed. "It's no secret that I miss Aaron. But I think he would want me to find love again, if it ever came my way."

Charlie lifted a silvery brow. "Oh?" Something hopeful twinkled in his blue eyes.

"I like you, Charlie. You are a good man." Her heart began to race. Her mouth felt dry. "And also quite handsome."

He grinned lopsidedly, his smile digging dimples into his cheeks. There was something boyish about him, which was endearing but also sexy. Even a woman at her age could appreciate that. "I think you're exquisitely beautiful. And I adore you. Whenever you decide it's finally time to leave your house, do you think we might go on a date? Or if you're not ready to leave, we can have a date here. If your yard is good enough for a wedding, it's good enough for a date."

Fear cooled her skin. But she was also excited. There was something about a wedding that made one feel so much hope. She'd always thought so. "When I am ready, which might not be for quite some time, I want to put on my best dress and go out to dinner. And I want to have a glass of wine," she added giddily. "Just one. I don't need another broken bone."

Charlie reached for her hand and gave it a squeeze. "I want to give you that. The date, not the broken bone."

Eleanor laughed softly. "I'm not sure if it will be here or at my favorite restaurant but it's a date. Next weekend?" she asked, promising herself she'd choose the excitement over her fear.

He lifted her hand and brushed a delicate kiss to her knuckles, lighting up every cell in her body. "Next weekend it is," he said.

Chapter Twenty-Four

Savannah

I shall take the heart," returned the Tin Wood-man; "for...happiness is the best thing in the world.

The Wonderful Wizard of Oz,
L. Frank Baum

Where is Evan?

Evan had been MIA the past fifteen minutes. Savannah guessed he'd gone home to check on June but surely he was coming back.

"Excuse me, Savannah?"

Savannah turned to face Charlie. "Oh. Hi, Charlie." She glanced around to see if Eleanor was nearby. "Everything okay?"

"Yes, yes. Ellie's just catching up with some of the Books and Blooms members who are here. And when they start talking books, the conversation can go on forever." He shoved his hands into his blazer pockets. "I saw you standing over here and thought I'd come see if you were up for a dance."

"A dance?" Savannah repeated. "With you?"

"Why not me? I may be an old man but I'm pretty smooth on my feet."

Savannah thought Charlie was perhaps the most charming man she'd ever known. "I would love a dance, Charlie. Unless you think Aunt Eleanor will get too jealous."

His laugh rumbled deep from his belly. "I don't think that aunt of yours gets jealous. If she did, she would have agreed to a date with me a long time ago." He held out his hand.

Savannah took it, and they walked out to the area where couples were dancing under a tent lined with fairy lights.

"Where's Evan?" Charlie asked.

"I believe he's next door. Probably checking on his daughter. She went home after the wedding."

"Ah." Charlie nodded knowingly. "I guess this isn't such a hip scene for a youngster."

"I guess not." Savannah placed her hands on Charlie's shoulders, and they swayed to the slow tempo of the music.

"Your aunt has agreed to go on a date with me next weekend," Charlie confided.

Savannah felt her eyes widen. "Wow. That's great, Charlie."

Charlie was absolutely beaming. "I knew eventually she would agree. I'm fairly hard to resist."

Savannah knew he was joking but she also thought that statement was true. Charlie was handsome for his age, and he was young in spirit.

"I want you to know that I promise to treat your aunt well," he said with a serious expression.

"I wasn't worried about that, Charlie."

"And I hope Evan treats you well. He's a good man. I've known him since he was a baby. Just like I've known you since you were in diapers. I think Ellie has been planning your match since you were about six months old."

Savannah shook her head on a stifled laugh. "I wouldn't be surprised."

"She just wants you to be happy. And most folks believe love is what brings happiness. Judging by my granddaughter's face today, I'd say that's at least partly true."

"I guess it all depends," Savannah said. "I actually think that a person has to be happy in order to find love. Not the other way around."

"I wholeheartedly agree. So?" he asked.

"So?" she repeated, furrowing her brows. It looked like he was waiting on an answer.

"So, are you happy? Are you in a good place to find love, Savannah?" he asked.

It was a very personal question for two people who really didn't know each other well. "You know, I think I'm maybe happier now than I have been in a long time. I've forgotten how much Bloom felt like home. I also forgot how wonderful it is to have a real garden, not a bunch of pots in a cramped apartment. I think..." She hesitated as she collected her thoughts. "I think I had forgotten how it felt to be truly happy. And now I remember."

Charlie looked pleased. "I understand what you mean. So you're saying you are in a good place to fall in love and that it's the right time? In which case, all you need is the right person."

As he said it, Savannah's gaze pulled to the far side of the lot, where Evan was dipping through the missing fence panel and returning to the reception.

Charlie followed her gaze, pulling his hands from her waist. "Speak of the devil." He looked at her again. "Thank you for the dance, Savannah."

"Thank you, Charlie." She lowered her own arms to her side, ready to go see Evan. He'd only been gone a short amount of time but she missed him already. She took a step in his direction but then stopped short, feeling a sharp, stabbing pain in her chest. It felt as if someone had plunged a knife through her. Savannah pressed a hand to the spot and hunched forward, moaning softly and trying to catch her breath. "Ohh."

Charlie stepped closer and grabbed her upper arm. "You okay?"

The pain took her breath away. *What is this?* Savannah had never felt pain to this degree before—sharp and sudden. She shook her head, trying to form words. "N-no. I'm not sure but..." She really didn't want to be overly dramatic. She didn't want to call unnecessary attention to herself either. This wasn't the kind of pain that could be ignored though. "I think...I may be having a heart attack."

Evan was suddenly standing next to her. "A heart attack?"

Savannah hurt too much to say anything more. All she could do was attempt to breathe past the blinding pain.

"She's too young for a heart attack, isn't she?" Charlie asked.

Evan wrapped his arm around Savannah's shoulders. "I don't know. I'll call an ambulance."

"No!" Savannah shook her head, working hard to muster words. "I don't...want to ruin Madison's wedding. Drive me there, Evan...Please."

He studied her face and then nodded. "Okay. Let's go."

"Dad?" June came running up. "Dad, what's going on? What's wrong with Savannah?"

Savannah opened her eyes just long enough to catch the fear in June's expression. Savannah hated that she was the reason. She hated that she was ruining the occasion.

"I'm not sure," Evan told her. "You stay with Ms. Eleanor tonight. Got it?" he asked.

June's eyes were wide with fear. "O-okay," she said, voice threadbare. "Savannah?"

Savannah opened her eyes to look at the young girl. "It's okay, June. I'm okay." At least she hoped she was. This was scary though. She felt helpless. Out of control. And some part of her wondered if she was dying.

"Promise that you'll be okay?" June asked.

Savannah grimaced as another bolt of pain ripped through her. Evan hugged her body more tightly to his as if sensing that the pain had intensified. "Promise," Savannah managed to say.

"All right, we need to get you to the hospital now," Evan told Savannah. "June, find Ms. Eleanor but don't tell anyone else about this. Got it? Don't tell anyone except Ms. Eleanor."

The girl's voice was small. The fear was palpable. "Got it."

The next fifteen minutes were timeless. Pain made seconds and minutes irrelevant.

"An ambulance could have gotten you there faster," Evan said, talking to Savannah as he drove.

Judging by the roar of the motor, Savannah was sure he was speeding.

"Are you okay?" It was the twentieth time he'd asked.

She'd only nodded and grunted in response to all of them. She hated that she was worrying the people she loved. That was the last thing she wanted. She was used to being the one that others could depend on. She was used to drawing as little attention to herself as possible.

"It's going to be okay," Evan said when she didn't answer him.

Savannah closed her eyes, feeling the wetness of tears on her cheeks. She would wipe them away but she needed to keep her hand applying pressure to the area above her heart. What was this? *What is wrong with me?*

Finally, Evan pulled into the emergency room parking lot. By this point, Savannah was certain she was having a heart attack, not that she'd experienced one to know. What else would cause such excruciating pain though?

Evan pushed his truck door open and ran around to the passenger side, opening her door. "Lean on me. Put all your weight on my body," he instructed.

As she got out of the vehicle, Savannah nearly collapsed into Evan's side. "Evan, I'm so s-sorry," she managed to say. This was exactly what Randall had said no to. He didn't want his life to be complicated by unplanned hospital visits. Neither did Savannah but she didn't have much choice in the matter.

"You have no reason to apologize. We'll get you to a doctor and they'll make you feel better."

The automatic doors to the emergency room opened and a blast of cold air-conditioning covered Savannah as they headed inside.

"My friend needs to see a doctor immediately," Evan told the receptionist.

"Here's the paperwork. Fill this out and bring it back up," she told Evan.

Savannah didn't look at the woman but she could hear the impatience in the receptionist's tone.

"This is an emergency," he said, raising his voice. "We can do paperwork later. My girlfriend needs to see a doctor now."

Girlfriend? Even in her condition, Savannah caught that word and somehow found comfort in it.

"Sir, this is an emergency room. Everyone in here is having an emergency."

Savannah thought she heard Evan growl. Had he growled at the receptionist?

"My friend is having a heart attack," he explained, biting back his words. "This can't wait for me to fill out paperwork that I don't even have the answers to."

"A heart attack?" the receptionist's tone completely shifted. "Well, that's different, sir. Why didn't you say so? Wait right there and I'll get your girlfriend a room."

Savannah cracked her eyes open long enough to see the woman disappear through a set of curtains. When she came back, she had a male nurse by her side. She handed Evan the clipboard. "Fill this out once you're back there."

Evan audibly exhaled. "Thank you."

Savannah could feel his relief even alongside her pain, which hadn't subsided in the least. If anything, it was getting more intense. She pressed her eyes shut, breathing past the nausea that was now also rolling through her. This better not turn out to be indigestion because if it was, she might die of embarrassment anyway.

"Go home, Evan." Savannah was exhausted but her chest wasn't hurting any longer. The physician who'd come in to examine her had already ruled out a heart attack, which was good news. He'd ordered a few additional tests, and in the meantime, he had given her an IV with something to alleviate her symptoms.

Evan looked tired as well. "I'm fine."

"June needs you more than I do," Savannah said. "And I plan on sleeping here in a minute. You'll serve us all better at home with June. You can sleep and come back in the morning." Savannah glanced up at the clock on the wall. It was nearly midnight. "Please," she added for good measure.

"Okay." He nodded. "But you have to promise to call me if you need me to come back. I don't like leaving you here alone."

"I won't know the difference because I'll be sleeping," she reminded him. "Go. Thank you for bringing me here and for staying this long. The hospital is no one's favorite place."

Evan leaned forward and kissed her forehead, his woodsy scent mixing with the sterile smells of a medical environment.

He was comforting, and she actually did want him to stay with her right now. She just couldn't admit that, because she didn't want to be a burden.

"Being next to you anywhere is one of my favorite places," he said. "I got a text from Hollis. No one at the wedding even missed us."

Savannah smiled, the simple gesture taking just about all the energy she had left. "Is that good news or bad?"

"Both, I guess." He reached for her hand, bringing it to his lips and pressing a kiss on the back of her fingers. "I'll be back tomorrow. Early."

"Hopefully it'll be to take me home." Before he left, she closed her eyes, unable to hold them open any longer, and fell asleep.

Chapter Twenty-Five

Evan

All human wisdom is summed up in these two words—'Wait and hope.'

The Count of Monte Cristo,
Alexandre Dumas

Evan quietly let himself into his home. June had stayed the night with Eleanor so his house was empty for the first time since June had come to live with him. Maybe it was only in his mind but the house felt emptier knowing she should be here.

He poured himself a glass of water and drank it while watching out his back window. There wasn't much to see in his yard. No magical garden or library that seemed to grow out of the ground. He could see the fairy lights that were still on in Eleanor's yard from the wedding reception. He finished off his glass of water while watching and imagining the fireflies were competing with Eleanor's fairy lights next door.

It'd been a great night—until it wasn't. Wasn't that always how things went? Perfect until some small catastrophe happened. Even though the doctors had ruled out the possibility that Savannah was having a heart attack, they were still concerned given Savannah's medical history. Evan was concerned too.

He guessed he'd kind of been in denial about how sick Savannah was. She didn't look sick—not usually. It was easy to forget that there was an invisible storm brewing under her surface, threatening to wreck her body like the storm had done to the Finders Keepers Library a few short weeks ago. Now the damage was fixed on the library or covered up well enough so that no one would ever know. It was invisible.

Evan guessed Savannah hid most of how she was feeling. Why wouldn't she? Her ex had shunned her for having a chronic illness. Evan wanted to meet that guy in a dark alley and pull out some of the defensive moves he'd learned in the military. Another part of him wanted to pity the guy because he would miss out on all the wonderful things that Savannah was. She was goodness and grace personified.

Exhausted but not sleepy, Evan turned and walked over to the dining room table and opened his laptop. He sat down and pulled up a browser. Then he spent the next half hour googling a variety of keywords:

Lupus and chest pain.

Lupus symptoms.

Lupus and prognosis.

The results of his search overwhelmed him. There was a spectrum of what to expect, ranging from cold-like symptoms to the worst-case scenario. After reading through his findings, Evan's mind was even less ready for sleep. In the past month, his feelings for Savannah had deepened, plunging to a level he'd never experienced in his lifetime. She was important to him, and he knew she was important to June as well.

June had seemed worried when Evan had taken Savannah from the reception. Hopefully, Eleanor had been able to talk her down. Knowing his neighbor, Eleanor had probably made June a cup of chamomile tea and quoted relevant books to comfort her. That's what she'd always done for him. His favorite quotes had come from books like E.B. White's *Charlotte's Web*.

A spider's web is stronger than it looks. Although it is made of thin, delicate strands, the web is not easily broken.

When Evan would be upset, missing his mom or wishing his dad had more time to spend with him, he would draw webs all over his papers, telling himself that he was stronger than he looked. He was not easily broken.

Closing his laptop, Evan headed to bed, knowing he likely wouldn't get much sleep but he had to at least try. Tomorrow, he needed to be functioning as close to 100 percent as possible. June would need him, and so would Savannah.

Evan stirred in bed as he listened to the sounds of someone shuffling around in the kitchen. That was odd. Typically, he woke up before June. He glanced at his bedside clock. It was still early. *What is June doing up?*

He sat up on the edge of his bed and stretched his arms overhead. Then he yawned as he made his way to the front of the house, stopping in his tracks to watch his daughter. "I must still be dreaming. Because there is no way that you're up at 6:00 a.m., cleaning my house without being asked."

June lowered her spray bottle and a roll of paper towels. "I couldn't sleep."

Evan somehow didn't think it was because she was at a different house. "Does Eleanor know you left and came back over here?"

"I wrote her a note. I didn't want to wake her," June told him. "Good."

June blew a breath upward to move a strand of hair that had fallen in her eyes. "How is Savannah?" she asked, wringing her hands.

Evan wasn't surprised by how worried June appeared. His daughter had watched her mother go through an illness. It had to be stressful for her, seeing someone else that she loved being rushed to the hospital. "She's under doctors' care. Everything will be fine."

"Mom was under doctors' care too," June countered.

"For something far different." Evan stepped toward her and put his hand on her shoulder, narrowing her eyes. "Your mom had cancer. Savannah has an autoimmune condition."

"I read that people die from lupus though," June said.

So she had been doing her own Google searches last night, when Eleanor had thought June was asleep.

Evan hesitated before responding. "People can die from anything. From crossing the street or going on an amusement park ride. From allergies. From chicken pox."

June frowned. "I don't think people die from chicken pox."

Maybe that was true. "My point is, if you search for something on the internet, you'll find proof of any worst-case scenario. Trust me. Savannah is sick but she'll get better."

June still didn't look so sure.

"You want to come with me to see her this morning?" Evan asked.

He expected June to jump at the chance. Instead, her worried expression grew even more anxious as she wove her fingers together.

"I'm sure she'd love to see you," he added, lowering his voice. "It might even make her feel better."

June avoided his gaze. "I-I don't know. Maybe I should wait until she gets home."

Was June scared of going to the hospital? Evan really didn't know how much time June had spent visiting her mom in the hospital in California. Had June looked at the doctors there and hoped that they'd make her mom well? He wished he'd been there for every visit to comfort his daughter and hold her hand. To quote *Charlotte's Web* the way Eleanor had for him when he was younger. "You don't have to go with me. I'd rather not leave you home alone though."

"I'm old enough," June said. "I'm almost thirteen."

Evan nodded. "I know but I still don't like it."

"You could leave me with Ms. Eleanor."

"I guess that's true. I'll ask her." He retrieved his cell phone from his bedroom and tapped on Eleanor's contact, knowing she was an early riser. She was probably sitting down with a cup of hot tea right about now.

"Evan," Eleanor said as soon as she answered. "I'm glad you called."

"Oh?" He wondered at the urgency he heard in Eleanor's voice. Had everyone stayed up worrying about Savannah last night?

"I want to go see my niece this morning, and I need you to drive me there," Eleanor said.

Evan glanced up at June, who was standing in his doorway watching him closely. "You want to leave your house and go to the hospital?" he clarified to Eleanor, repeating the request so that June knew what was going on.

"Yes." Eleanor's voice was shaky. "Savannah needs me, and I don't want to let her down. I can do this. I can do this," she repeated, as if trying to convince herself. "A spider's web is stronger than it looks. Although it is made of thin, delicate strands, the web is not easily broken," she said.

Evan was shocked. Eleanor hadn't left her home in months. There was no way he could turn her request down right now. "Sure. You can come with June and me," he said, keeping his eyes on June. "Give us thirty minutes to get showered and dressed."

"Thank you. And Evan," Eleanor said, "don't let me back out of this. I want to go. It's not comfortable for me but I need to do this. For Savannah."

"Okay. See you soon." He disconnected the call and waited for June to say something.

"I thought you said I didn't have to go if I didn't want to," June finally said, sounding defeated.

"I don't feel right about leaving you here alone, June. Not under these circumstances."

"Call Mallory then. She'll stay with me."

Evan grimaced. "Mallory will likely want to see Savannah this morning too. I can try to call someone else. Maybe Uncle Hollis."

June's lips pressed together. She folded her arms at her chest and looked away. "Whatever. I'll go with you." She shrugged. Then she turned and headed down the hall toward her bedroom.

"Where're you going?" Evan called after her.

"To get dressed. Hospitals are like iceboxes, you know." From someone who was familiar with being in hospitals. Evan wished he could take June's pain away. He wanted to do the same for Savannah too. All he could do was support them— and stay off Google. Those searches last night had done nothing to ease his mind.

Half an hour later, Evan knocked on Eleanor's front door.

"Her sign says to just walk in," June muttered, turning the knob and doing just that.

"But it's polite to make your presence known," Evan responded, following June.

"Nonsense." Eleanor walked toward the door. "My home is your home." She grabbed her purse from the table next to the door. Evan noticed that her hands were shaking.

"You sure you want to come along?" he asked.

Eleanor looked at him sternly. "I thought I told you to make sure I didn't back down. Not to offer to let me do just that." She pulled the strap of her purse over her shoulder. "I am sure. 'Get busy living, or get busy dying,'" she said.

Evan recognized the quote. "Since when do you read Stephen King books?"

A small smile formed on Eleanor's lips. "I read across all genres; you should know that by now. There are so many life lessons to be learned in that book. Have you read the novella *Rita Hayworth and Shawshank Redemption?*"

Evan shook his head. "I've seen the movie though."

Eleanor tsked. "The book is always better. No exceptions." She looked at June. "I especially like *The Hunger Games* book better than the movie."

June's jaw dropped. "You read the book?"

"Of course I did. We had a deal, didn't we? I'm channeling my inner Katniss right now. Yes, I know it's just a little drive to the hospital, and I'm not even the one behind the wheel but it's my own personal war." She stared at June a moment more. "I know in some cases, it's not healthy to slip into some fictional character's shoes. But sometimes it helps. My new counselor calls this a healthy dissociation." She looked at Evan. "Now let's go before I lose my nerve. And don't you tell me that it's okay if I do." She looped her arm with June's. "Fear will suck the life out of you faster than any illness."

"What book did that come from?" June asked.

Eleanor tilted her head while narrowing her eyes. "I do have some of my own words, you know? And I'm fairly wise, if I do say so." She laughed lightly even though Evan could see that she was nervous. Nervous, yet brave. He admired Eleanor maybe more than any other human on earth. He admired Savannah too. Both were strong women that he was lucky to have in his life. June was also lucky to have them.

"Ms. Eleanor?" June asked from the middle seat in Evan's truck as Evan backed out of the driveway.

Evan thought that maybe Eleanor was holding her breath as he reversed onto the street, leaving the boundaries of her yard.

"Yes?" Eleanor had one hand on the truck's door, her knuckles turning white as she gripped the handle.

"Do you think Savannah will be okay? I mean, really. I'm not sure my dad would tell me the truth."

"And you think I would?" Eleanor asked. "Why is that?"

"Because you remind me of Marilla. Sorry if that spoils your whole Katniss vibe."

"Marilla, hmm. Why is that?"

"Well, Marilla was no-nonsense even though she loved Anne very much. She told the truth no matter what. That's why I think you'd do the same for me."

"That's a high compliment then," Eleanor said.

Evan had read *Anne of Green Gables* at June's age. Eleanor put it on the summer reading list for both him and Savannah.

From the rearview mirror, Evan watched June squirm.

June nibbled at her lower lip. "I also think you wouldn't be leaving your house if you thought Savannah was going to be okay."

Eleanor seemed to momentarily forget that she was facing one of her biggest fears right then. She loosened her grip on the door, seemingly taken aback by what June had just said. Evan was taken aback too. "I've lost a lot of people in my life. My dear husband was one of them. I think Savannah will be okay but I still want to be there for her. Life is too short not to be there for the ones you love." Evan saw a smile flicker at the corners of Eleanor's mouth. "You remind me of Anne, you know?"

June's gaze dropped to her lap. "Why? Because my mom died too?"

"No; heavens no. Because Anne was brave. Stubborn and brave. And she had a beautiful heart, just like you."

Chapter Twenty-Six

Eleanor

Now that I knew fear, I also knew it was not permanent.

The Round House, Louise Erdrich

Eleanor felt clammy. She imagined this is how the characters in *The Hunger Games* felt being plunged into dangerous environments. Yes, she knew comparing herself to someone who was fighting for their life was a bit dramatic but that's what leaving home felt like for her.

She wanted to demand that Evan turn his truck around and take her back—right now. But Savannah was in a hospital bed. Savannah had been there for Eleanor this summer, helping to revive her precious garden and help with the Finders Keepers Library. She'd been there for Eleanor. So, even if it felt like Eleanor was in the midst of her own sort of hunger game, she was doing this. One breath at a time. One step at a time. She was almost in a meditative state by the time Evan pulled into the hospital parking lot.

"We're here," he said, putting the truck in park.

Eleanor felt Evan watching her as she sat stiffly in the passenger seat. Her hand was sore from her death grip on the door's handle.

"Ms. Eleanor?" June asked. "Are you . . . okay?"

Eleanor looked at the father and daughter. "Before doing things he wasn't sure about, Aaron used to say, 'I can do hard things.' He would whisper it under his breath. I must have heard him say those words a hundred times when he was alive. Maybe a thousand." Eleanor swallowed. Her throat was so dry. "I always wondered what the benefit of those five simple words was." She pulled a breath into her lungs. "I can do hard things. I can do hard things," she repeated.

June placed a hand on Eleanor's shoulder.

Eleanor looked at the girl. "It's just a little bit of fear. I can do hard things," she said again. "You know, those words do help a bit."

"You don't have to go in," Evan said. "I can take you home, Eleanor."

Eleanor gave him a stern look. "I told you not to do that. I don't need you to let me off the hook. I need you to hold me accountable. I can do hard things," she said adamantly. "Especially with you two beside me."

"Okay, then. Let's go in." Evan pushed his driver's side door open and headed around to the passenger side, opening the truck door for Eleanor.

She took her time stepping out, her body trembling. "I can do hard things."

June stepped out after Eleanor and reached for her other hand. Eleanor was proud of June. She had a good heart.

After Evan locked up the truck, they headed toward the hospital. One step at a time. One breath.

I can do hard things. Eleanor could hear Aaron's voice in her head, saying those words. Coaxing her along.

"Can we stop at the gift shop and get Savannah something?" June asked once they'd reached the lobby. "Please."

Evan glanced over at Eleanor.

"You two go on. Buy Savannah something pretty. I'm going to head up. Second floor, room eleven, correct?" Eleanor asked.

"I thought you wanted us beside you." Evan gestured between him and June. "We don't need to buy anything."

"Nonsense. Buy her a plant if they have one. That should lift her spirits." Eleanor patted her chest. "I'm not alone. I've realized Aaron's voice isn't just with me in the garden. I hear him clearly even here in this bustling environment."

"Aaron is talking to you right now?" Evan looked concerned.

Eleanor laughed softly. She imagined he was worried that she might get checked in to a room at this hospital as well. "My memory is full of words that I've read in the books I've loved. My heart is full of words I've heard from the man I still love. I can do hard things. It's just taking an elevator and walking down a hall by myself but I want to do it. I'll meet you up there."

Evan seemed to be deciphering what the right thing to do was.

"I'm still your elder and you still have to listen to me," Eleanor said more sternly. "Now go buy a plant for Savannah and meet me upstairs."

"Okay." Evan nodded. "Will do. Call me on my cell if you need me."

Eleanor had already turned and was heading toward the elevators. She was David, and this walk was Goliath. She was Katniss and this walk was her hunger games. Every great fictional character faced something that terrified them. She borrowed their courage as she pressed the elevator button for the second floor and stepped inside. As the doors began to close, her fear intensified. Her knees shook and threatened to buckle. She stifled a scream that wanted to erupt out of her.

"Hold the elevator," a familiar voice said.

A hand poked through the elevator's opening, stopping the doors and causing them to reopen.

Eleanor blinked past blurry vision, clouded by tears, as Charlie stepped in beside her. "W-what are you doing here?"

"Visiting Savannah. Same as you."

The elevator doors began to shut again.

"I was doing fine on my own," she lied, fighting back tears.

"I know, Ellie." Charlie stared forward, and she suspected he was respecting her privacy. "It's brave to face things on your own. But maybe it's braver if you allow someone to come alongside you."

"I wouldn't say I'm being brave." She sniffled. "I'm just trying to be there for my niece." Eleanor shook all over. It felt like her body might collapse beneath her. She didn't feel one inkling of bravery.

Charlie shrugged. Then, surprising her, he spoke her love language, talking in bookish quotes: "I have a theory that selflessness and bravery aren't all that different."

Her body calmed as she tried to place where she'd read that line before. Usually she knew immediately but she was out of her depth right now.

"*Divergent.*" He cast her a sheepish look. "I know, I know. You like your classics. I'm a fan of action though."

"I like all books," she said. "Veronica Roth is a popular author. She did very well writing that series."

"You are brave and selfless. You're a remarkable woman, Eleanor Collins." The elevator dinged as it came to a stop. "Don't mind me. I'm just here," he said.

"As always," she replied quietly. "You've always been there for me."

"And I always will be, assuming you let me." He glanced over, meeting Eleanor's gaze.

She breathed a little easier with him beside her, and she still heard Aaron's voice loud and clear. *I can do hard things.* Having Charlie didn't cancel out Aaron. She had both men with her, and that gave her the strength to keep going.

The elevator doors opened on the second floor. Charlie stepped out first.

"You're no less brave if you hold my hand, you know," he said.

"I'm probably braver if I do." She slipped her hand in his and took small deliberate steps onto the smooth hospital flooring. "Thank you, Charlie." She pulled her hand away but then looped her arm through his.

"I didn't do anything, Ellie."

"Oh, but you have, and I appreciate you." Appreciation wasn't the right word. No, the word she wanted to say was stronger than that but it frightened her too much to say. And her limit for facing her fears today was already spent.

Chapter Twenty-Seven

Savannah

We accept the love we think we deserve.

The Perks of Being a Wallflower,
Stephen Chbosky

Make it stop!

The sound of the machines beeping all around was driving her nuts. She'd barely slept a wink last night between the unfamiliar hospital sounds, the pain in her chest, and the dings coming from her iPhone. She had almost shut her phone off but then she'd noticed that June was one of the concerned people in her contacts who was checking on her at all hours of the night.

Guilt wove its way through Savannah's body. June had sent several texts, time-stamped as late as 3:30 a.m., when the girl should have been sleeping.

9:34 p.m.

June: *Are you okay?*

11:15 p.m.

June: *What do the doctors think?*

12:30 a.m.

June: *Is your chest okay? Are you in pain?*

3:30 a.m.

June: *I hope you're feeling better.*

The text messages broke Savannah's heart into many pieces. There were also messages from Evan and Eleanor. Mallory. And even Madison, who wasn't supposed to know that Savannah had quietly slipped away from the wedding to go to the hospital. Madison shouldn't have been thinking about anything on her wedding night except for her bright future with her new husband.

A knock on the hospital room door got her attention.

Savannah blinked as her mind tried to process how her aunt Eleanor was standing in the doorway. She had Charlie beside her. "Aunt Eleanor, you left your house."

"I did." She nodded shakily. "My favorite niece needed me, and I couldn't let her down. I wouldn't." She walked over to Savannah's bedside, bent over, and kissed Savannah's cheek. Then she took hold of Savannah's hand.

"You didn't have to," Savannah said, overwhelmed by her aunt's gesture.

"Yes, I did." Eleanor forced a smile but Savannah could tell that Eleanor was uneasy. Charlie stepped up beside Eleanor and looped his arm with hers. Eleanor glanced over and smiled warmly.

"So Charlie drove you?" Savannah asked.

"No. Evan did. He and June are downstairs at the gift shop."

Knowing Evan and June were here set Savannah on edge. She hated that she'd raised so much concern among her loved ones. That was the very last thing she wanted to do.

"So what's going on? Did the doctor figure out what was causing you so much pain last night?" Eleanor asked.

Savannah pushed herself up to a sitting position in the bed. "Yes. He said it was costochondritis." Savannah laughed at the look on Eleanor's face.

"That sounds serious. Why are you laughing?" Eleanor asked.

"It sounds scarier than it actually is. Although it was very painful in the moment." Savannah reached for her large plastic cup of water that the nurses had provided her. "The way they explained it, I had inflammation in the cartilage that connects my ribs to my breastbone. Apparently, it's common, especially with people who have an autoimmune disease."

"So it wasn't a heart attack?" Eleanor clarified.

"Not even close."

"Thank goodness." Eleanor blew out a breath. "I will be sure to update your parents once I return home. I spoke to them late last night and they were very worried about you," Eleanor told Savannah. "They send their best and would like to know if there's anything you need," she added.

Savannah hadn't told her parents about having lupus yet. She guessed that was part of her being in denial and thinking she would never need to. "I'll call them later," she said.

Eleanor patted Savannah's hand. "Take your time. The focus right now needs to be on getting well and returning home."

When Savannah thought of home, she thought of Eleanor's house now. It was clear that was what her aunt meant as well.

Savannah looked at Charlie. "If you didn't drive Aunt Eleanor, what brings you here?"

"You, of course." He looked sheepish as he added, "And Eleanor. She texted me earlier to let me know she'd asked Evan to drive her here. I knew it wouldn't be easy for her to leave the house, so I came to support her and check on you. I wanted to make sure you were okay too."

"That's sweet." Savannah took a breath. She had so many rampant emotions right now. "I'm okay. I think I'll be discharged around noon today if everything checks out. But I appreciate you coming, Aunt Eleanor. It makes me feel..." She swallowed and worked to steady her breath. Why was she so emotional? "It makes me feel loved."

"You are loved, dear," Eleanor said.

"Very loved," Charlie echoed.

Savannah felt it but at the same time, she felt guilty for causing the people she cared about to worry.

"I won't stay long," Eleanor said. "I know Evan and June will be up here soon, and I don't want to impinge on their time."

"You probably want to get back to your cottage," Savannah added.

Eleanor seemed to inhale deeply. "Actually, I was thinking Charlie might take me out for a milkshake or something first."

Charlie lifted his brows. "I'd be happy to. If that's what you want."

Eleanor nodded. Then she turned back to Savannah. "I'm glad you're doing better, dear."

Her aunt's concern touched Savannah's heart. "Thank you."

"See you at home tonight?" Eleanor asked. "I'll make us both a hot cup of tea."

"I'd like that." Savannah watched Eleanor and Charlie leave. Not two minutes later, Evan walked in. He knocked first, lingering in the doorway until she waved him inside. She waited for June to follow but June was nowhere in sight. "Hi."

"Hey." Evan stepped over to her bed and handed her a small plant in a decorative pot.

"Oh, wow. How beautiful, Evan. Thank you."

He took a seat in the chair beside her bed. His hair was disheveled, and he looked out of sorts, like a man who'd been up worrying all night.

She glanced at the doorway again. "Where's June?" she finally asked.

"Oh." He averted his gaze. "Well, she, uh, she sends her well wishes." He seemed to shift nervously in the chair.

Savannah wanted to ask why June had to send well wishes. Why didn't she just walk into Savannah's room? "I scared her last night, didn't I?" Savannah asked, a horrible feeling taking hold in the pit of her stomach.

Evan shook his head. "No. No, June is fine."

Savannah saw the truth in his eyes though. June wasn't fine at all. "Evan, I'm really sorry."

"Hey, no." He reached for her hand. "You don't need to apologize for anything. You didn't do anything wrong."

Savannah suddenly felt like she just wanted to curl up and cry. "Madison found out about me leaving the reception last night. I hope it didn't put a strain on her wedding."

Evan gently ran his hand back and forth over her skin in a soothing motion. "Things happen. It's okay."

She studied his face, where there were dark circles under his bloodshot eyes. "You didn't sleep well."

"Now is not the time to be worrying about me, Sav. It's you we're all worried about. We love you," he said quietly.

She wondered in what sense he had included himself in that word. *We.* Did he mean he loved her as a friend? Or more? She averted her gaze to keep him from seeing the tears she was desperately trying to hold back. This was the epitome of what she didn't want. She wanted lots of loved ones in her life but she didn't want to cause them undue distress. "Where's June?" she asked, deciding she wanted the truth. She needed to hear it.

Evan looked down at their hands. "She, uh, well, you know how kids are?"

"No, not really." Savannah could see Evan trying to figure out how to respond without admitting that June was here in the hospital. June was just too upset to come see Savannah. She knew that Evan was hoping June would choose to stay in Bloom. If June was uncomfortable around Savannah now, would that make June want to leave even more than she already did? The last thing Savannah wanted was to hurt either of them. "Evan, maybe this is too much right now."

He narrowed his eyes. "What do you mean?"

"Me and you. I'm not leaving Bloom for a couple more weeks but maybe it's time to distance ourselves." Savannah hadn't planned to have this conversation. It was just spilling out of her but as much as it broke her heart, it felt like the right thing to do—the only thing to do.

Evan shook his head quickly, squeezing her hand in his. "No. That's just it, Savannah. I don't want to distance ourselves. I don't want to say goodbye at all. I don't know how that looks.

Maybe we could do long distance for a while. All I know is how I feel about you."

Savannah didn't dare ask how he felt. She could hear her heart rate speeding up in the monitors that she was hooked to. "We both have a lot going on, and it's complicated. For both of us."

"No," he said again, shaking his head. "Every relationship is complicated. That's the nature of relationships. This is just a speed bump."

"This isn't a speed bump for me. This is my life." She hated feeling this way. Hated being in this bed and feeling so helpless. She hated loving Evan so much that she knew she had to let him go. What they'd had this summer was amazing but any reservations she'd had about saying goodbye to him had dissolved. The bubble they'd been caught up in had burst last night. She hadn't had a heart attack but she could have. Or she could have issues with her eyes, her kidneys, any part of her body. This was real life for Savannah.

She took a breath, doing her best to stay calm. If she broke down in front of him, he'd dissuade her from of what she was about to do. "Evan, maybe it's too much for me. I don't think I'm ready for a relationship right now." It wasn't the complete truth but she instinctively knew Evan would argue if she gave him any other reason. "I need to be focused on my health. Anything romantic is just...distracting."

Evan wore a pained expression. "I'm not sure I'm following."

"I've been spending a lot of time with you. Between hanging out with you and preparing for Madison's wedding, I haven't really taken care of myself the way I should."

"You think dating me is part of why you're in the hospital?" he asked.

Savannah avoided eye contact. This was for the best. For Evan. For June. For Savannah too, because it wasn't completely a lie. She could have focused more on her health instead of going off to the festival, working outside in the garden all day, and spending her evenings with Evan. She could have rested more and taken hot Epsom salt baths. "I need to concentrate on getting well and staying well, as much as I can. I think…" She hesitated. Her chest was hurting again but it wasn't the same pain as she'd felt last night. Last night's pain had been sharp and unrelenting. This one was a deep, penetrating ache—the kind that only love can cause. "I think we should take a break." Savannah didn't want to lead him on. She didn't want to allow herself to backtrack either. A clean break would be easiest. "The summer was fun, and I needed that after my broken engagement. But that's all this was for me."

Evan looked at her as if he was trying to determine if she was being sincere. His eyes had a sheen of tears making them appear glassy. "Why are you pushing me away, Sav?"

"I'm not. I still want to be friends. We probably never should have tried to cross that line. We work better as friends."

"Friends?" he repeated, looking numb—the way she felt.

"But we probably need to avoid each other for a little while. So that we can get back to where we were."

"What if I don't want to go back?" Evan asked. "I like where we are. Savannah; I like you. Maybe what I feel for you is stronger than like."

Savannah looked down. She couldn't look into Evan's eyes right now when he was implying that he might love her. She loved him too. Too much to allow him and his daughter to spend sleepless nights worrying over her like last night. "I have to think about myself. About my health." She knew he wouldn't be able to argue against this explanation. Not if he truly loved her.

And if she loved him, which she was pretty sure she did, this was exactly what needed to happen. She'd read enough Shakespearian tragedies and Nicholas Sparks books to know that love didn't always survive.

Mallory poked her head into Savannah's hospital room. "Hey, you! Ready to ditch this place?"

Savannah smiled at her friend. Mallory was still dressed in scrubs because she was coming off a nursing night shift. "So ready." Eleanor had already left with Charlie hours ago. Savannah assumed Evan had left as well. After she'd effectively broken up with him, he'd walked out, his head hanging low, leaving Savannah with a pit in her stomach. She wasn't sure if she'd done the right thing by cutting the cord and letting him and June live their lives free of medical baggage. She thought so.

Mallory wheeled a wheelchair into the hospital room doorway. "You have to ride this thing out of here."

"You're kidding, right?" Savannah did not want to draw attention to herself by sitting in a wheelchair when she could walk perfectly fine.

"Doctor's orders. Get in. I'll push."

Savannah dutifully stood and lowered herself into the sling seat. "For the record, I hate this."

"You hate depending on me or getting a free ride down the

halls? Because I for one wouldn't mind getting a joy ride down the halls." Mallory grinned widely.

Once Savannah was seated with her belongings in her lap, Mallory started pushing the chair, waving and saying hello to her coworkers as she passed. She seemed to know everyone here. "How long have you been working here?" Savannah thought to ask.

"This was my first job straight out of college. So about eight years now."

"Wow. That's impressive. I didn't think anyone stayed at their first job."

Mallory sighed. "That's the downside of a small town sometimes. Slim pickings for jobs. Sooooo, you should probably start putting out your feelers right away."

Savannah laughed. "Why is that?"

"Because hopefully you've realized that Bloom is the perfect place for you to stay. Eleanor needs you. I need you. And then there's Evan." She pushed Savannah up to the elevator and pressed the red button.

When Savannah didn't respond, Mallory walked around the chair and narrowed her eyes.

"And then there's Evan," she repeated, seeming to scrutinize Savannah's reaction.

Savannah looked down at her bag of belongings in her lap.

The elevator door dinged and opened. Mallory pushed the chair inside, tapped the button for the first floor, and faced Savannah again. "What happened with Evan?"

Savannah rolled her lips together. "We kind of…I guess you might say we broke up."

"He broke up with you?" Mallory practically yelled. "When

you were in the hospital?" Mallory's normally pale skin flushed with immediate rage. "I cannot believe that Evan—"

"Stop." Savannah held up her hand. "It's not like that."

"Your jerk of an ex broke up with you when he found out you were sick and now Evan does the same thing when you go to the ER," Mallory ranted.

"No," Savannah repeated. "He didn't break up with me, Mal. I broke up with him."

Mallory angled her face, looking at Savannah through her peripheral vision. "Why on earth would you do that? I thought you liked Evan."

The elevator came to a stop and the doors opened.

Mallory took control of the wheelchair but didn't push Savannah out to the front breezeway as Savannah expected. Instead, she turned to the right and pushed Savannah's chair down a long hospital corridor.

"Where are you taking me?" Savannah asked, trying to look at Mallory behind her.

Mallory didn't answer. "Why did you dump Evan?" she pressed instead.

"Dump seems like a harsh word to describe it. I just told him it wasn't a good time for me. I need to focus on my health."

"Uh-huh." Mallory continued walking.

"It's true. Dating him has been a distraction for me, and look what happened."

"Please tell me you did not blame your hospitalization on him when you dumped him."

Savannah rolled her eyes, reminding herself of June. "I didn't dump him. And no, I didn't blame him in so many words. I mean, I kind of did but I said it nicely."

"Evan is the sweetest guy, Sav. He's the kind of guy you deserve. He's *your* Sam and you're his Madison. I can't believe you would do that to him."

"Do what? Put myself first?"

Mallory stopped walking and stepped around to face Savannah again. She arched one brow high on her forehead. "Who do you think you're talking to right now? Are you honestly going to lie to my face and tell me that breaking up with Evan is putting yourself first?"

Savannah looked down again. "It's true," she said, but her voice came out weak.

"It's baloney." Mallory squatted to get to Savannah's eye level and forced her to look at her. "I have known you since we were kids. When we both had a crush on Pete Wilson that one summer and he liked you more than me. I knew it and so did you. But you pretended to hate his guts so that he would pay more attention to me. You put me first. Every summer when your parents left you at your aunt and uncle's house, I rode up on my bike and watched their send-off. You acted like they were leaving you at Disney World or something but I knew better. You were smiling and jumping up and down so that they didn't feel bad about leaving you behind when they went on one of their grand vacations. You never acted upset."

"Because I loved staying with Aunt Eleanor and Uncle Aaron."

"But you were sad too. I could always see it in your eyes, despite how you were acting. You put them first, Sav," Mallory said. "I assume you did the same with your ex-fiancé. His business is taking off and he's living his dreams because you put his needs ahead of your own. And as soon as you had needs, he ditched you."

Savannah took a shaky breath. "Maybe I learned my lesson and that's why I broke up with Evan."

Mallory shook her head. "No, I don't think so. You're still doing it. Savannah Collins chronically puts other people first, which is one of the reasons that I love you." Standing, Mallory walked over to the wall outside the door that they were stopped in front of. Savannah had thought it was random that they had stopped here but apparently not. Mallory lifted a brochure out of a clear plastic casing and handed it to Savannah. "Here. There is a support group for people with chronic illnesses. It meets here every Thursday night at 6:30 p.m. You're going."

Savannah stiffened. "What?"

"Don't worry. I'll go with you. Support groups are for friends and family too. Anyone affected by chronic illness. If you're truly putting yourself first, then this is what you need. You need to process what lupus means for your life and what it means for the lives of everyone around you. You need people to talk to." Mallory took hold of Savannah's chair again, turned it around, and started walking back down the hallway toward the outside breezeway.

"I had forgotten how pushy you are," Savannah said once they were outside.

Mallory used her foot to lock the brakes on the wheelchair. She motioned for Savannah to stand up. "Come on. The free ride stops here." She pointed to a sporty Lexus in the employee parking lot. "That's me. I'll drive you home."

Savannah watched as Mallory pushed the chair back inside the hospital and then walked back to where Savannah was standing. "Thank you," Savannah said. "You're pushy but a good friend."

"I'm okay. I mean, I didn't hesitate to talk to Pete Wilson even though you liked him." She winked at Savannah and started leading her to her car.

"What's Pete doing these days anyway?" Savannah asked, eager for a change of subject. There was too much to process in what Mallory had said since leaving her hospital room.

"He's a pharmacist here at the hospital, actually." Mallory pointed her key fob at her car, making it honk softly.

"Yeah? Any interest in him?" Savannah asked.

"Not one bit." Mallory ducked into the driver's seat.

Savannah took her time settling into the passenger seat. "Too preoccupied with Hollis Franklin, huh?"

Mallory slid her gaze over. Then she pointed a finger. "You're deflecting. We're discussing your love life right now, not mine."

Savannah sighed wearily. "It was so much simpler before we discovered boys, wasn't it?"

Mallory cackled as she cranked the engine. "In a way, I guess you could say that Pete Wilson ruined everything."

Later that night, Savannah lay in bed staring at the brochure that Mallory had given her. She was also thinking about what her friend had said. Mal was right. Savannah did put other people first, which she'd always thought was a good thing. Maybe it wasn't so good when it meant chronically putting herself last.

Savannah had always had a fear of being a burden to others, especially after her broken engagement earlier this year. She guessed that fear had been triggered when she'd seen how upset

June had gotten last night. Of all people to burden, a child was the very last she wanted to be that for.

There was a soft knock on the door.

Without asking, Savannah knew it was Aunt Eleanor, who was the second-to-last person Savannah wanted to burden. Some part of Savannah had thought being here this summer was a way for her to pay Eleanor back for all those summers of kindness. Savannah had thought that she was the one caring for Eleanor for once. This weekend flipped that on its head though, and once again, Eleanor was caring for her. "Come in."

Eleanor opened the door and peeked inside. "You okay? You've been in here for a long time. Are you reading?"

Savannah had to laugh. "No. I don't think I could if I wanted to."

Eleanor stepped inside the room. "Why is that?"

Savannah shrugged. "Tired."

"No one ever gets any sleep at a hospital." She laughed softly. "Mind if I sit?"

"Not at all." Savannah sat up in bed. "I'm tired but not sleepy. I can't read but I can't sleep either."

"I know the feeling. All you can do is worry," Eleanor said. "So what is it that you're in here worrying about?" She folded her hands in her lap. "I heard about you and Evan."

"He told you?" Savannah asked.

Eleanor looked sheepish. "Not exactly. He told the roses. I just happened to be sitting there very quietly on my bench. Almost like a garden statue."

"Ah." Savannah nodded. It was funny that she had been the

one to start talking to the roses and somehow it had caught on. Eleanor spoke to them. June. And now Evan. "Yes, I broke up with him. But I don't really want to talk about it right now, Aunt Eleanor."

"You love him, Savannah. I know love when I see it. In case you aren't sure of what you're feeling, it's love." Eleanor leaned forward and placed her hand over Savannah's. "I know I'm not your mother. I know that. But I have always thought of you like a daughter. I have always wanted the best for you."

"Thank you, Aunt Eleanor."

"I don't want to overstep but Evan is the best man I know. I've always thought of him as a son, and I've wanted the best for him. And that's you. Maybe I don't know all the particulars but I think it boils down to perspective. 'People generally see what they look for and hear what they listen for.'" Eleanor looked at Savannah expectantly.

"Is that a book quote?" Savannah asked, willing to bet it was.

"*To Kill a Mockingbird*. Harper Lee."

"I'm a little rusty." Savannah folded her hands on her lap. "How does that explain my breakup?"

"I think I'll let you determine the meaning behind those words. So if you broke up with Evan, I assume that means you've accepted the job in South Carolina."

Savannah was confused about so many things right now but for some reason, that wasn't one of them. "Actually, I've decided to decline. It's not the right job for me." She grimaced. "I hope you meant it when you told me I could stay here as long as I needed to."

Eleanor looked delighted. "Of course I did. I think you made a good decision. Following your heart is always the right choice." Eleanor stood, her movements slow. "If you need me, you know where I'll be."

"In the front room with a book in your lap," Savannah said with a small smile. "I love you, Aunt Eleanor."

"I love you too. I'm glad you're here."

"Me too." Savannah watched her aunt leave the room and shut the bedroom door again, leaving Savannah alone. Savannah looked around and found herself standing and walking over to the window where she could see the garden.

It hurt knowing that Evan had been out there pouring his heart out to the roses. She wanted to go find him, wherever he was, and take everything she'd said back. She couldn't though. She was so confused. All she knew was that she needed time to process her feelings about so many things. She needed time to heal.

Savannah glanced back at the brochure that was still on her bed. Maybe she needed time to attend that support group on Thursday night as well.

Chapter Twenty-Eight

Evan

Love is the longing for the half of ourselves we have lost.

The Unbearable Lightness of Being,
Milan Kundera

"Dad? Are you going to get out of bed or not?"

Evan cracked his eyes open and looked at June standing in his bedroom doorway. "Hmm? What time is it?"

She folded her arms over her chest, leaning in the doorway. "Way later than you normally get up. Are you sick or something?"

Evan stirred, stretching his legs under the covers. Then he erupted into an oversize yawn. "I was just up late last night." He sat up and cringed at the weight of his head on his shoulders. He hadn't even had anything to drink. What was wrong with him?

The memory slammed into his brain, and he felt like lying back down—just like every day for the past few. Right. Savannah had taken a step back from their relationship. She'd basically dumped him.

He blinked his daughter into view. "I'm okay. I'm getting up."

Her expression softened. "I was starting to worry."

"No need for that." He forced a smile that made his brain ache. He felt like he had a hangover, that was for sure. Or even the flu.

"So, are we going or not?" June asked.

"Where?"

"To church. It's Sunday."

Evan noticed that June was already wearing a nice sundress with silver sandals. "Do you want to go?" he asked, surprised.

"Kinley invited me, remember? She's expecting me to be there."

Had June really just said that? He felt like staying in bed all day but he really couldn't say no if his daughter wanted to go to church, especially if she was making friends. "Mind making me a cup of coffee while I shower?"

"The pot is already made. Hurry up." June turned and headed back down the hall.

Evan listened to her footsteps trailing off into the distance. Then he got up. There would be people at church. They'd all want to talk to him about this and that. They might want to talk about Savannah. It was a small town, and people had seen them together this summer. As far as Evan knew, Savannah didn't attend the main church in Bloom so at least he wouldn't have to run into her. They could still be friends, yes, but his heart wanted more. It would be easier for him to avoid Savannah for a while.

She wanted to focus on her health, and he understood that. He just didn't understand why she couldn't focus on it with him at her side. Maybe he'd fooled himself and her feelings for him hadn't been as strong as his were for her. Because if they had been, there was no way she could have walked away.

An hour later, Evan pulled his truck into the church's parking lot and glanced over at June. "Ready to go in?"

She pushed the truck door open and hopped out. Then she looked through the vehicle at him, still seated behind the steering wheel. "Are you going to be okay sitting in church alone while I go to the teen class?"

Evan pushed his own door open. "I'll be fine."

As they walked toward the church, Kinley called out to them. "June! You came!" She looked at Evan. "Hi, Mr. Sanders."

"Hey, Kinley. How are you?" he asked.

"Terrific now that June is here. Are you coming to the teen class with me?"

June's gaze flitted between Kinley and Evan. "Are you sure you'll be okay, Dad?"

How the cards had flipped. "Don't worry about me. Go have fun," he told June.

He watched June walk off with Kinley. Too bad they hadn't met earlier in the summer. That could have possibly changed everything. Then again, one good friend didn't erase June's home in California or her relationship with her grandmother.

Evan walked into the church and slid into the back pew where he was least likely to run into a million folks who wanted to talk. He wasn't normally an introvert but today, he needed space. He kept his head low and tried to draw as little attention to himself as possible. Then he heard a familiar voice entering the sanctuary.

"Morning, Eleanor!" the pastor said. "It's been a long time since you've walked in. I'm glad to see you."

"Morning, Pastor. It's a small miracle I'm here, huh?" Eleanor's laugh filled the sanctuary. "I had my lovely niece drive me here this morning. So it's a miracle and a blessing."

"Savannah, I hope you're feeling better," the pastor said.

Evan stopped breathing for a moment. *Savannah is here?* Of all Sundays, why had she shown up on this one? Had her hospital visit scared her to the point of making sure she came to church today? Or maybe she'd been coming, and he just hadn't realized.

"I'm feeling much better, thanks. Aunt Eleanor surprised me by asking me to drive her this morning," Savannah told the pastor. "What could I say?"

The pastor chuckled. "Well, I'm glad you're both here. It's good to see you."

Evan angled his body toward the opposite wall, hoping Eleanor and Savannah wouldn't spot him. If it weren't for the fact that June was in the Sunday school class, he would just slip out and leave.

In his peripheral vision, he watched Savannah and Eleanor walk down the middle aisle toward the front of the church. Once they were seated, he breathed a sigh of relief and settled in as the choir began to sing their hymns.

"Hey, buddy." Hollis scooted into the pew next to him.

Evan blinked. "Since when do you come to church?"

"Since my grandmother practically ordered me to when I visited her this summer. She kind of asked me to come and, I don't know, I guess I thought I should. I like church."

"You're late," Evan whispered.

"But I'm here." Hollis leaned back and folded one leg over the other. "Where's June?"

"Sunday school."

"Why aren't you sitting up there with Savannah?"

Evan hadn't exactly informed his friend of what was going on in their relationship. "We probably shouldn't talk in church," Evan said, not wanting to discuss the breakup here.

When the pastor started his message, Evan closed his eyes. It was as if the pastor were talking directly to him. The sermon title was "Letting Go." Evan didn't want to let go. He wanted to hold on and hold on tight. His gaze drifted to where Savannah was sitting, and he wondered if she was listening to the pastor and taking his advice. She'd already let Evan go though, and it hadn't seemed nearly as difficult for her as it was for him. This breakup was tearing him apart. The simple act of getting out of bed felt difficult lately.

When the final prayer was being said, Evan got up and slipped out of the church to avoid running into Savannah and Eleanor. He opened the church door as quietly as he could and took long strides toward his truck.

"Where do you think you're headed?" Hollis asked, following behind him.

Evan hoped Hollis had been as quiet in exiting the sanctuary as he had. "I'm going to sit in my truck and wait for June. I don't feel like talking to anyone."

"Does that include your best friend?" Hollis asked.

Evan sighed. "Do you want to sit with me in my truck?"

"Sure."

Evan climbed in his truck and closed the driver's side door behind him, exhaling as if he'd just dodged a bullet.

Hollis slid into the passenger seat. "Did you and Savannah have a fight?"

"We broke up," Evan said simply. "And I don't want to discuss it."

"You broke up?" Hollis asked, ignoring Evan's wish to not discuss it right now. "Why did she dump you? Because I'm guessing you weren't the one to dump her."

Evan pinched the bridge of his nose. "She needs to focus on her health. I guess focusing on me is what made her sick."

Hollis was quiet for a long moment. He blew out a breath and stared out the front windshield. "You don't really believe that, do you?"

"Why wouldn't I?"

"Well, I'm no expert in love but blaming you is obviously just a tactic to push you away. And you let her do it. Why's that?"

Evan shook his head. "You can't force someone to stay if they don't want to."

"Did you fall on your knees? Grovel?" Hollis asked.

"Of course not."

"Did you even tell her how you feel? Truly feel. Did you tell her that you love her?"

Evan looked at his friend. "You don't confess your feelings for someone when they're in the middle of dumping you."

"I don't know. Maybe some part of you was relieved that she dumped you, and that's why you let her. If I were dating someone with a chronic illness, it would scare me too. We're men.

We want to swoop in and take on all the battles for the people we love. You can't do that for Savannah though. That's pretty hard to accept." Hollis blew out another breath. "It's tough watching someone you love go through something that you can't help with."

"Savannah broke up with me," Evan reminded Hollis.

"But you let her. And you gave up easily enough to let her know that what the two of you had didn't mean all that much."

Evan didn't like how this conversation with Hollis was going. "Were you there?"

"No." Hollis shook his head. "I didn't have to be to know how it went down. I've known you since third grade. You assume you won't win most fights." He looked at Evan. "I have to say, I'm proud of you for not backing down on fighting for June."

Evan had considered backing down though, wondering if he was the right person for the job. "She's my daughter."

"You've fought for her, and I'd say you've won."

"Not yet. Margie is still going to take it to a judge."

"But you're going to fight like hell, and you're going to ensure that June stays exactly where she needs to be." Hollis leaned in. "With you." He rubbed his fingers over his cropped beard. "I just wonder why you aren't fighting for Savannah like that. You two are obviously good together."

Evan wanted to argue but Hollis was making sense. In fact, Hollis was telling Evan things that Evan didn't even realize were true. "I hate it when you're right."

Hollis chuckled. "Which is 99.9 percent of the time, right?"

"Right," Evan said sarcastically. He watched people begin to spill out of the church on their way home to Sunday dinners.

Then he spotted June exiting the building to the far left. "Want to grab a bite this week?" Evan asked his best friend.

"Yeah." Hollis pushed the truck door open and stepped out just in time for June to step in.

"Did you two skip church and sit in the truck?" she asked, looking between them.

Hollis chuckled. "No. Kind of. Do as we say, not as we do."

"Starting to sound like a parent yourself," Evan teased and then waved at his friend. He waited for June to get in and close the truck door behind her. "How was Sunday school?"

June sighed miserably. "The boys from the youth center were there."

"The ones who bullied you?" Was there no safe place from mean kids?

June held up a hand. "Before you go storming off to find them, I handled it."

"You did?" He couldn't hide his surprise.

"Mm-hmm." She folded her hands in her lap, looking pleased with herself.

"How?" Evan asked.

"I just ignored them. Kinley was with me so it wasn't so awful. She's pretty cool. I met some others that are friends with her, and now they're also friends with me."

Evan wasn't sure whether to be happy or disappointed, because June had gotten bullied but she'd also made new friends. "I'm sorry about those kids. It's a small town so it's hard to get away from anyone you might be avoiding." His gaze caught on Savannah as she crossed the parking lot.

June followed his gaze. "Oh, there's Savannah! I didn't

know she was here. Can I go say hi? Can I catch a ride with her instead?"

"No," Evan said quickly.

"Why not?" June's hand was already on the door's handle. "Just because you two aren't dating doesn't mean I can't still be her friend."

Evan ran a hand through his hair. "Of course not. I just don't want her to know I'm here, okay? I'm hiding," he admitted.

June furrowed her brows. "Why?"

Evan blew out a breath. "Because, according to your Uncle Hollis, I'm scared." He looked over. "But I'm working on it."

Evan wasn't sure how long he had spent in his garage wood-working. He'd made several spoons and was now working on one wooden bowl. That meant he'd been here for hours. Long enough for his hands to ache, but his thoughts didn't feel any clearer.

With a sigh, he put down his whittling knife and sat back in his chair. Even knowing it was a bad idea, he tapped the TikTok app on his phone and searched for Savannah's profile. Why was he doing this to himself? The answer came, quick and undisputed. Somewhere in the last month, he'd fallen in love with her. Maybe that was the thing that scared him most. Hollis had suggested it was because Evan was intimidated by Savannah's illness, because he couldn't help. Evan wasn't the type of guy who felt like he needed to fix situations for his loved ones though. That was Hollis.

Savannah's face came up on his phone screen. Behind her,

Evan could see dozens of little containers with some sprouts popping out of the soil. She was in the greenhouse that had once belonged to Aaron.

"New beginnings. That's what this summer has been about for me," she told the screen. "And, unfortunately, sometimes new beginnings mean painful endings. It's just part of the process." Her shoulders bounced lightly as she shrugged. "That's what someone said this morning."

She was talking about the pastor. Sometimes the beginnings themselves were painful. That was a truth that Evan knew well. People had a way of romanticizing new beginnings. A fresh start. New and exciting adventures, like the start of a marriage. Like graduating from high school or college.

The new beginnings that Evan had known, however, were more bitter than sweet. The first day after his mother's funeral. The day after June was born, which was both exciting and devastating because he had to live with this huge void, knowing his daughter was in the world and he wasn't spending most his life with her.

He hadn't really realized but his experience with love had been more painful than not. He'd lost his mom, and then he'd lost his father last year. This year, Juliana had passed away. Allowing yourself to love someone meant that you were opening yourself up to heartbreak. He was willing to take that risk with Savannah but when she'd ended things, he'd just accepted it, because, from his experience, that's what he was expecting to happen. Eventually, their love would break his heart so why not now?

Savannah's three-minute video was still playing as Evan's focus drifted in and out. "My life is a bit of a struggle right now," she told the screen, "so I'm going to focus on the plants that probably brought you to my profile. The seeds that promise the good kind of new beginnings." Her eyes looked shiny, and Evan wondered if she'd been crying—because of him? He tapped on the comments to see what Savannah's followers were already saying.

FlowerGirl97: *We love you. The plants brought us here but you're the one keeping us coming back.*

NumbThumb22: *New beginnings can be painful but the sun will eventually shine on you.*

HappyPlanter: *What happened with the guy? Did you two break up?*

Evan found it so strange that strangers across the world were interested in their relationship. He'd never been much for social media. He preferred real, face-to-face interactions. The social media community that Savannah had garnered seemed real though. "I'm sorry, Savannah," he whispered. As he held his phone, it began to vibrate with an incoming call, and Margie's name popped up on the screen.

Evan's knee-jerk reaction to seeing Margie's name was still dread but he at least understood where she was coming from now, and he could empathize.

"Hello?" he answered.

"Hello, Evan," Margie said with what sounded like forced cheerfulness. "How are you?"

"Good," he told her, even though it couldn't be further from the truth.

"Hmm. That's not what June told me."

Ah. He rubbed a hand along his forehead. "What exactly did my daughter tell you?"

"That you're staying in your bed much later than normal. That you're acting like a zombie. Her exact words."

Evan closed his eyes, wishing his daughter wasn't seeing him in this condition. "In that case, you should be jumping up and down," he told Margie.

"I don't want to see you unhappy, Evan. Nothing could be further from the truth. On the contrary, June needs a caregiver who is emotionally available."

Evan couldn't believe this woman was about to make another case for June to come live with her. He couldn't win with her.

"I've come to realize that you are that caregiver," Margie said, surprising him. "Juliana wanted it to be you, and I now understand why. I think when I visited last week, I wanted to prove to myself that you were not up to the job of raising June. I actually proved to myself the opposite, however. You are up to the job. You're a good father. June needs you. But, as a parent, you must protect her. Maybe you're going through a rough patch, and I'm sorry about that but—I say this lovingly—you need to buck up and put a smile on your face. June needs you to act like this is the happiest you've ever been. You need to do better. For her," Margie said sternly.

Evan wanted to take offense but there was truth in what Margie was saying. "I know," he said quietly. "I'll try."

"Don't try. Do." There was a long silence on the other end of the line. "Evan, I've decided not to hire a lawyer after all."

Evan was speechless for a moment. "Why?"

"Because June belongs exactly where she's at. I can't deny I wish she were with me but I'll be okay. So will she."

"Margie, if you're lonely or—"

"Hold on right there, Evan. I appreciate the sentiment but

I'll be fine. I've joined a senior citizens group that has meetings and outings. I suppose no matter how many friends I make, I'll always be lonely without Juliana to talk to."

"You still have June," Evan said. "You can talk to her whenever you want. And you can hop on a plane and come visit anytime."

"I appreciate that, Evan. After all I've said and done, I don't deserve your kindness. And you are welcome at my home anytime as well. Both of you. Talk to you soon, Evan."

"Bye."

Margie disconnected the call, leaving Evan sitting there numbly.

"Dad?" June peeked her head into his woodworking shop.

Evan stiffened and popped a smile on his face even though he felt lower than he had in a very long time. "Yeah, sweetheart?"

June wrinkled her brow. "Since when do you call me sweetheart?"

"Since always. Right?" He couldn't remember. That's how out of sorts he felt. "What's up?"

"Ms. Eleanor is here. She wants to talk to you." The expression on June's face told him it might not be a friendly visit.

What had he done now? He smiled wider at his daughter, following Margie's advice. Maybe he was letting everyone else down but he wasn't going to disappoint June—not if he could help it. Not anymore. "I'll be right there."

June stared at him a moment longer. "It's cool that she's leaving her property again. That's kind of a big deal."

"Yes, it is."

"And I think it's partly due to you. You're like her hero or something," June said.

Evan blinked. "I may have been the one driving but I didn't get her to leave. She did that all on her own. Sometimes healing takes time."

June fidgeted with her hands in front of her. "I still say you're a hero. And, no matter how I've acted this summer, you've always been my hero. And you always will be."

Evan thought that maybe that was June's way of apologizing. "Thanks."

June shrugged. Then she looked at the wood carvings that Evan had been working on. "Those are cool. Maybe you'll teach me sometime. Then I could sell at the farmers market too. You know, sell instead of steal."

Evan couldn't help but laugh. Things were getting better. Maybe not in every aspect of his life but in some. "Sounds good," he said, standing and following June out of the garage to go find out what Eleanor wanted.

Chapter Twenty-Nine

Eleanor

It is only with the heart that one can see rightly.

The Little Prince, Antoine de Saint-Exupéry

Eleanor crossed her arms over her chest and lifted her chin. "Where have you been?" she asked as soon as Evan entered his own kitchen.

He blew out a breath. "Nice to see you too, Eleanor. This is the first time you've come to my house for over a year now."

Eleanor could see through Evan's attempt to control the conversation. She wasn't here to discuss herself though. "I'm here now, and, in case you can't tell, I'm unhappy."

Evan pulled out a chair and sat down at his kitchen table where Eleanor was already seated.

Eleanor unfolded her arms, realizing there was an unsettling ache in her chest right above her heart. She wasn't having a cardiac issue. Instead, she felt brokenhearted. She'd been dreaming up this match between her niece and neighbor for decades, and it had finally happened. "Evan, you and Savannah belong together. You can't just disappear. And besides, even if you aren't together right now, I miss you. I take it very personally that you're not coming over anymore."

He massaged his forehead with one hand. "I'm just giving Savannah space. And need I remind you, she broke up with me."

"She's in love with you, Evan," Eleanor said.

Evan blinked. "She told you that?"

"Well, no. But I know love when I see it. And you're in love with her too. So, what's the problem?"

Evan ran a hand through his hair, giving it a disheveled appearance. "It's complicated. And, while I respect and love you, Eleanor, it's really not your concern."

"Nonsense!" Eleanor sat up straighter. She had known Evan since he was a small boy, and he'd never said such a thing to her. Even though, in this case, he was kind of justified. But so was she. "Savannah is my niece, and you are like a son to me. You always have been. That makes this my business." She reached out and grabbed Evan's hand, squeezing softly. "I care about both of you. You're both my business. I just want you to be happy, and, in my mind, that equals both of you being together."

"Happiness doesn't come from another person. Aren't you the one who taught me that?"

Eleanor pointed at him. "You're right. It doesn't. But once you're already in love, happiness is out of reach *without* that other person."

"You're happy though," Evan argued. "Even after Aaron has passed on."

Eleanor frowned. "Everyone keeps telling me he's gone but

he's not. He's just with me in a different way. It's not the same as a couple who has decided to part ways. That's different."

Evan leaned over his elbows on the table. "Is Savannah okay?"

Eleanor wanted to tell him to walk next door and see for himself. "She says yes but I know better. She's tired and her cheeks are red. I've read a little bit about lupus. Enough to know that stress can trigger a flare. I'd say a breakup counts as stress. Not saying this is in any way your fault. But it's our job to take care of her."

Evan offered a humorless laugh. "Don't let Savannah hear you say that. She doesn't want anyone to take care of her."

"Maybe that's true but we all need someone to care for us every now and then. We can't do this thing called life alone. We can't."

Evan looked down at his interlocked hands on the table. "Maybe it would have been better if Savannah and I had never crossed that line romantically."

"Nonsense." She lifted a finger in the air. "It is better to have loved and lost."

Evan side-eyed her. "You're tossing me softballs to make me feel better, aren't you?"

She shrugged while laughing.

Evan cleared his throat. "Despite popular belief, Shakespeare didn't say those words. It was Victorian poet Alfred Tennyson."

Eleanor clapped in applause. "You really are like a son to me."

He blew out a slow, heavy breath. "I don't know what to do about Savannah. I just don't want her to be hurting or sick, least of all because of me. I didn't realize that we would fall in love."

Did Evan realize he'd just admitted to being in love with Savannah? Did he even know that was how he felt? "Love happens when you least expect it and in the very last place you look," Eleanor responded. She opened the bag that she'd carried with her and pulled out a folded piece of paper. "This is for you."

Evan unfolded the paper and looked at what appeared to be a list. "Aren't I a little old for summer reading lists?"

"Nonsense. One never outgrows books. That is a reading list for the brokenhearted. It will help. I promise."

Evan released a soft laugh. "I don't know if a book will do the trick this time."

"Healing takes time. All those books listed are in the Finders Keepers Library. You are welcome to check them out."

"Thanks." He folded the list back up and tucked it in his front pocket. "I might continue to be scarce around your house for a while. I want to give Savannah space. Take care of her for me?"

"And she'll take care of me. That's what family is for. You're family too, Evan. I'll always be here for you and June."

"That means more than you know."

Eleanor scooted back from the table and stood. The ache was still in her chest, and she doubted it would lessen anytime soon. "I have to get home. I have a date to get ready for."

"With Charlie?"

"Who else?" she asked. "We're making up for lost time. Cheesy as it may be, once you find the person who completes you, you want to spend every moment you can with them. It's kind of like I'm reacquainting myself with me. Charlie brings out the person I was before all my hurts and disappointments. Except I'm older, wiser, and a much better version of her."

Emotion pricked Eleanor's surface. She felt her eyes stinging with unshed tears. Happy tears, mostly. They were also sad. She was disappointed that Evan and Savannah weren't going to work things out, at least not anytime soon. She'd always thought they belonged together. "Let me know if you need anything."

"I will. Thank you for the reading list," he said.

"Of course. You know I'm always good for a book recommendation. Or a hug."

"I'll take one of those too." Evan leaned in and wrapped his arms around her.

Eleanor melted into the hug, soaking it through all the way to her achy heart. When she finally pulled back, she gave him a long look. "Love has a way of working out. It never fails."

Evan looked skeptical. He hesitated before nodding. Eleanor got the distinct impression that he didn't think there was hope. Yes, she knew that love didn't always survive. There were a lot of things that love couldn't overcome but she didn't think that was the case here. "I'm happy for you and Charlie."

"Me too." Eleanor's face stretched into a wide grin. Charlie made her happy, and she was sure that Aaron would approve for that reason alone. Her late husband had only ever wanted to make her happy. If he couldn't be here to do so, he would want his friend to take on that role. She believed that in her heart. "Bye, Evan."

"See you later, Eleanor. Don't let my daughter be a nuisance over there," he said.

"Never," she said with a small laugh. "You have a cat lover on your hands. You might think about getting her one."

Evan made a disapproving noise from his throat. "I'm a dog man."

"My late husband said the same thing. Wouldn't you know, before he died, he discovered that he could be both and have both. His life was far too short but it was full."

She could be both too—a widow and a woman in love. And she could have both—a late husband, whom she still loved with all her heart and a new love, whom she also loved wholeheartedly.

Chapter Thirty

Savannah

*(Y)ou can never love people as much as you can
miss them.*

An Abundance of Katherines, John Green

Savannah had gotten fifty-two new followers on her social
media just since posting about her breakup with Evan. She had
also gotten twelve new sales in her online store. Mixing business with pleasure really did pay off sometimes.

Not that sales were the reason she'd posted. Talking to
strangers was good therapy. Venting. Releasing. And some of
her followers had left good advice.

GardenPop: *Stay single for a while and then try again. Always
try again.*

That sounded like a decent plan to Savannah. If she wasn't
going to be in a relationship with Evan though, she didn't want
a relationship with anyone. She wasn't sorry that she'd turned

down the assistant professor job in South Carolina. Not having a job scared her but having the wrong job scared her more.

Bloom was home, and she really needed a place to call home right now. She needed her friends and family, not just because she had a chronic illness but also because life was better shared with the people you cared about and who cared about you.

A noise from outside the greenhouse got Savannah's attention.

"Hello?" She waited for whoever was standing outside to show themselves.

June showed up in the greenhouse's entryway. "Hi." She swiped a lock of her hair out of her eyes, tucking it behind her ear.

"June. You okay?"

"Yeah." June took a few steps inside the greenhouse and looked around with interest. "I've never been inside a green-house before. This is kinda cool."

"It was my uncle's."

June sat on a wrought iron chair that Savannah used when she was trimming her plants. "I don't have any uncles. Or aunts. Both my mom and my dad were only children. All I have left for family is Dad and Grandma Margie."

Savannah placed her cell phone down on a shelf beside her, giving the girl her full attention. There was something weighing on June's mind. She could tell.

"I've always wished that I had a big family," June said.

"That's how life works, I guess. You wish for what you don't have. People who have big families would be the first to tell you that the bigger the family, the more conflict and drama."

June looked down at her interlocked hands. "I guess I came

in here because I miss you. You and Dad aren't hanging out any-more. You dumped him, and it kind of feels like you dumped me too."

Savannah hadn't meant to avoid June but she'd been avoid-ing Evan. She just didn't know what to say to him. She felt confused and overwhelmed. She was sure she was in love with Evan. So in love. She wanted to run into his arms and run away from him at the same time. "I'm sorry, June. I've missed you too. I love hanging out with you."

"Great," June said. "So let's hang out."

"What? Now?" Savannah looked down at her dirty clothes.

June hopped up from the wrought iron chair, smiling widely. "Yes, now. I'm in the mood for ice cream."

Who could say no to that smile?

"Did you ask your dad?" Savannah asked.

One corner of June's mouth pulled to the side in a grimace. "He's kind of been moping around because of you."

Ouch.

"He's spending a lot of time in his woodworking shed. I don't want to bother him." June nibbled at her lower lip. "I mean, you and I are still friends, right?"

Brushing her hands off on the sides of her shorts, Savannah stood. "Of course we're friends. And I would love to have ice cream with you. But you do need to tell your dad where we're going. I don't want him to worry."

"So your answer is yes?" June's expression brightened again. "Great! I'll go tell him now!"

"Meet me in the driveway when you're done," Savannah called after her. "I just need to wash my hands because dirt and ice cream don't mix."

June grinned as she ran out of the greenhouse. It was so nice to see her happy-ish. Savannah regretted that Evan was moping because of her. He should be enjoying time with his daughter. She took this as proof that breaking up with him was the right thing though. June needed Evan, and she didn't want to negatively impact their relationship in any way.

Ten minutes later, June crossed Evan's yard to meet Savannah at her car.

Savannah slid a pair of sunglasses over her eyes. "Your dad said it was okay?" she asked.

"Yep." June dipped into the passenger seat and pulled the door shut. "Thanks for agreeing to hang out with me," she said once Savannah was seated behind the steering wheel.

"You don't have to thank me. You are an awesome kid." As Savannah drove toward the ice cream shop in downtown Bloom, she listened as June rambled about little things that were going on in her life. In a week's time, she'd gone from doing nothing but reading to talking to a new friend and making plans to hang out. It was so nice to see things on the upswing for her.

Savannah pulled into the parking lot for the local ice cream shop and cut off the engine. Then she grabbed her purse and got out. "My treat," Savannah said, eyeing June's purse.

"I won't argue." June had a pep in her step that Savannah envied. As they neared the entrance, Savannah noticed the plant nursery a few shops down. She'd been meaning to drop in like Leanne had told her to. She would also love to peruse that place and see what kinds of plants were inside. She doubted June would want to though.

A blast of cold air hit them as they entered the ice cream parlor and walked up to the counter. There was a young teen boy manning the register. He had long dark hair, pulled back at the base of his neck and a hat that read *Two Scoops or Three?*

Without saying a word, he pointed at his hat with a goofy grin.

"Oh, um, I'll have two scoops of vanilla, please," Savannah said. "With chocolate sauce if you have it."

"We do." He looked at June and pointed at his hat again.

Savannah thought June might roll her eyes but instead, she seemed charmed by the boy. "Two scoops of s'mores ice cream, please."

"Fancy," Savannah said, wishing she'd made a more adventurous choice than plain old vanilla. Maybe next time.

After paying, they took their bowls to an empty table lining the wall.

"Want to know a secret?" Savannah asked as she slid into her seat.

June lifted her brows in question as she spooned ice cream into her mouth. "When I was a kid during the summers, I would beg my aunt Eleanor to take me here several times a week. The ice cream was okay but there was this guy who worked behind the counter that I had the biggest crush on."

"Was he your boyfriend?" June dipped her spoon back into the bowl.

Savannah laughed. "No. I'm sure he never saw me as anything more than a goofy kid. Sugar Scoops was the place to be when I was your age though. There wasn't a whole lot to do back then."

"Back in the olden days," June teased, popping her spoon into her mouth.

"Heyyy." Savannah looked up from her paper bowl. "I'm not

so old. Hanging out with you makes me feel younger though. I'm glad you invited me."

June's smile slipped at the corners. "Are you . . . sick again?"

Savannah's hand paused midway to bringing another bite of ice cream to her mouth. "Why do you ask that?"

June tapped a finger to her cheeks. "Because you have that butterfly rash on your face. Isn't that what you call it? I kind of looked up what you have on my phone."

Savannah looked down for a moment, navigating a multitude of feelings. "Yes, I'm going through a mild flare." She never wanted to hide what was going on with her health again. People couldn't help her or understand if she kept her symptoms a secret. "It's nothing for you to worry about though."

"You told Dad it was his fault that you got sick."

Savannah's lips parted. "Who told you that?"

June twisted her mouth to one side of her face. "I overheard at the hospital. I couldn't bring myself to go in your room. I don't know why. Dad told me to stay in the waiting area. But then I changed my mind and went to see you. When I walked up to your door, you were telling Dad that hanging out with him is why you got sick." She twirled her spoon in her ice cream. "So is it true?" She looked at Savannah with worried eyes.

Savannah lowered her spoon back to the bowl of plain vanilla. "No. No, of course not. I never should have said that." And she felt horrible that June had overheard that conversation. "The truth is, my illness is no one's fault. Not even my own." That was something she'd internalized over the last couple of weeks.

After Randall had broken things off, she'd blamed herself. Maybe she could have done something more to keep her body healthy. Exercised more often. Ate healthier. After educating herself on lupus, though, she'd realized that, while those things can help her feel better, they wouldn't have prevented her auto-immune condition or taken it away. "Stress can increase my symptoms but your dad isn't to blame."

"I mean, if stress can increase your symptoms, wouldn't it make sense that being happy could make them better? Dad made you happy, right?"

Savannah gave a slight nod. "Yeah."

June shrugged. "Then breaking up with him wasn't exactly a smart thing to do."

Savannah spooned another bite of ice cream into her mouth. "If only it were that simple."

June was quiet for a moment. "All I know is you love him. And he loves you." She spooned a creamy marshmallow past her lips. "And my dad is miserable right now."

Savannah wished that weren't the case, for June's sake and Evan's. "I remember a time when you didn't want us to date. What's changed?"

June shrugged. "I guess I was worried that if my dad fell in love with you, there'd be no one left for me." June licked her lower lip. "I was wrong. My dad is solid. He's not going any-where, no matter if I steal or slam doors. When he loves some-one, he's in it forever. He doesn't leave." She looked at Savannah.

Savannah got the feeling June was talking about her. For a girl who was only twelve, she was wise beyond her years. Grief and loss sometimes did that to a person. "It's not a good time for me or your dad to be in a relationship."

"That's just an excuse adults use. But really, adults can be so stu…" She stopped herself and gave Savannah an apologetic look. "Silly," she said instead. "Because my mom always said we'd hang out and do more stuff together later. She was always working or dating some new guy." June was quiet for a long second. "But we ran out of laters."

"June, I want you to know I'm here for you, always. If there's ever anything you need, don't hesitate to ask."

"Thanks." June took another big bite of ice cream. "I'm glad you said that, because I do need something. I need for you to give my dad another chance."

"Where are you off to?" Eleanor asked Savannah the next day.

Savannah was up, dressed, and eager to head out and explore the plant nursery that she'd spotted yesterday. "Love in Bloom Nursery. Come with me?"

Eleanor seemed to consider the invitation. She'd gone out a handful of times now with other people, mostly Charlie. "I would but my Books and Blooms Club is meeting at noon." She sat up straighter and lifted her chin, looking proud. "And guess who is attending in person?"

Eleanor had been attending the meetings via Zoom for months. "You?" Savannah asked.

"Indeed."

"Is Charlie driving you there?"

Eleanor shook her head. "It's just a few miles down the road. I'm driving myself."

Savannah wondered if that was such a good idea. "Would you like for me to come with you? For moral support?"

Eleanor tsked. "I am perfectly capable of going on my own.

Say hello to Leanne for me. She's a good friend of mine, you know."

"So I've heard." Savannah grabbed her purse and keys.

"Here's something I bet you haven't heard. She dated Aaron before me. On paper, she was probably better suited for him, because they both loved plants. The chemistry just wasn't there though. Sparks only come around once or twice, if you're lucky. When they happen, they shouldn't be ignored."

Savannah knew Eleanor was making a pitch for Evan. "I'm glad Aaron found you. I'll tell Leanne you said hello. Enjoy your club meeting."

"Oh, I will. Charlie will be there. Before him, I would have said sparks only come around once. He made me a believer that love can happen more often than that."

A few minutes later, Savannah's thoughts couldn't help drifting to Evan as she drove to the nursery. She missed him. Her heart ached for him. There was a thin line between selfless and selfish. Maybe she was being selfish in breaking up with him because she didn't want to feel like a deadweight. Or maybe she was being selfish in wishing that they were still together.

Why was love so hard?

Savannah parked in front of Love in Bloom Nursery and got out. Excitement swelled inside her as she opened the front door and took in all the plants. She breathed in the air around her, invigorated by the freshness of it.

"Savannah! What a pleasant surprise! I was beginning to think you weren't coming while you were here in town," Leanne said as she approached.

Savannah smiled back at the nursery owner. "Sorry that it's taken me a while. Things have been a bit hectic." To say the least. Between the wedding, being in the hospital, and her breakup, things had been rough. "I'm so glad I was able to make it here today though. And I'm staying in town longer than I had expected." Savannah looked around. "This place is an absolute haven. You'll probably see me in here a lot."

Leanne was wearing a pale green shirt with the store's name and logo. "You haven't posted a new vlog lately. I've been watching for one."

Savannah couldn't hide her surprise. She'd thought Leanne was just being nice the other day when she'd raved about Savannah's vlog and social media pages. "Really?"

"You know your plants, just like your uncle did." Leanne stepped forward. "Come on. I'll show you around."

It took a half hour to walk the entire store, and Savannah could have walked it several more times to admire all the plants. When they were back at the front, Leanne turned to her.

"Excuse me if I'm being too forward but I meant it at the festival when I said you could have a job here if you ever wanted one. I think you're the person I've been looking for."

Savannah wasn't sure how to respond. "I'm sorry?"

"I'm ready to slow down. I should be at the Books and Blooms Club meeting right now but I can't just leave my store with anyone. I've been looking to hire a full-time employee for a while now. Someone I can trust to run this place so that I can more fully enjoy my golden years."

Savannah felt speechless. "You want to hire me full-time?" she finally asked.

Leanne shrugged. "I'm not even sure if you're looking for a job. You can certainly make your vlogs from here. We're busy but there is also a lot of downtime. That's when I read the books that your aunt loans me. Think about it." She offered her hand for Savannah to shake again.

Savannah slipped her hand into Leanne's. "Thank you. I will."

When Savannah got back into her car, she was shaking. She pulled out her phone, tapped on her TikTok app, and started recording. "Do you believe in fate? Because I just got offered a job that was made for me. *Eek!* Should I say yes? It involves plants. Lots of plants." She laughed excitedly. She hadn't felt this excited when she'd gotten the assistant professor offer. That must mean this is right for her. "I think I might take it." She ended the video and looked at the nursery. Everything inside her was screaming yes right now—and the one person she couldn't wait to tell was the one person she didn't feel like she could call. Evan.

A comment popped up on her video. That was quick.

@GardenGrandma: *Always listen to your heart. Say yes!*

Another comment came through:

@FlowerChild101: *Say yes! And go find that hot guy again.*

Tempting. Apparently, her followers couldn't get Evan off their brains either.

Chapter Thirty-One

Evan

*Love is holy because it is like grace—the wor-
thiness of its object is never really what matters.*

Gilead, Marilynne Robinson

The summer was quickly dwindling, and soon Evan would be
back to teaching in the classroom. He didn't want to spend the
rest of his vacation time sulking. June needed him to be present,
and that's what he was going to do.

"Where are we going?" June asked, sitting in the passenger
seat of his truck.

"The park." That was the best idea he had. There wasn't a
ton for kids to do in Bloom. Bloom Park was a great place for
fresh air and fun. It had lots of benches to sit and people-watch,
which was one of Evan's favorite pastimes. It also had a pond
for good fishing, and usually there was a vendor set up on either

side of the park, selling iced coffee or Italian ice. "It's one of the best places in Bloom."

"That's what you said about the farmers market."

"And it's true." Even though Evan was having a hard time with the breakup, he was enjoying spending time with his daughter. He was especially glad that she wasn't pushing him away anymore. Now that she knew her grandmother wasn't too lonely in California, she was relaxing into her life here.

Evan pulled into the parking lot and cut off the engine. Then he pushed his truck door open and stepped out.

"There are dogs here?" June said, springing out of the passenger seat at the sight of people walking dogs ahead.

"Yep. We can get our dog fix while we walk around," Evan said.

"Or you could just get a dog," June suggested.

"First you want a kitten, now you want a dog?"

"I still want a kitten but Savannah has one so I guess I can get my kitten fix over there." June met him around the front of his truck. Then they headed toward the park. It was a wonderland of nature, almost as enchanted as Eleanor's garden. June chattered nonstop as they made their way around. It was nice to listen to her. She sounded almost like her old self again.

"Look at that dog, Dad." June pointed at a couple walking a small, bushy dog ahead. Evan thought it looked like a mixed breed, maybe an Australian shepherd mixed with a dachshund.

Evan nodded and smiled, waving at the couple as they approached.

"Can I pet your dog?" June asked, making a visible effort to restrain her hands until the pet's owners agreed.

Evan watched the interaction and how much June loved on the animal. The same thing happened with each dog that passed by. "My theory is proven. You are a dog person, like me."

"I'm an animal person. I like all animals," she corrected. "Maybe I'll convince you to open a small zoo," she teased.

Evan slid his gaze to hers. "If that's truly what you want, we can discuss it." He loved how happy June looked this morning. He loved the feeling it ignited in his chest, watching her enjoy her afternoon with him. It almost made him forget the void that Savannah's absence had made.

"Can I pet your dog?" June asked someone else as they approached.

Evan looked at the person, recognizing the teen as a former student of his from maybe three years ago. "Devin. Hey, how are you?"

"Hey, Mr. Sanders." The boy had grown several inches since the last time Evan had seen him. Devin looked at June. "You can pet her. She's nice."

June dropped to a squatting position and laughed as the Labrador licked her cheek.

"Yeah, I forgot to let you know, Rufus gives kisses," Devin said, grinning.

"Kisses?" June laughed again, dodging another lick. After a moment, she stood. "So, my dad was your teacher?"

"Favorite teacher of all time," Devin said. "He's your dad?"

Evan felt like a fly on the wall.

"Favorite dad of all time," June said.

Evan had to catch his breath. Whatever hard times he'd had this summer with June, they were all worth it to hear her describe him in that way.

"See you later, Mr. Sanders," Devin said, continuing past them.

Evan and June began walking again. After a few steps, Evan cleared his throat. "So, iced coffee or Italian ice?" he asked.

June shrugged. "Italian ice for me and iced coffee for you. Maybe we can share?"

Evan struggled to breathe again. "Yeah. Good idea."

"Look," June said as they walked.

Evan thought she would be pointing to another dog but this time she pointed to a large pink butterfly. Evan watched it flutter around for a moment.

June held out her index finger.

"It's probably not going to land—" He stopped talking as he watched the butterfly land on the tip of June's finger.

"Dad! Look!" she whispered. "Mom loved butterflies." June's eyes filled with tears. "She had a pink butterfly tattooed on the back of her neck."

"She did?" Evan never remembered seeing that but Juliana had long hair that would have covered the back of her neck.

One tear slipped down June's cheek as she held her finger very still. "She got it last year before she got sick. She said butterflies lived half their lives in cocoons and then struggled to break out. But when they finally did, they were gorgeous and free."

"That's beautiful." Evan watched in awe as the butterfly opened and closed its wings.

June sniffled quietly. "Mom wasn't perfect. But she was gorgeous and free, and I miss her. A lot."

"I know." Evan placed a hand on June's shoulder. "You'll always miss her but it does get easier."

June gasped as the butterfly fluttered up above her hand. It seemed to stay suspended in the air, watching them. Then it flew away.

"Dad?" June wiped at a tear beneath her eye. "Is it stupid if I say that I think that was a sign from Mom?"

Evan lifted his brows. "It's not stupid. What do you think the sign means?"

June sniffled softly before putting on a small smile. "That we're going to be okay. Me and you."

Now Evan had tears in his eyes. "I think so too."

"And so you know, I'm going to get a tattoo just like hers one day," June said.

He wrapped his arm around her shoulders, chuckling softly. "Not until you're eighteen. And no boyfriends until then either."

She pulled back and looked at him. "Jeez. You're a little overboard with the whole overprotective dad act, don't you think?"

He slid his gaze over. "Is that a bad thing?"

"Nah. It's kind of cool," June said, leaning into the crook of his arm still resting around her shoulders.

On Saturday morning, Evan arrived at the farmers market downtown just as the sun was rising above the distant tree line. He laid out all his wood carvings for passersby to see. Then he sat on his metal foldout chair, pulled his ball cap over his head, and reached for his cup of coffee.

"Maybe I'm warming up to Bloom," June said, sitting in a chair beside him, "but I still think the farmers market is kind of boring. I mean, being here an hour or two is okay but for four whole hours? That's way too long."

Evan was tempted to wish for the days when he'd come here alone—when these early mornings had been peaceful. He loved having June with him though. "Once you get the hang of wood carving and you're ready to sell, you'll think differently about being here." He grinned at her over his cup. "Making money is fun." He bounced his eyebrows.

She smiled back. "If you say so. Can I walk around?"

"If you pay for what you take," he teased.

June rolled her eyes. "One lapse in judgment. No shoplifting," she promised.

Evan watched June wander off. Then his gaze turned to all the folks setting up around him, displaying their own talents. Someone was selling fresh eggs from their farm. Homemade soaps. Crocheted items. His gaze reached farther until he saw someone new to the row of vendors. Without thinking, he got up and moved in that direction, leaving his table unoccupied.

"Hey," he said, approaching Savannah. "What's all this?" He gestured at the display on the table.

Savannah ducked her head, looking a little shy. "Books. Eleanor sent me with a few boxes full. She's going to meet me out here later."

"She's selling her books?" Evan was shocked by this information.

"Of course not. They're free to a good home. You know Eleanor. She just wants to spread her love of reading." She pulled up a plastic bin. "And I'm selling plants. Plants and books do kind of go together. Did you know that some people read to plants?"

The conversation felt awkward, like they were only just

getting to know one another again. "And some," he said, "talk to plants."

"Touché." Savannah's skin was already turning pink even though her table had a tent over it, like most of the other tables there.

Evan cleared his throat. "I hear you and June had ice cream the other day. Thanks for doing that."

"You know how much I adore June. Just because you and I aren't…" She trailed off.

Evan nodded, understanding. Just because they weren't dating didn't mean she was abandoning June. It just meant that she was avoiding him. They'd crossed a line and now they could barely even be friends, it seemed. "So, when are you leaving?" he asked.

Savannah bit down on her lower lip. "Actually, I got another job offer."

Evan's heart took a deep dive. He already knew that she'd never intended to stay in Bloom. He shouldn't be disappointed. And honestly, if she moved, it might help him get over her more quickly. Seeing her, wanting her, and not having her in his life was hard. Much harder than he'd ever thought it could be. "That's great. Where?"

"Love in Bloom Nursery."

Evan took a moment to process what she'd said. "Leanne's place?"

"That's the one," Savannah said excitedly. "Turns out she wasn't kidding when she told me to come see her if I ever wanted a job. I stepped inside to look around and she hired me on the spot. She's ready to retire in the next couple years but she hasn't been able to cut back her hours because she didn't have anyone capable of caring for her babies." Savannah grinned. "Her plants."

"I remember." Evan nodded. "Wow. You'll be great at that job," he said, genuinely happy for her. And somewhere inside, he was also selfishly happy for himself. The job was perfect, and it would be reason enough to keep Savannah in Bloom.

Savannah laughed with excitement. "It's like fate handed me exactly what I needed. Aunt Eleanor said I can stay with her indefinitely. Normally I would want to find my own place but I kind of think Aunt Eleanor needs me right now."

"Whether she admits it or not," Evan agreed.

Savannah shrugged a shoulder. "I like being close for June too."

"She needs you as well." And he needed her, more than he cared to admit. She wasn't ready to hear it. They'd dated too soon after her broken engagement. Too soon after she'd received her diagnosis. Their timing was never right, and maybe it never would be, but he still couldn't stand the thought of losing her. "I'm happy for you, Sav."

"Thanks." She tilted her head to one side. "Earlier this year, it felt like my life was crumbling all around me. Now, it feels like it had to crumble for me to build my life back up to something even better. Does that sound crazy?"

"Not at all," he said.

"Dad!"

They both turned to the sound of June coming toward Savannah's table. Evan's heart took another deep dive.

"What is that and where did you get it?" he asked.

June continued walking toward Savannah's table. "I didn't steal it, if that's what you're asking." She hugged the wiggling puppy more tightly. Consequently, it lifted its head back and licked June's chin. "Ewww."

Savannah laughed. "How adorable is that? Is that a silver lab?"

"It is," June confirmed. "Mr. McGrew has five puppies, and he said I could have this one. As long as you say yes, Dad."

"Have it?" he asked. "Aren't puppies expensive?"

"Mr. McGrew said he could tell that I would give this little guy a ton of love. So he's giving him to me. Pleeeease, Dad. You said you're a dog man. Prove it." She lifted a defiant chin.

Evan shared a glance with Savannah, catching the humor in her eyes.

"Well, I think he's precious. I can't wait for Fig to meet him," Savannah added.

"You're not helping," Evan said sarcastically. He faced his daughter. "Are you going to feed him and give him water?"

"And walk and bathe him," June promised, bobbing on the balls of her feet. "And I've already named him too."

"Uh-oh," Savannah said. "Once you've named it, it's basically yours."

Evan could see he wasn't going to have any choice but to say yes. "What's his name?" he asked.

June looked between them, taking her time to build suspense. Then she looked down at the little puppy in her arms. "Monday."

Evan searched for some obvious explanation for the name but today was Saturday.

"Dog Monday is the dog that belonged to Anne and Gilbert's son in the *Anne of Green Gables* series," Savannah explained.

"But Dog Monday is a mouthful to say," June said. "That dog

was very loyal. It waited at the train station when his master went off to war and didn't leave until he came home. It's a good name," she said with conviction.

"Great name," Evan agreed.

"So the answer is yes?" June bounced some more.

Evan used one hand to massage his forehead while the other reached out to pet the dog behind his ears. "Yes."

June squealed and then squealed again as Monday licked her chin. "I'll go tell Mr. McGrew! Thank you, Dad! Thank you, thank you, thank you," she said as she turned and raced off.

Evan faced Savannah. "Am I going to regret this when he wakes me up in the middle of the night?"

"Doubtful. Because it'll make June so happy that you'll be willing to sacrifice a little sleep for the greater cause." She folded her arms on the table in front of her. "You're a good dad, Evan. Better than you even know."

"Because I said yes to a puppy?" he asked, warmed by the compliment.

"Because you can't help being a good dad."

Evan locked gazes with Savannah, and even though he knew he should look away, he couldn't. All he wanted to do was walk around that table between them and pull Savannah up into his arms. Why weren't they together?

She tipped her head toward his own table. "It looks like you have a customer over there."

"Right. I better, uh, head back," he said reluctantly. "Good to see you, Sav."

"You too." She rolled her lips together. "Maybe we'll get Fig and Dog Monday together sometime soon."

"Sounds awful," he teased. "I mean, yeah. That sounds fun." He grinned and waved before starting to walk off.

"It's not true that cats and dogs can't be friends," Savannah called behind him.

He turned and smiled back at her. It was true that two people couldn't remain friends after breaking up though. At least for him. The hurt was too fresh. Too raw. Too painful. "Goodbye, Savannah."

Chapter Thirty-Two

Eleanor

*Whatever our souls are made of, his and mine
are the same.*

Wuthering Heights, Emily Brontë

It had been nearly a year since Eleanor had been to the farmers market. She'd thought she was perfectly happy at home but she had just been in denial. Being here brought back so many memories. This was her late husband's favorite place away from his own garden in their backyard.

"Aunt Eleanor!" Savannah waved her over to the table that she'd set up for them. Half of the table was set up with books and half was set up with Savannah's potted plants.

"This looks so nice." Eleanor ran her gaze over the spread. "Any customers yet?"

"Three of your books have already gone to a good home," Savannah told her. "And I've sold two plants."

"That's a good start. Shall I get us a coffee?" Eleanor asked. "Or would you like to?" She lowered her voice. "Maybe you can find a few wooden spoons to buy too while you're at it? I always need a new spoon for cooking."

Savannah narrowed her eyes. "You have more than a dozen of Evan's carvings. And besides, I've already spoken to him. He stopped by earlier."

Eleanor lifted her brows. "Oh? Was it a good conversation?"

Savannah shrugged. "It's hard talking to someone after you've broken up. Suddenly you have to act differently around each other. You were together and then you're just friends but it's hard to be friends because now things are awkward. It's just weird." Savannah lowered her gaze to the table.

"It's weird because you still have feelings for him," Eleanor said.

"Of course I do. You can't just turn those off." Savannah looked frustrated.

"And why should you? I still don't understand why you broke up with him to begin with."

"Because I'm not ready. What if I get sicker? I don't want Evan to take care of me. What if he eventually resents me because I can't do the things that he can?" Savannah was talking quickly, letting the thoughts that had been occupying her mind run out as if in one long run-on sentence. She took a breath and looked up at Eleanor. "Why aren't you saying anything?"

Eleanor raised a finger in the air. "'The world breaks everyone and afterward many are strong at the broken places...' *A Farewell to Arms*. Ernest Hemingway. You know a book is my answer to everything."

"I do know that. I'm working my way down the reading list

you gave me, by the way. But I'm not sure any of your suggested books will fix my life."

"That's exactly what Evan said when I gave him the same list. Do you want to know what I think?" Eleanor leaned back in her foldout chair and crossed one leg over the other.

"What?"

"I think that only love can make a completely sane woman feel like she's losing her mind. That's how it feels, and there is no cure for that feeling. And why would you want to cure it? Evan loves you. When you love someone, it's a privilege to care for them. Did you resent me for needing help in the garden?"

"No."

"Did you resent me for needing you to buy my groceries?" Eleanor asked.

"Of course not. I love you, Aunt Eleanor."

Eleanor winked. Then, having made her point, she stood up. "I will go get my own coffee. You stay here and reflect on what I just said. And while you do, find some more homes for these books. Nothing brings me greater joy than helping others find their book mate. I do it for me as much as I do it for them. That's how love works, Savannah. See you in a bit."

Savannah gave a slight nod, looking a bit dazed—like a woman in love wondering where her head and heart were.

Love wasn't easy, no. But it was worthwhile. That was Eleanor's experience. First with Aaron and now with Charlie. *Love?* Who would have thought a woman in her seventies would find such a gem? Maybe in the past, she was a bit guilty of thinking the way Savannah had. Eleanor had wondered why Charlie wanted to date her when she wouldn't even leave her own home. She'd thought she would drag him down when he wanted to go out and have fun because all she wanted to do was stay home.

Charlie had never made her feel that way though. Her fears had mostly been in her head. The obstacle between her and Charlie was internal, and there was nothing Charlie could do to change her mind. *She* had to do the work herself. And she had been doing that work. She'd started talking to that counselor Savannah had located for her, and, lo and behold, it was helping.

Eleanor hoped Savannah would do her own work too.

"For you." Charlie stepped up beside Eleanor and offered her a bouquet of fresh wildflowers.

She immediately inhaled the floral scent. "I have a whole garden of these in my backyard so why am I so delighted when you give me them?"

"Because they're from my heart." Charlie chuckled at himself. "Who knew I was so cheesy?"

"So charming, you mean."

"You equate laughter with charm?" He tapped his temple. "Making a mental note of things that my Ellie likes. In addition to books, of course."

A book quote popped into her mind. There was hardly ever a conversation where she didn't think of a line from one of her favorites. She lifted a finger in the air. "'There is nothing in the world so irresistibly contagious as laughter and good humor.' *A Christmas Carol.*"

"By Charles Dickens," Charlie said. "I always knew I liked that guy, and not just because we share a name."

Eleanor always found herself laughing with Charlie. Their relationship was different than what she'd had with Aaron. At one point, she might have pointed to that as proof that Charlie wasn't her type but that would have been reaching for an excuse that she was no longer looking for. Instead of excuses, she reached for his hand. "Thank you. Do you have a table out here today?"

"Mallory is running it on her own this morning."

"Savannah is running one for me too. The younger folks are becoming us a couple decades ago. Mallory, Savannah, Evan."

"It's fine by me if the younger generations take over. You see, there's this woman who is occupying all my thoughts and time anyway."

"Mm. There's this man occupying mine as well. I could barely finish a book this past week. That hasn't happened to me in years. At this rate, I may never finish reading a book again." Eleanor was only teasing, of course. The thought of never completing a book for real was unthinkable. She squeezed Charlie's hand and met his gaze, her smile faltering. "Thank you for the flowers."

"You're welcome. Since the younger generations are running the market for us, how about you and I catch a bite to eat? And then maybe a movie."

"Dinner and a movie. Why, that sounds like a date, Mr. Blue."

"What do you say?" he asked.

Eleanor breathed in the floral scent from her bouquet, the smell as intoxicating as the endorphins running through her bloodstream. "I say love is all abloom and there is nothing sweeter."

Chapter Thirty-Three

Savannah

There is no greater agony than bearing an untold story inside you.

I Know Why the Caged Bird Sings,
Maya Angelou

Savannah couldn't sit still as she sat on a hard, metal chair in a cold, sterile room. The support group hadn't started yet. A few people had already arrived and were chatting among themselves. Savannah didn't know them. She didn't know anyone here. *Where is Mallory?*

A woman with long, dark braids stepped over to Savannah, a pair of glasses perched on her nose. "You must be Savannah," she said with a friendly smile.

Savannah gave the woman a questioning look and then

realized where she was. Mallory worked here, and her child-hood BFF apparently knew everyone. "You know Mallory?"

"I know and love her, like everyone else here." The woman grimaced slightly. "Except Walt. He openly loathes her. I don't know what she did to that man but he's never going to forget it."

This made Savannah smile. "I've never known anyone who didn't like Mallory." Savannah glanced at the door. Mallory had said she'd meet Savannah here to serve as Savannah's moral support.

The woman held out her hand. "I'm Sheila Price. I lead the support group, kind of. The support group really leads itself. I'm just here to unlock the door, let everyone in, and lock it again after we leave."

Savannah shook Sheila's hand. "It's nice to meet you."

"You as well. Mallory didn't tell me much about you. Just that you have been recently diagnosed with an illness."

Savannah nodded. She was about to say something more but Sheila held up her hand.

"I can't wait to hear your story but I want the whole group to hear it. When you're ready, that is. It's helpful to share your story with others who have similar experiences. It helps us to not feel so alone."

Savannah noticed how Sheila included herself in that group.

As if reading her thoughts, Sheila said, "I have a heart con-dition that's chronic. The group knows my story so I can give you a little spoiler." She winked. "We are glad to have you here. There's a coffeepot in the back. Help yourself. We'll get started in about five minutes."

As Sheila went to talk to someone else, Savannah fidgeted nervously.

"Sorry I'm late." Mallory slid into the chair next to Savannah's. "One of my patients pulled out their catheter right before I got off shift. The bed was a mess."

"On purpose?" Savannah didn't think she had the stomach to ever be a nurse. They were so patient and caring, and they dealt with a lot.

Mallory moved her head side to side in a quick motion. "Yeah, it was on purpose. I think he was just trying to make me mad." Mallory's smile grew. "He didn't succeed. I don't get mad if I can help it. So, sorry I'm late."

"Excused," Savannah said, glancing around again.

There were ten chairs formed in a circle with more piled high in the corner in case other people came. Sheila took a seat in a chair across the circle from Savannah. Taking their cue, the others in the room stopped talking and took a seat as well.

"Good evening, everyone." Sheila made a point of looking at everyone as her gaze scanned the circle. "We have a new person with us today. Everyone, meet Savannah. Let's go around and introduce ourselves, shall we?"

Savannah had never enjoyed being the center of attention. She waved and smiled politely but part of her wanted to shrink away and exit the room. After everyone had introduced themselves, Sheila opened the circle for anyone who wanted to talk. People seemed to jump at the opportunity. One guy discussed not wanting his wife to have to do the yard work when he was feeling bad. Another woman talked about how one of her friends suddenly didn't want to hang out with her anymore. Everyone seemed to sympathize. Even Savannah sympathized, and she hadn't been dealing with any of her symptoms for decades like some.

Savannah worried that she might be put on the spot and asked what her story was. She wasn't ready to talk about having lupus yet. As Sheila wrapped up the hour-long meeting, she caught Savannah's gaze and nodded as if she understood that Savannah didn't wish to share tonight.

"All right, everyone. Good meeting. I'm proud of all of you." She looked at Savannah again. "I look forward to seeing you next Thursday. Same time, same place."

Everyone joined in to say a final closing line. "Same pretty face," they all said with laughter.

"See?" Mallory leaned in. "It wasn't so bad, was it?"

Savannah looked over. "It wasn't. I kind of feel better, actually. The people are nice."

Mallory stood and looped her bag over one shoulder. "I'm glad you came."

"Me too," Sheila said, walking over. "And please join us again."

Savannah intended to do just that. She could use all the support she could get. And friends too. Making friends was important when you were the newbie in town. It was important for June, and Savannah as well. "Same time, same place, same pretty face."

Sheila's lips stretched into a wide smile as she turned to Mallory. "Look at that. She's already one of us."

A happy sigh tumbled off Savannah's lips. She closed the book in her lap and shut her eyes for a moment, reveling in that feeling of completing something. It had been a long time since she'd read a book in its entirety. She'd forgotten that satisfied feeling that came along with following a character through their journey until the end.

Opening her eyes again, Savannah hugged the copy of *Eat, Pray, Love* against her stomach. She'd also forgotten the power of a good book. Standing, Savannah slipped her feet into a pair of shoes and headed down the hall toward the back door. She intended to place the novel in the library and find one of the books on the reading list that Eleanor had recently given her. If reading the books helped her heal in any way, she'd read every recommendation.

The house was quiet. It was only 9:00 p.m. but Savannah guessed that Eleanor had fallen asleep in her chair. She didn't want to disturb her. Truthfully, Savannah just wanted to be alone. The support group had helped, and she intended to keep going. She was still struggling with her feelings for Evan though. They weren't going away. If anything, they were growing stronger.

Why had she broken up with him again?

Savannah slowed her pace as she walked under the rose arbor and breathed in the floral scent.

Lupus was a very real illness that she dealt with every day but her condition had the power to knock her off her feet and put her in a hospital bed at any unexpected moment. She'd known that in the back of her mind but some part of her had been in denial. Falling in love with Evan this summer had made her feel invincible. Then *bam!* She was admitted to the hospital, and she feared she was becoming the party pooper that she never wanted to be.

In her life thus far, she had always been the person who'd

lifted others up. She'd enjoyed helping Randall start his dream business. She'd enjoyed buoying him on the hard days. She didn't hesitate to stick around and help Eleanor when she'd arrived this summer either. Being needed felt good. Being the one who needed the help felt...foreign.

Savannah approached the bench along the garden path and sat. Evan had looked so scared at the reception. She'd been terrified too. She'd really thought she might be having a heart attack. The doctor had diagnosed her with costochondritis but they'd made a point to tell her that she should always go to the hospital with chest pain, because a heart attack was a very real possibility, especially for someone with a chronic illness like hers. Lupus could attack and cause inflammation anywhere in the body—and if she let it, it could attack things outside the body, like her relationships with others.

Fig playfully swatted her paw against Savannah's shoe.

Savannah watched the kitten find her tail and chase it for a few minutes, running circles until she finally lay down at Savannah's feet. "I'll get you a few toys next time I go to the dollar store," she promised.

The kitten lifted her head to look at Savannah and then her ears twitched, and she looked down the path as if hearing something that Savannah couldn't.

A moment later, a puppy came running toward them. Savannah immediately recognized it as Monday, the puppy that June had gotten at the farmers market over the weekend. Whoever was out with Monday this evening was yet to be seen. Would it be June or Evan? Savannah wasn't sure which person she was hoping for as she waited, holding her breath.

"Monday!" Evan rounded the corner, slowing when he located Savannah on the bench.

Savannah waved. "Hi." Her gaze dropped to Monday, who was sniffing Fig. The two hadn't officially met yet. Fig had her back arched high and her hair was standing up. "It's okay, Fig. Monday is a nice puppy."

"Naughty but nice," Evan added, continuing in Savannah's direction. He had a book in his hand. Savannah guessed he was returning it to the Finders Keepers Library.

Fig hissed softly and Monday backed up but continued to wag his tail.

"It's all right, buddy. She's just playing hard to get," Evan said.

"She's being cautious," Savannah argued, having a feeling they were talking about more than the animals. "Which is completely understandable. She's been hurt."

Evan nodded. "Sorry, uh, for interrupting you out here."

"You're not. I was just on my way to return a book." She held up the memoir in her lap.

"Ah. That one is not on my current reading list." He held up a copy of a Nicholas Sparks book.

"Aunt Eleanor recommended *A Walk to Remember?*" Savannah was surprised. "That's an interesting choice."

Evan shrugged. "I guess she wanted me to cry myself to sleep last night."

Savannah lifted a brow. "You cried?"

"I challenge you to read this book and not shed a tear."

Savannah shook her head as she laughed quietly. "I've read it and I've seen the movie. I understand. I think Eleanor understood that I didn't need any more reasons to cry this summer. I'm glad it wasn't on my list."

"I think Eleanor understood that I did need to cry." Evan's smile slipped away. There was something vulnerable in his gaze as he looked at her. "Sometimes a guy needs a good excuse."

Savannah swallowed past a dry throat. Her heart was suddenly beating hard and fast. There were so many things left unsaid between them. So many feelings left unexplored. "Evan, I'm sorry," she blurted out.

He took a step closer and then sat down on the bench beside her. "You have no reason to apologize for anything—but what exactly are you sorry for?"

"Not trusting you with my heart, I guess. Not trusting myself. I don't know. I got scared," she admitted, her words coming out quickly and completely unfiltered. If she slowed down long enough to censor what she was saying, she might not be so honest. She wasn't sure if she could live with that. She certainly wouldn't be able to sleep with that hanging over her head.

Evan reached for her hand. The feel of his skin against hers was warm and inviting. Familiar. Everything about him invited her to come closer and stay. She longed to be held in his arms. She'd missed the feel of him so much.

"Me too," he said quietly, looking deep in her eyes. So deep that she couldn't blink, much less look away. "The night of the reception scared me out of my mind," he admitted.

Savannah shivered, even though the night was warm. "You don't deserve to feel that way."

When she finally lowered her eyes, Evan dipped his head to catch her gaze again. "I was going to tell you how I feel about you that night. I was on my way. I didn't want to let you go without telling you that I had fallen in love with you."

A tear slipped down her cheek. She went to wipe it away but Evan beat her to it, wiping it with the tip of his index finger. Her breath hitched as she watched and waited for what he'd do or say next. It felt like her future, their future, suddenly hinged on these next few moments. It could go either way. They could be friends. They could decide to hate each other instead. Or they could be exactly what she wanted more than anything.

"If you don't have feelings for me, if you don't see a future together, that's one thing. It'll hurt but I'll accept it and I'll try to pretend like I'm not absolutely in love with you, Sav," he finally said. "But if you do have feelings, if you envision a future where we're happy and in love, and you're only pulling away because you think somehow that you're doing me a favor, I can't accept that. I'm sorry but I won't pretend like I'm not absolutely in love with you because it would be a lie." His eyes searched hers.

"It's harder than I thought it would be," she said quietly.

"What is?"

She hesitated to say the word because saying it made it real. "Love."

His lips curved in a small smile. "It's easier together though."

Taking a shaky breath, she nodded. "There'll be more ER trips. We might miss out on romantic dates."

He held her hand in his own. "Do you think I care about that?"

"No, but I do," she said honestly.

"Then I'll recreate whatever dates we miss. I'll do whatever I need to, Sav, if it means having you in my life, and not just as a friend."

She rolled her lips together. "I don't want June's life to be affected. She deserves the world after what she's been through."

Evan traced a finger along her cheek, taking his time. "In my mind, having you in our lives would be giving her the world. If you could see yourself through my eyes…"

Savannah fought back tears. She really didn't want to cry in front of him. She didn't want to need him as much as she did. She knew she could trust him though. He wouldn't leave and he wouldn't abandon her. "If you could see yourself through my eyes, you'd see that I'm completely and hopelessly in love with you too, Evan. Even a few thousand strangers on the internet can see that."

He leaned in toward her, his woodsy scent catching in the air. "Are we getting back together? I really hope you say yes."

Savannah hesitated. She wanted to be completely honest with him. That's the only way this was going to work, and she wanted it to work. "I'm still scared."

"Me too," he admitted. "But I'm not scared because of the doctor appointments or ER visits. I want to be there for you, Savannah. Loving someone is an honor, not a burden."

"Then what is it that scares you?" she asked in a small whisper.

He looked around. "I hope these roses can keep a secret." His gaze returned to hers.

"They seem pretty good at that," she said.

He narrowed his blue eyes. They were the exact shade of blue as a cornflower. "I'm scared of letting you down. Of letting June down. Of not being the man I know I can be. The one I want to be. The one you and everyone I love deserves."

"You're the best man I know," she told him.

Evan took both of her hands in his. "That's one of the things that scares me: you waking up one day, tomorrow or ten years from now, and realizing I'm not the best man. Seeing my flaws and weaknesses for what they are."

"I think I'll love you more for your flaws and weaknesses. I think that's what love is," she said, realizing she should be listening to her own advice.

Evan seemed to understand that she'd just made a convincing argument against her own deepest fears and worries. "I love you, Sav. You're the Daisy to my Gatsby. The Elizabeth to my Mr. Darcy."

The tears were streaming down her face even as she laughed. "You're my Mr. Rochester. My Augustus Waters," she added.

Evan lifted a brow. "*The Fault in Our Stars?* If I'm Augustus, I hope I get to live."

Savannah sniffled as more happy tears fell. "I hope you get to live a long, happy life and I hope it's with me. Even though I broke your heart and tried to push you away. If you give me another chance, I'll probably break it a dozen more times."

"That's usually how the good love stories go," Evan said. "I love how we speak in books, just like Eleanor."

"Not exactly like Eleanor. There's no one quite like my aunt." Savannah felt relieved and overwhelmed, and most of all happy. Being with Evan felt right.

"June will probably turn into one of us too. It's unavoidable if you live at or around Eleanor's cottage."

"Then she's the second luckiest girl in Bloom, if you ask me. With me being the luckiest."

Evan squeezed her hand. Then he turned to the roses and

made a show of talking to them. "If you don't mind, no eaves-dropping on this next moment, please. I'm about to kiss the woman of my dreams and I'd like a little privacy, if you will." He faced Savannah and his gaze dropped to her mouth. Before he could make a move, Savannah leaned in and brushed her lips to his in a soft kiss that lingered and intensified.

"My Anne. My Juliet," he whispered between kisses.

"Except I get to live too," Savannah teased. "My Peeta."

"How about this?" Evan pulled back, framing her face in his hands as he looked at her. "You're the Savannah to my Evan."

She smiled. "I think I like that story best."

"Just wait. It gets better." He leaned in and kissed her again.

Savannah lost herself in the next kiss but that was okay, because she'd found herself this summer. She'd also found the man she was meant to be with—forever.

Epilogue
Savannah

Life offers up these moments of joy despite everything.

Normal People, Sally Rooney

The following summer.

The day was made for love.

The sun was shining against a clear blue sky and the garden was as alive and vivid as Savannah thought she'd ever seen it.

Charlie turned to Savannah as she stepped out onto Eleanor's back patio. He was wearing a cobalt-blue suit and holding a bouquet of colorful wildflowers.

"Are those for Eleanor?"

Charlie's smile made deep wrinkles on his face. "Your aunt deserves all the flowers in the world. All the books. And all my love."

"Aw. That's sweet. I'm glad she has you."

"What are the odds that your aunt is going to be a runaway bride today?" he asked.

Savannah raised her brows. "Slim, I hope. First of all, Aunt Eleanor can't run."

Charlie shook his head, a thoughtful expression on his face. "I might not have a whole lot of life left but I want to spend it with her."

"And she wants to spend it with you. Trust me. I saw Aunt Eleanor just a few minutes ago, and she's not running."

Savannah had been shocked when Eleanor had agreed a couple months back to marry Charlie. She'd been shocked but so happy for the two of them. They were getting married in Eleanor's backyard, just like Madison and Sam had last summer, and saying "I do" at the entrance of the Finders Keepers Library.

Savannah used to wonder if the love in storybooks was true but now she was a believer. Evan had a lot to do with that. She'd realized she hadn't known true love until she'd remet him last summer. His love was true and unconditional. He'd seen her through several flares this year, and his feelings never seemed to waver. If anything, they grew stronger.

And Savannah's feelings for him, in turn, had also grown. The fact that June was part of the package with Evan only made their relationship that much sweeter. Savannah wasn't June's mom and never would be but she enjoyed being a female role model. She liked that June came to her for all the things she needed help with in life, like boys.

Once school had started back up, June hadn't had any trouble making friends, and some of them were of the opposite sex. Yeah, she was only thirteen—she'd had a birthday in May—but already, Savannah had caught the girl scribbling boys' names in her notebooks. She was talking on her phone with peers more these days than reading books but Savannah thought that was typical.

Life had found a new rhythm in the last year, full of ebbs and flows, seeds and harvest. Savannah loved her job at Love in Bloom Nursery. It was made for her and allowed her to continue vlogging, making TikToks, and writing gardening articles for various publications. She also continued to sell plants online from her little store. Her green thumb was very busy and that's how she liked it. But when her body demanded rest, all these venues afforded her time to heal. It was the perfect situation.

"You look lovely," Charlie told Savannah, gesturing at her pink bridesmaid dress.

Eleanor had chosen pink because of a butterfly she'd seen in her front yard last year. It had come to visit her, or so she said, several times since. She credited the butterfly with leading her to taking that first step off her property.

Savannah was going sans her wide-brim hat today but the ceremony promised to be brief. She, June, Mallory, and Madison were Eleanor's bridesmaids. Evan, Hollis, Sam, and Charlie's oldest grandson, Gus, were the best men.

"I'd better go take my place," Charlie said, still holding the flowers.

Savannah gave him a funny look. "Do you want me to bring those to Aunt Eleanor? As her wedding bouquet?"

He looked a little flustered. "I guess I'm not used to getting married."

This made Savannah laugh. "I should hope not. It's not

something one does every day. It's more of a one-day kind of thing."

"She probably has a bouquet already, huh?" he asked.

Savannah tilted her head. "I think she'd prefer this one though." She reached for it. "I'll give it to her. See you in front of the library in a couple minutes."

Charlie blew out a breath. "I've already been married once, you know," he said. "I never thought I'd catch lightning in a bottle once, much less twice." He turned and started walking, not giving time for Savannah to respond.

She looked down at the wildflowers. They seemed to match the bridesmaids' dresses with the perfect shades of pink dispersed throughout the arrangement. Turning, she went back into the house where Eleanor was standing in the kitchen, wearing a cream-colored dress that flowed around her feet. Her strawberry blonde hair was pulled back with a pair of rhinestone clips, a few strands of hair curling around her face.

"Are those for me?" She looked delighted as she reached for the bouquet. Then she looked at June, Mallory, and Madison. Savannah took her place behind Madison, whose wheelchair had been decorated with pink satin ribbon and strings of pearls for the occasion. "Well, then," Eleanor said, raising a finger.

Savannah waited for what she suspected was coming.

Eleanor lowered her hand. "I suppose you ladies are expecting a bookish quote from me. Well, I'm afraid I don't have one this morning. There are only two words to say today, and they belong to Charlie."

With that, she opened the patio door. The wedding music began to play softly, coming from speakers that Evan had set up near the library. Eleanor seemed to hesitate momentarily but Savannah wasn't worried. Slowly, Eleanor led her wedding party down the steps, across the garden stones, and through the rose arbor.

As they came to a stop in front of the library, Savannah caught Evan's gaze. Her heart swelled with so much love. An impossible amount. His gaze didn't waver until the preacher began to lead Eleanor and Charlie through their vows.

"I do," Eleanor said simply at the end of the long list of promises.

"I do too." Charlie leaned in and kissed his new bride as the crowd broke out into applause.

Savannah looked down at the ring already on her left hand. Evan had proposed last week, and they had been batting around potential dates. She looked up at him again, and this time it was like seeing into the future. Their future. Suddenly, she could imagine it all perfectly.

Next summer.

This very spot.

She also had two small words that she couldn't wait to say to him.

Two very simple words that had echoed through all the greatest love stories ever told. And they belonged to Evan. *I do.*

Acknowledgments

I like to think that each book I write is the book of my heart. I put a little piece of myself into each story, and *The Finders Keepers Library* is no different—although perhaps it carries a slightly bigger piece. This book would not have been possible without so many.

First, I would like to thank my editor Alex Logan and my publisher family, Grand Central Forever, for saying yes to this story and making a way for this book to find virtual and physical shelves. My editor always takes my stories and shines a light on the areas that need work—and sometimes the initial project looks more like a disaster site instead of a work-in-progress. Often, those books are the ones that I'm most proud of. So, a big thanks to my editor for shining her light.

Thank you to Grand Central's copyeditor, proofreader, and talented cover artist as well.

Without publicity, there are no readers; and without readers, there is no next book. Therefore, I would also like to acknowledge and thank my publicist at Forever, Estelle Hallick, for helping this book find its audience. You are appreciated!

All the hugs go out to my super-agent, Sarah Younger at

Nancy Yost Literary Agency. I am so thankful to have you on my team. You always lift me up and have my back, and I will always sing your praises.

Thank you to my invaluable assistant, Kimberly Bradford Scott. You make my author job SO much easier. You lighten my load and allow me to do more of what I love most, which is writing.

As always, I want to shout out to the ladies in my small writing critique group: April Hunt, Tif Marcelo, Rachel Lacey, and Jeanette Escudero. I never feel alone doing one of the most solitary jobs there is. Even in my dark writing cave (aka a comfy chair in a dark corner), you ladies are only a text away—and for that, I am so grateful.

Thank you to all my readers, especially those on my review team. I know that it is no easy task to read a book, review it, and pass the word on to other readers. I love my readers and appreciate all your efforts for every book. I see you, and I am grateful for you!

Last but never least, thank you to my family! It is not lost on me the sacrifices you make to help me follow my dreams and create these books that I am so passionate about. I could not do any of this without you, and I would never want to.

No chronic illness is experienced the same, even if it's labeled with the same name. I would like to thank everyone who has shared their personal experiences of lupus with me, including Kenia and Tina. Sending you much thanks and love.

About the Author

Annie Rains is a *USA Today* bestselling contemporary romance author who writes contemporary love stories set in fictional places in her home state of North Carolina. After years of dreaming about becoming an author, Annie published her first book in 2015 and has been chasing deadlines and creating happily-ever-afters for her characters ever since. When Annie isn't writing, she's living out her own happily-ever-after with her husband and three children. Annie also enjoys spending time with her two rescue pets, a mischievous Chihuahua mix and an attention-hungry cat, who inspire the lovable animals in her books.

Learn more at:
AnnieRains.com
X @AnnieRainsBooks
Facebook.com/AnnieRainsBooks
TikTok: @AnnieRainsBooks
Instagram: @AnnieRainsBooks